STOCKPORT
METROPOLITAN BOROUGH COUNCIL

Ambitious Stockport,
creating opportunities
for everyone

CH 11/24

Withdrawn
from Stock

Please return/renew this item by the last date shown.
For information about renewing your library books
please scan QR code or visit:

www.stockport.gov.uk/libraries

Bernardine Kennedy

'A quaint, British cozy, complete with characters

MURDER AT THE CROOKED HORSE

LESLEY COOKMAN

ACCENT

First published in 2024 by Headline Accent
An imprint of HEADLINE PUBLISHING GROUP

1

Cataloguing in Publication Data is available from the British Library

ISBN 978 1 0354 0571 8

Typeset in 10.5/13pt BemboBookMTPro by Jouve (UK), Milton Keynes

Printed and bound in Great Britain by Clays Ltd, Elcograf S.p.A.

Headline's policy is to use papers that are natural, renewable and recyclable
products and made from wood grown in well-managed forests and other
controlled sources. The logging and manufacturing processes are expected
to conform to the environmental regulations of the country of origin.

HEADLINE PUBLISHING GROUP
An Hachette UK Company
Carmelite House
50 Victoria Embankment
London
EC4Y 0DZ

www.headline.co.uk
www.hachette.co.uk

To my family

The village of
Steeple Martin

Allhallow's Lane

to Canterbury

High Street

Oast House Theatre

The Pink Geranium

Manor Drive

The Manor

Maltby Close

Steeple Farm

to Nethergate

S. Alison

Character List

Libby Sarjeant
Actor and director of the Oast Theatre, Steeple Martin. Part-time artist.

Fran Wolfe
Actor and occasional psychic.

Ben Wilde
Libby's significant other. Owner of the Manor farm and the Oast Theatre.

Guy Wolfe
Fran's husband and father to Sophie Wolfe. Artist and owner of a shop and gallery in Harbour Street, Nethergate.

Peter Parker
Freelance journalist, part owner of the Pink Geranium restaurant. Ben's cousin and Harry Price's civil partner.

Harry Price
Chef and co-owner of the Pink Geranium. Peter Parker's civil partner.

DCI Ian Connell
Local policeman and friend.

Hetty Wilde
Ben's mother. Lives at the Manor.

Flo Carpenter
Hetty's oldest friend.

Lenny Fisher
Hetty's brother. Lives with Flo Carpenter.

Jane Baker
Editor of the *Nethergate Mercury*.

Reverend Patti Pearson
Vicar at St Aldeberge.

Anne Douglas
Librarian and Reverend Patti's friend and partner.

Edward Hall
Academic and historian.

Alice Gedding
Sheep farmer and friend of Edward.

Tim Stevens
Landlord of the Coach and Horses, Steeple Martin.

Mavis
Owner of the Blue Anchor café.

Joe Wilson
Friend of Lenny, Flo and Hetty.

Simon Spencer
Manager of the Hop Pocket, Steeple Martin.

Beth Cole
Vicar at Steeple Martin.

John Cole
Beth's husband.

Adam Sarjeant
Libby's son.

Sophie Wolfe
Guy's daughter.

Ron Stewart
Retired pop star.

Maria Stewart
Ron's wife.

Barney
A dog.

Ricky Short
Barney's owner.

Debbie Pointer
Ricky's mother.

Linda Davies
Ricky's grandmother.

Judy Dale and Cyd Russell
New residents of Steeple Martin. Singers.

George
Landlord of the Red Lion, Heronsbourne.

Philip Jacobs
Barrister.

Lewis Osbourne-Walker
Owner of the Creekmarsh estate.

Edie Osbourne-Walker
Lewis's mother.

Sid Best
Landlord of The Poacher, Shott.

Richard Brandon
Actor and new resident of Steeple Martin.

Stan Hadley
Landlord of the Fox and Hounds, Shittenden.

Inspector Rob Maiden
Detective.

Rachel Trent
Detective.

Trisha
Stan's daughter.

Zack
Landlord of the Gate Inn, Felling.

Wallace Mayberry
Owner of Beer and Bargains.

Malcolm Hodges
Owner of an Antiques Barn.

Fay Hodges
Malcolm's wife.

Acting DI Clare Stone
Detective.

DC Bodie
Policeman

George and Bert
Captains of The Dolphin and The Sparkler.

Dan and Moira Cruildhank
Residents of Steeple Martin.

Tara Nichols FSA
Archeologist.

Jim Frost
Antiques dealer.

Bren
Landlady of The Fox, Creekmarsh.

Sir Andrew McColl
Theatrical Knight.

Susannah
Musical Director at the Oast Theatre.

Portia Havilland
Executive at Marsham's Brewery.

Graham
Landlord of The Sloop, Nethergate.

Ginny Mardle
Libby's next door neighbour.

Livia Renshaw
Works at Marsham's Brewery.

Chapter One

The boat rocked gently against the small jetty, moonlight sporadically highlighting its empty interior. Eventually the cut rope pulled away from the stanchion and the boat, freed from its mooring, began to drift away on the rippled grey satin of the sea.

'Did you hear about the old Crooked Horse?' said Lewis Osbourne-Walker, handing Libby Sarjeant a large mug of tea.

'The what?' Libby, seated at the large kitchen table with Lewis's mother, Edie, looked startled.

'It's a pub, dear,' said Edie. 'Over on the marshes.'

Libby's brow wrinkled. 'I don't remember a pub on the Flats.'

'Not Heronsbourne Flats,' said Lewis. 'The marshes over towards Felling.'

'Oh. No, then. Why would I have heard anything about a pub all the way over there?'

'Because it's made the news, lovey.' Edie offered a plate of biscuits. 'On the telly.'

'No – I must have missed it. What's happened to it?' Libby ignored the biscuits.

'It burned down,' said Lewis.

'Oh no! How sad. Anyone hurt?'

'No.' Lewis frowned and sat down. 'All a bit odd, actually. It burned down – or nearly – at the weekend, and then yesterday a digger turned up to demolish what was left.'

'Oh dear.' Libby gave a rueful smile. 'Insurance job, was it?'

'Dunno. The police stopped the digger – something to do with permissions. They're looking into it.'

'We wondered, see,' said Edie, 'if it was to do with all that other stuff about the pubs.'

'Oh?' Libby frowned. 'Why?'

Edie shrugged. 'Just because it's a pub, I s'pose.'

'And it was over near Marsham's. It was sold, see,' said Lewis. 'It didn't say on the news, but we wondered if it was one of the ones that got sold off last year.'

A local brewery, Marsham's, had sold off several pubs and got themselves into a good deal of trouble in the process over the past year. Libby and her friend Fran had helped look into the circumstances.

'Could be, I suppose,' she said, 'but if it was sold to become a private dwelling, why burn it down?'

'Development,' said Lewis darkly.

'Where, though? There isn't anything over that way. Near the Dunton estate, is it?'

'Well, yes, sort of,' said Lewis, not very helpfully. 'Well, part of that's been bought up, and they want to turn it into houses. And the pub's just up the road. Right by the nature reserve.'

'Who wants to? The new owners?'

'Oh, I don't know,' said Lewis. 'Someone does, anyway.'

'Well, it's nothing to do with me, and I've got enough on my plate at the moment,' said Libby, leaning back with a sigh. 'I'm rehearsing this play at the theatre.'

'What play?' asked Lewis.

'Oh, it's lovely. It was written by some friends of mine years ago, and has never been performed since, so I'm going to revive it. It's great, and really local.'

'Steeple Martin local?' asked Lewis.

'No – Kent local. It's called *Contraband*.'

'Oh, smugglers!' Lewis beamed. 'That'll go down well.'

2

'Yes, it will. And it's a musical, even better!' Libby grinned back at him.

'What I meant was, the Crooked Horse was a smugglers' pub.' He raised both eyebrows and waited for her to speak.

'So?' Libby frowned.

'You could be researching smugglers while you look into it!' Lewis leant forward eagerly. 'Perfect!'

'Oi!' Libby banged her fist on the table. 'I'm not looking into anything! I said I'm far too busy. Anyway, the police will be doing it. And the insurance company, I expect.'

'Oh, Lib! Come on. For the locals.' Lewis looked down at his hands and shook his head. 'I sort of said . . .'

'I told 'im,' said Edie. 'I said you wouldn't want to. Not after that last lot.'

'What?' Libby looked from one to the other. 'What have you done, Lewis?'

Lewis looked defensive. 'It wasn't my idea! It was George.'

Libby narrowed her eyes at him. 'Which George?'

'How many do you know?' he asked.

'Don't try and muddy the waters.'

'George at the Red Lion,' muttered Lewis.

'And it was his idea to ask me, was it?'

Lewis sighed. 'We was talking about it, see. And George said you ought to look into it, seeing as you'd helped with the whole Marsham's Brewery thing.'

'And the silly fool said he'd ask you,' said Edie, with a positively witch-like cackle.

'Oh, bloody hell.' Libby let out her breath in a whoosh.

'What?' Lewis said after a moment.

'I can see what he meant,' said Libby. She sat staring at her now empty mug for a long time.

Eventually Edie stood up. 'Shall I go, duck? I'll wait for you in my sitting room.'

'No, it's all right, Edie.' Libby sat up straight in her chair. 'I'm just being feeble. I can quite see why George said what he did, it's just that people seem to treat me and Fran like proper private detectives, and we really aren't.'

'You might as well be,' said Lewis. 'And I looked it up. You don't even have to take exams, you know.'

'I know, but the police prefer it if you do.' Libby smiled wistfully. 'Ian said he'd love to see my answers to the questions.'

'Ian is a rare thing among policemen,' said Lewis. 'Never known one like him.'

'As I'd never known one before, I can't say the same,' said Libby, 'but he's a very good friend. I wonder if he's in charge of this investigation.'

'It isn't a murder, so probably not,' said Lewis.

'He doesn't only do murders,' said Libby, 'although now he's part of this MIT, or whatever it is, I suppose he mainly does.'

'What's that, duck?' asked Edie. 'MIT?'

'Major investigation team,' said Libby. 'DCI Ian Connell is one of the top bods in this area now. I think he's only got a superintendent above him.'

'Anyway,' said Lewis, 'he might be in charge of this fire thing, as it's raised such a stink locally.'

'And why exactly is that?' asked Libby. 'You just said it was an old smugglers' pub.'

'Well, see, it was on a route from where stuff used to be landed,' Lewis began, settling himself more comfortably now that danger was past. 'Called the Pack Horse then, it was, so the iggerant masses knew it was a safe house by the picture.'

'Oh, yes – they had the pub signs for people who couldn't read, didn't they?' said Libby.

'That's it. But then there was the coal mine.'

'Eh?' Libby and Edie both looked startled.

'You know about them, Lib,' said Lewis. 'I remember you learnt about the miners when you first heard about their reunion service at St Aldeberge Church.'

'Oh, yes, Betteshanger and Chislet and all of them.' Libby nodded.

4

'Well apparently, so George and some of the others was saying, they tried a few others, which didn't work.'

'Oh yes, I remember – Woodnesborough was one, wasn't it?'

'Yeah – so they drilled right near that old estate, and the pub slipped.'

'Oh!' Libby clapped her hands. 'So it became the Crooked Horse! Lots of places suffered like that when they dug the coal mines in the north, didn't they?'

'I dunno about that,' said Lewis, 'but that's what happened, apparently. And the council was supposed to protect it or something.'

'Wasn't it listed?' Libby frowned. 'Must have been. I bet it was at least a couple of hundred years old.'

Lewis and his mother exchanged smiles. 'So you will look into it then?' said Lewis innocently.

'I'll think about it,' said Libby, standing up. 'Now come on, Edie. I came over to take you to see your mate at Temptation House, not sit here gossiping.'

Creekmarsh Place, the venerable estate owned by Lewis, bordered the sea on one side and the Heronsbourne Road on the other. Libby drove Edie through Heronsbourne itself to Nethergate and on out the other side, where Temptation House stood alone on a cliff overlooking Nethergate Bay. Last winter, Edie's friend Chloe Vaughan had moved into the house to join Miss Dorothy Barton's group of what she called 'indigent ladies'. She loved her bed-sitting room with kitchenette and shower room, and rather revelled in her status as widow of a notorious London crook. Not, she and Edie both assured Libby, that Mickey Vaughan had been particularly notorious; he just 'got in with a bad crowd', as Chloe put it.

'What are you going to do about this pub, then, duck?' Edie asked as Libby pulled up outside.

'Find out a bit more about it first,' said Libby. 'We're all going over to the reopening of the Fox and Hounds at Shittenden tonight – I told you, didn't I? – so I'll ask a couple of questions while I'm there.'

'That was one o' them pubs they sold, wasn't it?'

'Not quite. They threw poor Stan, the landlord, out but never got round to selling it, so they let him have it back when the whole bad business came out. So now he's reopening. And he might know if the Crooked Horse was a Marsham's pub.'

At six o'clock, the minibus pulled up at the foot of the Manor drive in Steeple Martin high street and collected Libby, her partner Ben Wilde and their friends Fran and Guy Wolfe from Nethergate; Peter, Ben's cousin, and his partner Harry; Ricky (and Barney the dog) and his grandmother, Linda Davies. They stopped at the corner of New Barton Lane to collect Anne Douglas and her wheelchair.

'It's a proper Libby's Loonies outing,' said Harry, *chef patron* of Steeple Martin's vegetarian Mexican restaurant, the Pink Geranium, leaning over between Ben and Libby. 'Are we going to play hunt the murderer?'

'As no one's been murdered recently, no,' said Libby.

'Well, that's a relief.' Harry sat back and nudged Peter. 'We can relax.'

It was nearly a quarter past seven by the time the minibus arrived outside the Fox and Hounds, due to the usual heavy rush-hour traffic in Canterbury.

'Looks pretty, doesn't it?' said Fran as they climbed out.

'Stan's already got his lovely hanging baskets out,' said Libby, smiling happily. 'I'm so pleased he got the pub back.'

'Thanks to you,' said Ricky, coming up behind them.

'The brewery saw sense,' said Libby. 'And your mum helped.'

'Least she could do,' said Ricky with a sigh, and went to help with Anne's wheelchair.

Libby and Fran looked at one another.

'Oh dear,' said Fran.

The Steeple Martin contingent were welcomed into the pub – which looked a lot brighter than the last time Libby had seen it – by Stan Hadley and his daughter Trisha. Ricky's mother, Debbie Pointer, was

6

sitting looking rather self-conscious on a stool at the bar. Ricky and Linda both went forward to give her a kiss. Libby noticed the slightly disparaging glance that Trisha sent after them.

'Well, Trisha's not happy with the situation, that's for sure,' Fran murmured in Libby's ear.

'A bit dog-in-the-manger of her,' said Libby, as they both smiled and nodded to acquaintances. 'After all, Debbie did help Stan restore the pub to its former glory.'

'Hmm,' said Fran. 'And usurped Trisha's position, perhaps?'

'Look, we aren't here to carp about the situation,' said Libby. 'We're here to celebrate with Stan – he looks really happy, doesn't he?'

Stan did indeed look happy. A small man, with grey hair and a cheerful, wrinkled face, he was positively bursting with excitement.

'I'm so pleased to see you two,' he said confidentially, handing the women glasses of champagne. 'It's all down to you, this.' He waved a hand around the bar.

'And Debbie, surely,' said Libby with a smile.

'She wouldn't have done it without you,' said Stan firmly. 'And that's another thing I've got to thank you for.' He looked quickly at Debbie and her family, a slight frown on his face.

'Nothing to do with us,' said Fran.

'Have all the clubs come back?' asked Libby, hastily changing the subject. 'The Vintage Drinkers?'

'Oh yes.' Stan beamed. 'And old Joe Wilson has brought all his old codgers, as he calls them, back here. And the ladies – even the book club. They didn't much like the Hop House Centre.'

'No, it was a bit soulless, wasn't it?' said Libby, remembering the converted oast houses in Shittenden.

'Yeah – anyway, I got to go and talk to that TV chap now, but I wanted to ask you something. Catch you later?' He looked hopefully from Libby to Fran.

'I wanted to ask you something too,' said Libby. 'See you later.'

Stan beamed and blew a kiss before turning and plunging once more into the crowd of appreciative drinkers.

7

Chapter Two

'Lib – can you spare a moment?'

Ben appeared at Libby's elbow with a large man in a rather shabby three-piece suit, who held out his hand.

'Hello! I'm Wallace Mayberry.'

'Oh, hello.' Libby took the outstretched hand with a tentative smile. 'I'm Libby Sarjeant.'

'I'm Beer and Bargains!' continued Wallace Mayberry.

Fran and Libby exchanged puzzled glances.

'Wallace wants some advice.' Ben looked slightly uncomfortable. 'If you don't mind.'

'Advice?' Libby frowned.

'Er – yes.' Wallace straightened up and wiped a perspiring brow.

Ben sighed. 'It's about a friend of his.' He looked at Wallace, obviously waiting for him to speak. He didn't.

'What about him?' asked Libby, aware of a sinking feeling somewhere under her ribcage.

'Well,' Wallace said. 'He's disappeared.'

'Ah,' said Libby.

There was a rather awkward silence, which Ben eventually broke.

'You see,' he said, 'Wallace sometimes buys his – er – antiques from someone who has a barn out at Shittenden, and now the Fox and Hounds has opened again, he pops in here for a drink.' He looked at her hopefully, as if this explained everything.

'And?' she said.

'Well, he got talking to Stan, you see.' Ben turned to Wallace. 'Go on, you tell her.'

Wallace heaved a sigh and settled back against the table, which creaked alarmingly.

'It was like this. My mate's got this barn, you see. And he's got a boat.' He scratched his head, getting redder in the face than ever. 'And his missus gives me a ring, see. And she says he went out on the boat last week and he hasn't come back.'

'Hasn't she told the police?' asked Fran.

'No.' The red was turning, alarmingly, to puce. 'She – er – didn't like to.'

Dodgy dealing, Libby thought to herself. 'So what advice can I give you?'

'It was Stan, see,' said Wallace, giving her a pleading look like a starving bulldog. 'He says it's mostly down to you he got the old Fox back, and you're like a sort of private eye. So we – that's Fay and me – we thought we'd ask you what you thought.'

'I'm not a private eye, Wallace,' said Libby. 'I sometimes help with inquiries. My friend and I are' – she flicked a quick look at Fran – 'civil consultants. And really, I think you should report this to the police. Have the coastguard been informed? I assume it was at sea, not on a river?'

'Yeah.' Wallace looked at his feet. 'Channel.'

Of course, thought Libby. The illegal trade in 'antiques' from the Continent had increased in the last couple of years, since the gentrification of the area and the growth in the holiday-rental and second-home markets.

'Is Fay his wife?' she asked, more gently now.

He looked up. 'Yeah. We're sort of – mates.'

'Well, I really think you should tell the authorities. I honestly don't see what we can do.' Fran smiled sympathetically. 'I'm sorry.'

Wallace sighed and shrugged. 'Oh well, it was worth a try,' he said and gave Ben a lopsided grin. 'Thanks, mate.'

9

He wandered off and Harry took his place, indicating an empty table by the door.

'Pete's getting drinks,' he said. 'So what did old Wally want?'

'He said he was Beer and Bargains,' said Fran.

Harry laughed. 'He's one of your customers, isn't he, Ben? It's an antique shop in Nethergate.'

'Antiques? With beer?' Libby looked puzzled.

'It's more – what do they call it? – collectibles, that's it. And Wally's turned it into a micropub. You can buy practically everything that isn't nailed down, and he's doing much better now, with Ben's beer.'

Ben had become quite the entrepreneur over the last few years, reviving his family's hop garden, starting up a microbrewery and restoring a small village pub, the Hop Pocket.

Peter appeared with a tray of glasses and Guy carrying a bottle of champagne.

'Well, it might run out,' he said, topping up Libby and Fran's glasses. 'I thought I'd make sure we had enough.'

'Heaven forbid,' said Ben.

'So what was that all about?' Harry asked.

'Your Beer and Bargains man just asked us for advice,' said Libby. 'Cheers.'

'Wally?' Harry's eyebrows shot up. 'What's he done?'

'Nothing. A friend of his has gone missing, that's all.'

'In the trade?' Harry was frowning now.

'Owns an antiques barn, apparently, near here.'

'Ah.' Peter nodded. 'Malcolm Hodges. You certainly don't want to get mixed up with him.'

'I don't?' Libby looked surprised.

'Definitely dodgy,' said Harry firmly.

'How do you know?' Libby squinted at him suspiciously.

'Word gets around,' said Harry evasively.

'But you're nothing to do with antiques.'

'But I've got a business, dear heart. And like it or not, there is a business community in the area – mainly on social media these days, of

10

course. Mind you,' Harry looked thoughtful, 'I've heard nothing about Hodges going missing.'

'Apparently Fay didn't want to go to the police and Wallace talked to Stan.' Ben shrugged. 'Fatal.'

'Stan recommended you, did he?' Harry chuckled. 'And who's Fay?'

'Hodges' wife. And a "mate" of Wallace. Oh – and he went missing on his boat in the Channel, which definitely sounds dodgy to me.'

'Smuggling stuff over from the Continong?' said Harry. 'So she hasn't asked the coastguard, either?'

'No. We told him he should go to the police,' said Fran.

'Good girl.' Guy patted her on the shoulder. 'You're learning.'

'Don't patronise,' said Fran.

Libby and Fran were sitting outside the pub with Ricky and Barney when Stan and a woman Libby would describe as 'well preserved' approached them.

'Nice speech, Stan,' said Libby.

Stan went pink. 'Never was much good at speeches. 'Specially having to do it to bloody TV cameras. Dread to think what'll happen if Trish gets married.' He cleared his throat. 'This is Fay. I think Wally Mayberry mentioned her to you.'

'Oh yes.' Libby nodded. 'Ben introduced us earlier.'

'He said.' Fay looked rather ill at ease. 'He's just – er – had to pop out for a bit.'

She had the voice of a lifelong smoker, thought Libby.

'I'd better get back,' said Stan. 'I'll see you later, all right, Libby?'

Libby nodded and smiled. 'Well, sit down, Fay.'

Fay's form-fitting orange and purple dress creaked a bit at the seams as she perched on the bench next to Ricky, who promptly stood up.

'I'd better leave you alone,' he said. 'Come on, Barney.'

Barney gave Libby a last lick and followed his master, his tail whirring like a helicopter.

'What can we do for you, Fay?' asked Fran. 'I'm Fran Wolfe, Libby's colleague.'

11

How confidently she said that, thought Libby. I'd still be struggling with how to introduce us.

Fay darted a narrow-eyed stare between them. 'Wally told you. My hubby's disappeared.'

Libby suppressed a wince. 'Yes, he did. He said he went out on his boat and didn't come back. This would be the week before last, now, wouldn't it?'

'Have you told the police and the coastguard?' asked Fran.

'No.' Fay looked away. 'Didn't want to make a fuss.'

Libby and Fran exchanged glances.

'Then I really don't see what we can do,' said Libby gently. 'We haven't got the resources the police have.'

'You work with them, though. Stan said.' Fay sent a penetrating glare in Libby's direction. 'You can find out.'

'How?' asked Fran reasonably. 'Ask them if they've heard of a man out on a boat who's missing from home? I think they might want to know why.'

Fay frowned down at her green-painted nails. 'What do I do, then?'

'Tell the police,' said Libby firmly.

'What's the name of his boat?' asked Fran suddenly.

Fay glanced up, hopeful. 'The *Jan Bishop*, named after his mum.'

'We'll ask around,' said Fran. Libby looked surprised.

'You still ought to tell the police,' she said.

Fay creaked to her feet. 'You let me know if you – er – hear anything.' She nodded at Fran. 'Thank you.'

Libby waited until Fay was out of earshot.

'Well?' she said. 'What was all that about? Are we going looking for a boat now?'

'I just thought we could ask George and Bert if they know it.' Fran stood up. 'Nethergate was always a smuggling port, wasn't it? I bet it still goes on – only probably not wool any more.'

'No,' agreed Libby, thinking of Skinner's Alley and Slaughterman's Cottage. 'Are we going back inside?'

'I thought we ought to help Stan with that champagne,' said Fran, with an innocent look. 'Don't want it to go to waste.'

Peter met them as they re-entered.

'Wondered where you'd gone,' he said, eyeing them suspiciously. 'Ben's friend Wally was asking for you.'

'Well, as we were talking to his so-called "mate", I'm surprised he needed to ask,' said Libby. 'And we need more champagne.'

Libby managed to corner Stan a little while later on her way back from the smart new ladies' room.

'Very nice,' she said, indicating the rather twee 'Vixens' sign.

'Debbie's idea,' said Stan with a sigh. 'You said you wanted to speak to me, didn't you? Sorry, I got Fay in first!'

'That's OK,' said Libby. 'I just wanted to know if you'd heard anything about the Crooked Horse?'

She didn't need to explain.

'Oh, bloody hell, yes!' Stan scowled. 'Terrible business.'

'Was it a Marsham's pub?'

'Ah – that's why you're interested, is it?'

'Somebody suggested it might be, that's all. Was it?'

'Still is,' said Stan. 'Well – not exactly. New owners were about to take it over.'

'I thought they already had?' Libby raised her eyebrows.

'Hadn't been signed,' said Stan, leaning in confidentially. 'That's why they reckon it was fired.'

'They? Who's they?'

'People. In the trade. After all that business before, Marsham's were a bit wary. Word was that the new owners wanted to sell out to the developers, see, so they – Marsham's – put a halt on the sale.'

'Oh! I didn't hear that.'

'No.' Stan nodded wisely. 'You wouldn't. Funny, though.' He paused, frowning.

'What is?'

'Well, you know it was a smugglers' pub?'

Libby nodded.

'The antiques boys used it too.' He slid his eyes sideways. 'Get me?'

'Yes. Avoiding the red tape and coming in under cover of darkness?' Libby grinned. 'And was Fay's husband doing the same?'

'You got it.' Stan grinned back. 'Not a word.'

'Course not.' Libby tried to look innocent. 'No wonder Fay's worried.'

'Yeah, well. I'd better get back to the rabble. See you before you go,' and Stan hurried off.

The sky was turning itself purple and gold when Libby and Ben found a corner of the pub garden to hide in.

'It's lovely that so many people want to thank us for saving Stan's pub, but so embarrassing,' said Libby with a sigh. 'It wasn't us, after all.'

'If Ian hadn't asked you to help, it wouldn't have happened,' said Ben. 'Give yourself some credit.'

Their friend DCI Connell tended to treat Libby and Fran as unpaid members of the force. Not always with the approval of their nearest and dearest, or the force itself for that matter. Although he also had a habit of telling them off when they got too involved.

'But people start expecting things.' Libby gazed out at the sunset. 'Even Joe Wilson introduced me and Fran to his Vintage Drinkers mates as the ones who are going to find Malcolm Hodges.'

'They'll forget about it soon enough,' consoled Ben.

'Not if he's not found,' said Libby. 'They'll go on and on, you know they will.'

Ben frowned down at his feet. 'I wish I hadn't introduced you to Wally now.'

Libby smiled and patted his hand. 'You could hardly have avoided it, could you?'

'I suppose not.' He looked up and gave her a rueful grin. 'So what are you going to do now?'

'Now? I'm going to go and find a last drink, courtesy of Stan, then I'm going home with you to start thinking about *Contraband*.'

Ben helped her to her feet. '*Contraband*'s about smuggling, isn't it?'

'Clue's in the title,' said Libby.

'Well, we decided that Hodges could have been smuggling, didn't we?'

'But what's that got to do with a play about smugglers two hundred and fifty years ago?' Libby looked at him in surprise.

'What were they smuggling, and why?' Ben started walking slowly back towards the pub.

'You *know* what they were smuggling! Brandy, tea, tobacco . . . Nothing that was illegal in itself.'

'It was stuff they thought they had a right to, wasn't it? They objected to the government saying they couldn't. Not like smuggling drugs or people.'

Libby stopped with a hand on his arm. 'So you agree Hodges could be smuggling antiques?'

Ben tucked her arm into his own and resumed walking. 'These dealers have been bringing stuff in from Europe for years. Nothing really expensive – no Old Masters, or priceless Greek vases, or anything like that. Just silly stuff – kitchen artefacts, old posters, that sort of thing. And from what I can gather, they all resented the fact that Brexit tried to stop that by imposing exorbitant duty and forests' worth of paperwork. Not to mention the problems getting in and out of the country via the ports.'

'So they just started doing it on their own? Taking little boats out from places like Nethergate?' She paused. 'That's what Harry said. Smuggling things over from the Continong, as he put it. And Stan was saying the antiques boys used the Crooked Horse pub.'

'Yes. And it was your idea in the first place. I'm only following up on it.' Ben gave her a kiss on the cheek. 'Come on, let's go and beard the rabble. And why don't you ask Hodges' missus if you can go and have a look at their barn sometime?'

★

15

Applied to, Fay looked wary, but acquiesced.

'Do you think it will help?' she asked.

'Yes, will it?' Fran came up behind them.

'It'll help understand Malcolm,' said Ben, and smiled at Fay, who preened slightly.

'OK,' she said. 'When do you want to come?'

'We can be available any time,' said Fran. 'Just give one of us a ring and let us know.'

Wally Mayberry came up behind Fay and put a proprietorial hand on her shoulder. 'Tell me, love,' he said, 'and I'll call old Ben here.'

Trisha saw the Steeple Martin minibus off.

'Sorry if I seemed a bit – well, grumpy,' she said to Libby.

'That's all right.' Libby smiled at her. 'At least you've still got your nice flat in Canterbury and you can get out of the way.'

Trisha sighed. 'Trouble is, I quite miss the old bugger now he's come back to the pub.'

'And he's happy,' said Libby.

'Not happy enough for her,' said Trisha with a nod over her shoulder. 'And yes, I know I'm being ungrateful – after all, she's spent money on the place – but it was your investigation that made the brewery give it back to Dad.'

'Oh, I don't know about that,' said Libby modestly. 'We just helped the police.' She paused. 'She hasn't actually moved in, has she?'

'Not for want of trying!' said Trisha with a laugh. 'No, she's still got her nice little place in your village.'

'Let's hope she stays there, then,' said Libby. 'She looks after Ricky's dog while he's at uni, so she can't really move here while she does that, can she?'

'He's a lovely boy, isn't he?' Trisha peered into the minibus.

'Ricky or Barney?' asked Libby.

'Both.' Trish gave her a good-natured grin. 'Well, have a good trip back, and let me know when you're coming over again and I'll come

16

and meet you for a quieter drink.' She stepped back and Libby climbed in to take a seat.

'What was all that about?' asked Fran from behind her.

Libby explained. 'So we'll have to call her when we go over to see the barn,' she concluded. 'We can have a drink afterwards.'

'We'll be driving,' said Fran with a sniff. 'Or I will, at least. You can buy me lunch.'

Libby smiled. 'It's a deal,' she said.

Chapter Three

'Well, it won't be lunch,' Libby told Fran on the phone on Wednesday morning. 'Ben just called. Apparently Fay's invited us over this afternoon. So I wondered if you'd like to stay to dinner and come to the pub this evening?'

'I'd say yes, but Guy would want to come too, which means two cars and no one can drink.' Fran sounded unusually petulant. Libby sighed.

'There's nobody in the spare room at the moment, so stay over – if Balzac can spare you.'

Balzac was Fran's black and white long-haired cat.

'Of course he can. And I didn't mean to sound – well, miffed.'

Libby laughed. 'Apology accepted. I shall have to do an hour with *Contraband* before we go to the pub – is that OK?'

'Of course, as long as I can come and watch.'

Libby went to tell Ben at the brewery.

'And did you know,' she said, 'National Shakespeare have asked if they can book the Glover's Men in for *Merry Wives* later in the year.'

The Glover's Men were an all-male company of actors recreating Shakespeare's works as they were originally performed, and had had notable successes when they played at the Oast Theatre.

'At this rate we ought to charge them an annual rent,' said Ben, climbing down from the top of the shiny mash tun. 'They're already bringing the *Dream* in a couple of weeks.'

'Oh, come on, they're no trouble,' said Libby. 'And if it introduces people to our theatre, it's a bonus. Do you know how many people who came to see *Woman in Mind* said they came because they'd seen *Much Ado* last year?'

'Your most recent triumph, my love,' said Ben, patting her on the shoulder.

Libby looked at her feet. 'I wasn't too bad, was I?' She had played the lead in the famous play and was still slightly amazed at her own success.

'No false modesty, please,' said Ben, shrugging off his brown overall. 'So we're hosting the Nethergate waifs and strays this evening, then?'

'I thought you'd be pleased to have a drinking companion,' said Libby, as they left the brewery and made for the Manor and Ben's office.

'I had several drinking partners last night,' said Ben, 'and I usually have several on a Wednesday, too.'

'Don't quibble,' said Libby. 'Are you staying here for lunch?'

'Yes, Mum's done sandwiches. Want some?'

'No, I'll go back – I've got to put something in the slow cooker for tonight, as I don't know how long Fran and I will be over at Shittenden.'

'So where exactly is this barn?' asked Fran, as she turned down the lane that led to the Fox and Hounds. 'Didn't Fay give Ben a postcode?'

'No. She just said keep on past the pub and we'll come to it.' Libby peered through the windscreen. 'And frankly, as I keep saying, I'm not sure what we hope to find out by coming here.' She looked back at her friend. 'Or what you needed to know the name of the boat for, come to that.'

'To find out if anyone knew anything about it, I told you.'

'I know, and you said you'd asked George and Bert.'

George took his boat, the *Dolphin*, chugging round the uninhabited island in the centre of Nethergate Bay every other day, and Bert took the *Sparkler* to the little cove round the point. The next day they changed over. Tourists asked them if they didn't get bored doing the same thing all summer from Easter to September, but they just shrugged and smiled. The sea was always different, they said, the people were always different, and the weather – well, the weather could be even more different.

'And they did know it, I told you,' said Fran, sounding exasperated.

'And they'd seen it?' prompted Libby.

'Oh, for goodness' sake! I told you almost as soon as you got in the car! Yes! Bert saw her going past the St Aldeberge Cut last week.'

'What was Bert doing all the way over there?' asked Libby.

'They're taking trips all along the coast this season, not just round the bay. And George said he'd seen her moored at the cove a couple of times.'

'Hmm.' Libby returned her gaze to the front. 'That's suspicious. Landing the goods in a quiet little cove, would you say?'

'I don't know, Lib. And look – there's the barn.'

'Well,' said Libby, peering. 'It's *a* barn, anyway.'

Standing completely on its own in a flat landscape, the traditional barn, with its boarded exterior and steeply hipped roof, looked rather sad. Fran pulled up in front of it, on a partially gravelled surface.

'Well, it looks as if we're on our own,' said Libby, climbing out of the Smart car.

'There's a van round the side,' said Fran, joining her. 'Shall we go in?'

But before they had gone a step further, Fay appeared from behind the van.

'Didn't want to go inside on my own,' she muttered. 'Haven't been in since – well. You know.'

'A couple of our friends have seen the *Jan Bishop*,' said Fran, as Fay tried to fit a key into the large padlock securing the big double doors. 'But not since a couple of weeks ago.'

'Oh, where?' Fay turned to look at her.

20

'Near St Aldeberge, and Nethergate Bay.'

'He moors up at Nethergate sometimes.' She shrugged, and pushed at the doors, which gave a protesting shriek. 'Don't know what he was doing at the other place, though.'

Finally, with all three women adding their weight to the doors, one of them finally opened.

'Here we are then,' said Fay. 'Help yourselves. I'll stay here, if you don't mind.'

She pulled out a battered chair and sat down at the small table obviously doing duty as a sort of reception area by the doors.

'Is there any lighting?' asked Libby. 'Only it's a bit difficult to see.'

'Nothing much *to* see,' said Fay, with another shrug.

Libby and Fran looked at one another, then went to the other door and managed to pull it open.

'Bit better,' said Libby quietly. 'Do you think she didn't want us to see properly?'

'She wouldn't have agreed to us coming if that was the case,' Fran replied, peering at a pile of what looked like logs.

'Hmm,' said Libby.

In fact, there was very little to interest anybody as far as the friends could see. Kitchen paraphernalia, a few metal advertising hoardings, stone garden ornaments, a horse trough and, further back, a selection of what could possibly be Victorian furniture.

'What's back there, Fay?' called Fran, indicating what looked like old stalls.

'Nothing much. Used to keep tools and such there. You know, for repairs. You don't want to bother about them.' Fay dismissed them with yet another shrug.

Fran raised her eyebrows and looked at Libby.

'I think she's right. We don't want to bother with them.' Libby stepped towards the doors. 'I don't think there's anything to find out, frankly.'

'I'll just have a quick look,' said Fran. 'You never know.'

Libby turned back with a sigh, and saw Fran stop. There was a long pause.

'Libby,' she said quietly. 'Call the police.'

And Libby knew.

'What?' Fay was on her feet, lumbering towards them. 'Police?'

'Police,' Libby was saying into her phone. 'A body. A barn near Shittenden.'

Fay tried to snatch the phone, but Libby stepped out of reach behind a large table.

'Yes,' she continued, grabbing hold of a distinctly wobbly Fran and forcing her onto a dilapidated iron bench. 'Near the Fox and Hounds.' She moved the phone away from her ear and spoke quietly to the other two women. 'I have to stay on the line,' she explained. 'Fay, do you want to take Fran outside?'

'Are you mad?' hissed Fay, once more making a grab for the phone. 'We ain't paid duty on none o' that stuff.' Her accent had slipped, Libby noticed. She cast a wild, panicked look beyond Fran.

'Is it your husband?' Fran asked, making an effort to sound normal. 'Aren't you worried?'

Fay paused, looking confused. 'Malc?'

'Your husband,' reiterated Fran.

Fay suddenly seemed to understand, and without warning slumped heavily onto the bench beside Fran. 'Can't be,' she whispered. 'He went off in the boat.'

'Yes, I'm still here,' said Libby into the phone. 'Shall I do anything?'

Fran stood up and took Fay's arm.

'Come on,' she said. 'Let's go outside.'

The police operator was still talking, although Libby had ceased to take any notice. Suddenly, the voice stopped and someone else took over.

'Is that Mrs Sarjeant?' asked a light female voice.

'Er – yes?'

'I don't know if you remember me, Mrs Sarjeant, my name's Clare Stone.'

'Oh! DS Stone! Of course I remember!' Libby felt a wave of relief wash over her.

'You've found a body, I gather?'

'Er – yes,' said Libby again.

'Oh dear! Well, don't worry, someone's on their way to you – Shittenden, wasn't it? – and the message has been passed up the line to DCI Connell.' DS Stone sounded quite cheerful.

'Oh, OK,' said Libby. 'Um – nice to hear from you.'

And that was singularly inappropriate, she said to herself as she ended the call.

She made her way between various piles of junk and arrived outside the barn almost at the same time as two police cars drew up. Fay was leaning against the wall and Fran was taking deep breaths.

The next ten minutes were a confused jumble of questions, overt suspicion and anger. The officers could not understand why Libby and Fran had been looking in the barn and were alternately suspicious of them and of Fay, who was furious. Both Libby and Fran realised that as soon as a more senior officer arrived things would be sorted out, and wasted a good deal of energy trying to calm Fay down.

'Another reason why we should give up this whole investigation business,' muttered Fran, as they perched on a sagging wooden bench and watched Fay arguing with an officer who was trying desperately to keep her temper.

'And Ian knows,' Libby muttered back.

'So we'll get told off,' said Fran with a sigh.

'Remind me again – why did we want to look in this barn?' asked Libby, watching as Fay was ushered into the back of one of the police cars. 'They're not arresting her, are they?'

'No, they're just making her comfortable.'

'They're not doing that with us,' grumbled Libby.

'It's not our husband lying in there, is it?' said Fran, going rather pale again.

'Was it horrible?' Libby slid her a nervous look.

23

'Yes!' snapped Fran. 'Shut up.'

Libby shut up.

Eventually one of the officers came over to them with a friendly smile.

'Acting DI Stone says she knows you.' He looked from one to the other. 'Which one's Fran and which one's Libby?'

They introduced themselves.

'We did give our names to that other officer,' said Libby. 'Acting DI now, is she? Wow! Good for her.'

'Yes, she is, and she'll be along soon, with all the rest of the circus. I gather you know a bit about police investigations?'

'Yes,' said Libby, 'although we don't usually find bodies.'

'And I would rather not do it again,' said Fran, somewhat shakily.

'Would you like to sit in one of the cars?' The officer looked concerned. 'I'm sorry we can't let you go yet.'

'I don't think I could drive anyway,' said Fran.

Libby cast her another worried glance. Fran gave her a weak smile.

'Don't worry – I'm not going to keel over.'

The arrival of several other vehicles signalled an escalation of activity, and the friendly officer scurried off to join in. Within a minute or two, a tall redhead with enviably long legs hurried over to them, accompanied by a schoolboy in long trousers.

'Hello, Libby, Fran! How are you? Silly question, I suppose!' Clare Stone gave them a rueful grin. 'This is DC Bodie.'

Libby and Fran murmured hello.

'So what happened here exactly? And can you tell me anything about the background?' Clare asked. DC Bodie took out a tablet and prepared to take notes. 'I can record it if you like,' Clare said, 'but I prefer to leave that for the interview room.'

Libby frowned. 'Have we got to go to the station?'

'I doubt it.' Clare grinned. 'Just give me the basics.'

This wouldn't have taken very long had Libby not got entangled in details of the last case.

'That really isn't relevant, Lib,' said Fran eventually, exasperated, and gave Clare a precis of events since the reopening of the Fox and Hounds. 'And we'll have to do it all over again now anyway.'

'Why?' said Clare and Libby together.

'Because I'm here,' said DCI Connell.

Chapter Four

Libby was interested to note that Acting DI Stone did not look over-joyed to see DCI Connell, despite the faint pink that crept into her cheeks. DC Bodie melted away.

'Hello, Ian,' said Fran. 'What are you doing here?'

Ian's satanic eyebrows leapt up into his hairline.

'What?'

'He's MIT,' said Clare in slightly strangled tones.

'Yes.' Libby eyed him curiously. 'But not on the ground, we thought.'

Ian gave an exasperated sigh. 'You know perfectly well that as soon as I saw either of your names I would attend. And in this case – both of your names.' He turned to Clare. 'I'm sorry, DI Stone. I don't mean to interfere.'

This time both Libby and Fran's eyebrows shot up in surprise.

'No problem, sir,' said Clare, clearing her throat and looking at the floor.

'So what are you doing here?' Ian looked first at Fran, then at Libby. 'Presumably you were invited here?'

'Yes,' said Libby. 'The lady over there, Fay Hodges, asked me – us – to look into her husband's disappearance. He'd gone out on his boat, apparently.'

'So why look in a barn?'

'We thought we might find something that would help. This is his business.' Fran gave Ian a weak smile.

'Junk?' Ian's mouth twitched in an answering smile.

'Antiques, please!' corrected Libby.

'How did you meet this lady?' asked Ian.

Clare Stone uttered an audible grunt of protest. Ian turned back to her.

'Sorry, Clare. Shall I leave you to it?'

She sighed. 'No – carry on, sir. I'll go and talk to Mrs Hodges.'

She turned and stalked off to the car where Fay drooped unhappily in the back.

'You've upset her,' said Libby.

'I know.' Ian scowled at her. 'No need to point it out.'

'Well, to satisfy your curiosity,' said Fran, 'Ben introduced us to someone called Wallace Mayberry . . .'

'Of Beer and Bargains,' put in Libby helpfully.

'. . . and he told us about Fay, and Stan from the Fox and Hounds introduced her. She told us about her husband, Malcolm.'

'Who had gone missing on his boat?'

'Yes,' said Libby. 'He's an antiques dealer.'

'At the lower end of the market, I gather,' said Ian, casting a quick look into the barn, where various figures could be seen milling around in the gloom. 'I still don't see why you came here if she said he'd gone missing on his boat.'

'I thought it might help,' muttered Fran.

'Ah.' Ian nodded slowly. 'I see.'

Occasionally Fran had been known to have the odd 'moment', as her friends called them, where she seemed to know something outside of her own experience. The police had made use of this on occasion.

'No, I didn't see anything,' she said. 'Just felt . . . I don't know, that I should look.'

'And you were right,' said Ian. 'As I understand it, you actually found the body. Are you all right?'

Fran gave him another weak smile. 'I will be.'

Ian looked round the yard. 'Have you got your car?'

'Yes – it's hidden behind the Forensics van,' said Libby.

'Come on, then. I'll take you home,' said Ian.

'You can't do that!' gasped Fran. 'We're supposed to stay here. And it's Clare's crime scene.'

'I shall leave that entirely to her,' said Ian with a grin. 'But I *am* the boss, and I shall take you both home.'

'What about my car?' Fran stood up.

'One of the officers can drive it home. Guy wouldn't want you to be driving after you've had such a shock.' Ian held out an arm to usher them both forward. Neither of them moved.

'I'll drive Fran's car home,' announced Libby. 'If Clare lets us go, of course.'

Fran nodded. Ian looked bewildered. Libby marched past him to where Clare stood beside the patrol car.

'Clare – I mean, DI Stone – DCI Connell says we can go. I thought we ought to ask you. I'll drive Fran's car.'

Clare stifled an involuntary giggle.

'I bet he didn't like that!' she said. 'Yes, of course you can go. We know where you both live, and we can always send someone to take statements.'

Libby beamed at her and went back to Fran.

'Clare says we can go,' she told Ian. 'She'll make sure statements are taken.'

Ian stood quite still, looking astonished, before bursting out laughing, laughter that he quickly suppressed.

'Sorry, inappropriate,' he said. 'Right. Perhaps I'll see you both this evening?'

'Me, probably,' said Libby. 'I doubt Fran will want to come.'

'Right.' He smiled at them both and stood back. 'See you when I see you, Fran.'

The two women made their way to Fran's little Smart car, followed by curious looks from officers and technicians.

'Am I insured to drive this?' Libby murmured as Fran passed her the keys.

'Yes – you and Guy are both named drivers.' Fran sighed. 'I could have done without this.'

Libby unlocked the car and gave her an old-fashioned look. 'So could we all, dear.'

Fran shook her head and opened the passenger door. 'I know. And it's my own bloody fault.'

Libby climbed in beside her and peered at the controls. 'How do you make that out? You didn't kill the man.'

'I suggested asking about the boat, didn't I?'

'That's got nothing to do with it,' said Libby. 'And it was Ben who suggested coming to look at the barn. He's going to be right teed off.' She grinned. 'He won't be able to tell us off this time.'

As Libby drove very carefully back towards Nethergate, Fran called Ben and asked him to come and fetch Libby from Coastguard Cottage.

'You were right,' she said to Libby after she'd ended the call. 'He wasn't happy.'

'But with himself, not us?' said Libby.

'Sounded like it.' Fran smiled wearily. 'I should have driven really.'

'Don't be daft.' Libby gave her a quick sideways grin. 'It's not often I get the chance to do something for you. Anyway, I wanted to ask you what you thought about the Crooked Horse.'

'Eh?' Fran looked startled.

'You know – that pub that burnt down.'

'Oh, yes. Why?'

'I told you it's an antiques pub, didn't I? Well, in case you need reminding . . .' She launched into the tale of the Crooked Horse. 'So, I wondered if it had anything to do with Malcolm Hodges.'

'Why would it?' Fran frowned out of the windscreen.

'Well, Stan said it was used by the antiques boys. It was him who linked them up. And now Malcolm's dead.'

★

29

Ben collected Libby from Coastguard Cottage, where they left Fran being tended by her slightly bemused husband.

'I cancelled your *Contraband* rehearsal – I hope you don't mind. Would you like to join Patti and Anne at Hal's tonight instead of cooking?' asked Ben, as he turned up Nethergate's steep high street.

Libby's friend Patti Pearson, vicar of St Aldeberge, a village on the coast, came to Steeple Martin every Wednesday, her day off, to visit her friend and partner Anne Douglas. They always had dinner in the Pink Geranium and joined Libby and Ben in the Coach and Horses afterwards.

'I don't think so,' said Libby. 'I'll only have to repeat the whole story all over again in the Coach. I'd sooner eat at home and go down a bit later.'

'OK,' said Ben, sounding surprised. 'Are you sure you're all right?'

She gave him a rueful smile. 'Bit shocked, if I'm honest. Think I need a couple of hours' rest.'

Ben drove the rest of the way home very carefully.

Libby and Ben arrived at the Coach and Horses later that evening to find various friends already at the round table in the small bar. Edward Hall, tall, elegant and black, stood up immediately.

'Sit down,' he said, bestowing on them his wide white smile. 'I'll get the drinks. You've had quite a day, I understand.'

Patti and Anne manoeuvred Anne's wheelchair aside to make room at the table and Peter leant over to give Libby a kiss on the cheek.

'You OK, petal?'

'Yes, I'm all right, Pete.' Libby smiled round at everyone. 'I take it you all know what's happened.'

'You know,' said old Richard Brandon, one of the most recent residents of Steeple Martin, 'I don't think I really believed there would be any more murders.' He looked at the others present for confirmation. 'Did you? Any of you? I mean, the first one I knew about was when the pantomime cat got murdered, and I thought that was a once-in-a-lifetime event!'

'And then you made the mistake of joining the cast of this year's panto,' said Libby. 'I'm surprised you didn't turn tail and run!'

Brandon beamed comfortably. 'I told you – I haven't been so happy in years. My cottage is perfect, and I've got some real friends. And you'll solve all the murders, so what could be better?'

Everyone laughed.

'Well,' said Anne, '*you* have to help solve the murders too, you know that. We all do.'

Edward returned with a tray of drinks. 'Ian says he'll pop in if he has time,' he said, putting Libby's glass in front of her.

'Oh good.' Libby pulled a face. 'I don't think he was too happy with us earlier.'

'He didn't give me that impression.' Edward raised an eyebrow. 'And I think he was quite pleased to see Clare Stone.'

There was a murmur of interest round the table.

'A detective sergeant we met briefly before and now an acting DI, like our Rachel,' explained Libby.

Brandon looked confused. Libby smiled at him. 'I'll explain later,' she said, just as the street door burst open.

'Well blow me down with a sausage,' said Harry, entering with a flourish, followed by Ian. 'You've done it again, dear heart. I said, didn't I? When we went on our Loonies outing? I asked if we going to play hunt the murderer.'

Ian went straight to the bar, shaking his head.

'Shut up, Hal,' said Peter. 'Not helpful.'

Harry stood still, looking at Libby's unnaturally pale face.

'Oh bugger,' he said. 'I'm sorry, petal.' He pushed round to the back of her chair and bent down to kiss her. 'I'm a thoughtless sod.'

'Never mind, Hal.' Libby patted his arm. 'You were quite right.'

Chairs were fetched and room made for Ian and Harry.

'Nothing to ask, Anne?' Ian lifted his glass to her.

Anne went a faint shade of pink. 'All right, I'm nosy,' she said. 'Sorry.'

31

'She's not the only one.' Libby smiled at her friend. 'I am too, which is why I get into these scrapes.'

'I wouldn't call finding a dead body a scrape, exactly,' said Ian.

'And we know all about it anyway,' said Patti. 'Edward told us before Libby and Ben came in.'

'And we won't ask if there's any more news,' said Ben, 'so you can have a nice relaxed drink.'

'That'll be the day,' said Ian. 'Cheers.'

A slightly awkward silence fell.

Libby shifted in her seat and cleared her throat. 'What do you know about the Crooked Horse, Ian?' she asked a little desperately.

He sighed and gave her an unreadable look. 'What do *you* know about it?'

'What's the Crooked Horse?' asked Brandon.

'It's a pub, isn't it?' said Harry.

'It was,' said Ian.

'Was?' asked Anne.

Patti, Ben and Peter sighed.

'Here we go again,' muttered Ben.

'Just tell me why you had to bring that up as a change of subject?' Ian glared at Libby.

'I couldn't think of anything else,' she mumbled. 'Sorry.'

'It's a pub and it burnt down,' said Peter. 'No mystery. Is there, Ian?'

Chapter Five

'Yes, it's a pub, and it burned down.' Ian picked up his glass and stared at the contents.

Libby frowned at him. 'Great shame,' she said. 'Nice old pub, apparently.' She stood up. 'Anybody ready for another drink?'

Ben and Peter, acknowledging another brave attempt to change the subject, stood up too and began collecting glasses.

'Nicely diverted,' Ian said quietly to Libby as she sat down again. 'I take it you know something about it?'

'Only a little,' said Libby warily.

'I'll ring you tomorrow.' He looked up and accepted a fresh drink. 'Thanks, Ben.'

Thursday morning Libby spent on the phone explaining and apologising to her *Contraband* cast and waiting for Ian to ring, which he did, finally, at almost midday.

'What do you know about it, then?' he asked, after pleasantries had been exchanged.

Libby repeated what Lewis had told her, and why.

'So we blame George at the Red Lion, do we?' She heard Ian chuckle. 'And we blame Stan at the Fox and Hounds for your interest in Malcolm Hodges. What is it about you and pubs?'

'I don't know.' Libby frowned at Sidney the silver tabby, who was stretched out beside her. 'They're such a good source of gossip, I suppose.' She thought for a moment. 'When you come to think about it, all the pubs I know I've originally been in to ask for information or directions. Except the Coach.'

She heard Ian sigh. 'And I've even taken you myself. So go on, tell me what you know.'

Suppressing the urge to ask him why, Libby obliged.

'And then when we found out it was an antiques pub, we thought of Malcolm Hodges,' she concluded.

'Antiques pub?'

'The – er – antiques boys used it,' said Libby, feeling uncomfortable.

'It's all right, we know about the so-called antiques boys. I'm afraid we've been leaving it to HM Revenue and Customs to chase them up. It really doesn't seem to be worth wasting resources on missing duty on questionable antiques.' Ian sighed again. 'What we're more concerned with is the attempt to knock the building down.'

'Surely that's the council's problem, isn't it?' asked Libby.

'Of course. Unless there's a secondary motive.'

'Eh?'

'For a start,' said Ian, 'we can't find out exactly who gave the order to demolish it. We assumed at first that it was the new owners, but we then found out Marsham's had put a stop on the sale because the owners were planning to sell it on to the developers. But the developers are denying any involvement.'

'Yes, that's what Lewis said.'

'But . . .' Ian paused for effect, 'suppose it was to be demolished to prevent something being discovered in the building?'

'Like . . . Oh.' Libby stopped in surprise. 'You mean like a body?'

'Possibly.'

She fell silent.

'Come on, Lib. Surely you've got something else to say?' She could hear the smile in Ian's voice.

'To be honest,' she said slowly, 'it sounds more like one of my flights of fancy.'

Now he laughed out loud. 'And that's exactly why I wanted to know what you'd heard! I was surprised you hadn't come up with the same idea.'

'Oh. Bloody hell, I'm a nuisance, aren't I?'

'Sometimes, yes,' agreed Ian, 'but actually this is a theory we are working on, and I wanted to know what the general public thought about it.'

'Ah.' Libby paused again. 'So what you're asking me is . . .?'

'To do your well-known pub crawl in search of opinion and evidence. Of course.'

Now Libby laughed. 'You've got a cheek, Connell! And I thought you were MIT — surely the possible demolition of a pub doesn't come under your remit?'

'But if there's a body . . .'

'So are you actually agreeing with me that Malcolm Hodges' death might be connected with the pub?'

'It's not beyond the bounds of possibility, is it? But I wouldn't get sanction to link it as things stand. Yes, his death will be investigated by MIT, with Acting DI Stone and Sergeant Riley on the ground, but in order to get a warrant to search the remains of the Crooked Horse, I need a bit more evidence.'

Libby sighed. 'You do know I've got a play to rehearse, don't you? And it's the start of the season, so I'm supposed to be looking after the Huts.'

'Yes, I do know, Libby. I also know that nothing's stopped you interfering — oh, sorry — *investigating* before.'

'Hmm,' said Libby. 'And you'll get told off by the powers-that-be — *again* — for involving me and Fran, I suppose?'

'If I could put you on the payroll, I would,' confessed Ian. 'We're still being investigated ourselves, you know. If I didn't think it would look suspicious, I'd leave the service and set up on my own.'

Libby was shocked into silence.

'Well, say something!' Ian sounded irritated.

'I just can't believe you said that.'

'I can't believe I've been driven to even thinking about it,' he grunted.

'All right,' Libby said eventually, 'of course I'll ask around. You knew I would anyway, didn't you?'

'Let's say I hoped.' The smile was back in Ian's voice. 'You said it was George's suggestion that you looked into it?'

'His and Lewis's. I'll go down to the Red Lion this afternoon. And ask Fran if she'll come too.'

Fran, unsurprisingly, was not keen to accompany Libby on today's fact-finding mission.

'We're not going to find a dead body in the Red Lion,' protested Libby.

'But you're going to get involved,' said Fran, 'and quite frankly, I don't want anything to do with it.'

'What – *nothing*?'

'Exactly. Tell me when you're coming to Nethergate and you can have a cup of tea and tell me all about it. Otherwise – no.'

So Libby arrived at the Red Lion in Heronsbourne alone, shortly after two o'clock. Two elderly couples sat at tables near the windows and one solitary man pored over a newspaper at the bar. George slipped off a stool and came towards her.

'This is a surprise,' he said. 'If you want Kayleigh, she's not here.'

'No, it's you I want to speak to,' said Libby, climbing inelegantly onto a bar stool of her own. 'Kayleigh's not needed at lunchtime, I suppose?'

George grinned broadly. 'No – she's left.'

'Left?'

'I said we'd never keep her, didn't I? Well, we haven't. Going to uni, she is!'

'Uni? Gosh!' George's former barmaid had always struck Libby as being bright, but this was a surprise.

'It's your mate Edward's fault.' George gestured towards his under-used coffee machine. Libby shook her head. 'He started coming in here with Alice and they got talking.'

Edward was a lecturer at Kent University and spent a good deal of his free time with his girlfriend, Alice, a sheep farmer on Heronsbourne Flats.

'Is she going to read history?' Somehow Kayleigh didn't strike Libby as history material.

'Fashion and design,' said George with a grin. 'Got a name for it where Edward works, apparently.'

'University of the Creative Arts, yes,' said Libby. 'Well, good for her.'

'So what do you want to talk to me about? And if you don't want coffee, do you want a nice cuppa? I can put the kettle on.'

'No, I won't, George, thank you. I shall go and have one with Fran after I've talked to you.'

George heaved himself back onto his stool. 'Go on, then.'

'The Crooked Horse.' Libby raised an eyebrow at him. 'You told Lewis you thought I should look into it.'

'Well, of course!' George looked surprised. 'After all the Marsham's business – stands to reason. Could be part of the same thing, couldn't it?'

'It could, but what about the houses? The ones the developers want to put up?'

'All part of the same thing,' said George.

'No, I don't think so,' said Libby. 'No one wants those houses built there – it's right next to the nature reserve, and while the pub was still standing, there was no hope of planning permission.'

'Yeah, I know.' George shrugged. 'But we do need houses.'

'Yes, but not there,' said Libby, who had done a whistlestop online tour of all available information on the prospective building site, 'and not those sort of houses.'

'Oh?'

'Think about it, George. Miles from a town, or even a village, no public transport, no infrastructure of any sort and only executive homes. No affordable or social housing – heaven forbid!'

'So it's not just the "not in my backyard" crowd, then?'

'No – and think about it. The pub was crooked because of the unstable ground.'

'From mining, yeah.'

'And it's on a marsh. You know how unstable the land is round here? Well, it's the same over there. Why on earth they thought it would be a good idea to build there beats me.'

George frowned. 'Don't look like they'd've got planning permission anyway, then?'

'I don't like to cast aspersions, but I suspect a few brown envelopes would have been circulating, don't you?'

'Ah!' George slid off his stool. 'Well, I'm going to have a drink, even if you aren't.' He took a glass from the shelf above the bar and poured himself a half-pint of Ben's Best Bitter. 'Doing well, this is,' he said with a wink. 'So you reckon the old Horse was fired to clear the way?'

'And then when it didn't burn down completely, they sent in the diggers.'

'So it's the new owners who did it?' George was frowning again.

'No idea, but Marsham's had stopped the sale,' said Libby, 'because the word is – and you know this, George – the new owners had been going to sell it on to the developers.'

George nodded. 'Couple from London, apparently. Don't know much about them.'

'Who would know?' asked Libby.

'Marsham's, of course.'

'They'd never tell me.'

'Your Ian could find out.'

'Yes.' Libby looked down at her hands.

'And you don't want to ask him?' George laughed and tapped the side of his nose. 'Doing it on the QT again, are we?'

Libby smiled. Easier to let him think Ian knew nothing about her investigation.

'What about the Gate at Felling?' he said. 'I bet Zack knows, even if he isn't a Marsham's landlord. He knows most of what's going on.'

'Oh yes! What a good idea, George!' Libby beamed at him.

'Full of 'em, me.' George beamed back. 'And I bet he knows about the antiques boys, as well.'

Libby's mouth fell open.

George raised his eyebrows. 'Well, we've all been wondering about that, haven't we?'

'Have we?'

'Come on, Lib! You know about them. Straight up from the sea. Land where those people-smugglers landed – everybody knows that.'

'Actually, I didn't until just this week,' admitted Libby.

'Oh, ah. Hodges.'

'You heard?'

'Course. 'Spect it's on the news, but we've got WhatsApp.' George looked faintly proud of himself.

'Course you have,' said Libby with a sigh.

'Well, old Zack'll know about the antiques boys as well, so you might as well go and see him, eh?' George took a healthy swallow of his beer. 'And ask him when he's going to host the quiz night while you're at it!'

The pubs in their area of Kent had formed their own games league, and the Gate was notorious for only ever hosting bat-and-trap games.

'I will.' Libby slid off her stool and smiled. 'Thanks, George. I'll go and see Fran now. And send my love to Kayleigh if you speak to her.'

Libby was thoughtful as she drove from Heronsbourne to Nethergate. She hadn't learnt much that was new, other than the information that the local publicans had a WhatsApp group, and even they had linked the antiques boys, in a nebulous fashion, to the fate of the Crooked Horse.

'I thought you were going to ring me first?' said Fran, when Libby arrived at Guy's gallery.

'I forgot,' said Libby.

'Go on, go home,' shouted Guy from his studio at the back. 'But put the kettle on first.'

Fran cast her eyes to heaven but did as she was told, and the two women left to walk down Harbour Street to Coastguard Cottage. Libby began explaining what she'd learnt from George, and continued while Fran made tea.

'So there you are,' she said, settling in the window seat with Balzac the black and white cat on her lap. 'What do you think?'

'I think you ought to take Ben over to see Zack at the Gate and then turn the whole thing back to Ian,' said Fran, handing her a mug.

'But I told you, he can't investigate—'

'Without evidence. Yes, I know.' Fran sat down beside the fireplace. 'And he's placing you in danger trying to find it.'

Chapter Six

Libby stared at her friend.

'Danger?' she repeated eventually.

Fran nodded, gazing into the fire.

'And you have come to this conclusion – how?'

Fran heaved a sigh. 'You've done all the research for *Contraband*, haven't you?'

'What's that got to do with anything?'

'The smugglers turned to wholesale murder in order to protect their livelihoods, didn't they?'

'Yes, but as Ian said, these smugglers are only depriving the government of a small amount of duty, nothing like the seventeenth-century lot.' Libby frowned. 'What aren't you telling me?'

Fran looked up, all innocence. 'Nothing!'

'This isn't a "moment", then?'

She looked back at the fire. 'I don't think so.'

'You don't *think* so?' Libby repeated, exasperated. 'What does *that* mean?'

'I just think it's a dangerous enterprise.' Fran gave her a half smile. 'I'm pretty sure Hodges' death is to do with smuggling.'

'Well – duh!'

'Yes, I know, but it's not just to do with him, is it? If he was just cheating someone in the business, I doubt they'd kill him. There's something bigger going on.'

Libby pondered for a long moment. 'And this is simple deduction, is it?'

'Yes. Nothing more.'

'But Ian doesn't want me to look into the murder,' said Libby after a minute. 'He just wants information about the fire and the attempted demolition. And any connection there might be.'

'And how are you going to find that out?' asked Fran. 'You've asked George, and you're going to ask Zack. There isn't anything else you can do without digging really deep and . . .' She stopped.

'It *is* a moment,' stated Libby. 'Otherwise you wouldn't mind.'

Fran put her mug down on the hearth beside her. 'Honestly, Lib, I don't know. And I really don't know if the two cases are linked. It's just such a coincidence.'

'Yes, that's what Ian thinks,' agreed Libby. She shifted, and earned herself a glare from Balzac. 'Look, I'll go and see Zack, and if I find anything out, I'll tell Ian and leave it at that, OK?'

Fran nodded and frowned. 'But what about the boat?' she said.

'The boat?'

'Yes. Hodges' boat.'

'But he wasn't on the boat – he was in the barn,' said Libby.

'Fay thought he was.'

'What was it called?' Libby asked.

'The *Jan Bishop*.' Fran stood up abruptly. 'Come on, let's go and ask Bert and the other George. I told you they'd both seen it, didn't I?'

Libby scrambled to her feet, dislodging Balzac. 'They might be out.'

'They might not. We can always leave a message with Mavis.'

Mavis owned the little café, the Blue Anchor, at the end of Harbour Street, beside the Sloop pub.

'Five minutes ago you were telling me not to get involved because it was dangerous,' Libby grumbled, taking her mug into the kitchen. 'What happened?'

Fran collected her keys and smiled over her shoulder.

'I don't know,' she said. 'I never do, do I?'

*

42

Bert and the other George sat outside the Blue Anchor, their tourist boats, the *Dolphin* and the *Sparkler*, rocking gently at anchor beside the jetty.

'No trips today?' asked Libby, as she and Fran approached.

'Teatime,' said Bert laconically.

'Going out this evening,' said George. 'You wanting to go out?'

'No thanks,' said Fran. 'We wanted to know if you can tell us anything more about the *Jan Bishop*.'

Bert and George both looked up, startled.

'What do you want to know for?' asked Bert, narrowing his eyes.

'You do, then,' said Libby. 'Where does she go out from?'

'Not here,' said George. 'We told you that, Fran.'

'You know her owner?' Fran sat down beside him.

'Might do.' He turned away, picking up his packet of cigarettes.

Libby and Fran exchanged looks.

'Seen the news?' asked Libby.

George and Bert both looked at her.

'Why?'

'Malcolm Hodges is dead,' said Fran.

'Murdered,' added Libby.

'Ah.' Bert stood up. ''Nother cup, George?'

George nodded, and Bert waddled off to the Blue Anchor.

'So Hodges is dead.' George scowled down at his unlit cigarette.

'Go on, George, you can light up. Don't mind us,' said Libby, ignoring Fran's disapproving face. 'What do you know about Hodges?'

'Antiques, ain't he?' muttered George. 'Like Wally Mayberry.'

'Beer and Bargains,' said Libby. 'Where is that exactly?'

'End of Marine Parade. Near where Skinner's Alley comes out.'

'And where did Hodges keep his boat?' asked Fran.

George cleared his throat noisily. 'Don't rightly know.'

'But presumably he tied up here sometimes?' suggested Libby.

'Might have done.' George stared over at his own boat. 'At night mostly.'

'Ah.' Libby nodded wisely.

Bert came back carrying two mugs.

'Did you want summat?' he asked the women, who shook their heads. He nodded and sat down. 'Now,' he said, 'the *Jan Bishop*. Told 'em anything, George?'

George shrugged.

'He said Hodges used to moor up here at night sometimes,' said Fran. 'Was he unloading?'

'Never said.'

'It was here up till last week,' said Bert. 'Then one morning it was gone. Told you, saw him at the cove and over at the St Aldeberge Cut.'

'I think we'll have to tell the police that,' said Libby.

Bert looked worried. 'Don't get us involved.'

'Nothing to get involved in,' said Fran. 'You didn't know what he was doing, did you?'

'Only he used to go and see Wally. Nothing else.' George stubbed out his cigarette in Mavis's tin ashtray. 'Whatever it was, wouldn't do it here. Too many people around.'

'He had a barn,' said Bert.

Libby frowned. 'But his barn was near Shittenden.'

'Used to moor up over that way,' said George. 'Near your mate.'

'Mate?' Libby frowned. 'Which mate.'

'The telly bloke.'

'Oh – near Creekmarsh?'

'That'll be on the creek,' said Fran. 'But the Crooked Horse is near Dunton, not Creekmarsh.'

'Ah.' Libby, Bert and George all nodded.

'Terrible thing, that,' said George.

'That's where you ought to look,' said Bert. 'Law-abiding folks we are, round here.'

'We know,' said Libby, grinning. 'And yes, I'm going over to talk to Zack at the Gate.'

'Felling.' George nodded again. 'Course, the old Horse was a Marsham's house, wasn't it?'

'Yes, but it's nothing to do with that,' said Libby firmly.

'So, you working with the police again?' asked Bert. 'They paying you yet?'

Libby gave an unconvincing laugh.

'Yes, she is, and no, they aren't,' said Fran, amused. 'Come on, Lib. Time we left these people to themselves.'

'Don't worry about us,' said Bert, opening his eyes wide. 'Glad to help.'

'Eventually,' muttered Libby, as they walked back towards Coast-guard Cottage.

'Any actual help, do you think?' asked Fran as she opened her front door.

'A bit,' said Libby. 'Do you think we should go and see Wally Mayberry?'

'No,' said Fran. 'I still think it's dangerous. But go and see Zack and let me know what happens.'

'I've forgotten – why am I going to see Zack?'

'*You* told *me!*' Fran shook her head. 'Honestly. You're supposed to be finding out what Zack knows about the Crooked Horse and the new owners.'

'Oh yes. And the antiques boys too, I suppose. It's a whole new world.'

'Pubs aren't,' said Fran.

Libby grinned. 'Certainly not!'

'Well,' said Ben later, when she told him about the day's events, 'I think I'll come with you to see Zack in the morning. There's nothing pressing for me to do at the brewery, and we've got no guests in the Huts yet.'

The Huts were a row of hoppers' huts, so called because they were erected to house the hop pickers who used to come down from London every year for the hop harvest in September until the late 1950s. In fact, it was how Hetty, Ben's mother, had met his father, Greg, who was the son of the estate owner. Now the Huts were let out as holiday

45

homes – a little basic, but Libby consoled herself with the fact that they were not in the least suitable for permanent residents.

She looked at Ben with a quizzically raised eyebrow.

'You're keen. You don't usually want to involve yourself.'

'Yes I do. Recently, anyway.' He carried his dinner plate to the kitchen table. 'I could hardly object to you getting involved with the homeless – or the sale of pubs, for that matter.'

'True. And you came to see Zack with me last time, didn't you?'

'Yes, I did – and he said he was going to join the quiz league.'

'Well, he did at first,' said Libby.

'But he's never once hosted it,' objected Ben. 'George was right. I shall tackle him.'

Libby sat down at the table. 'So what is it this time? There's hardly a humanitarian crisis in this affair, is there?'

Ben shook his head. 'No, but I feel guilty. If I hadn't introduced you to Wally Mayberry—'

'Stop right there,' said Libby. 'Stan was the one who told Fay and Wally about me, not you. So it's not your fault.' She reached over and patted his hand. 'And I shall enjoy having you with me.'

Felling was a small town inland from St Aldeberge, at the head of a small, unnavigable creek leading from the St Aldeberge Cut, where smugglers of all shades had landed their craft in the past. A tunnel led from the cave there up to the Dunton House estate. Felling itself could only be reached by land through the Sand Gate, next to which stood the Gate Inn, in whose small car park Ben drew up on Friday morning.

Zack, the landlord, small, wiry and cheerful, was wiping down tables outside the pub and looked up with a surprised grin.

'Hello, hello!' he said, holding out a hand. 'To what do I owe this honour?'

'I've been told to find out why you haven't hosted a quiz night yet!' said Ben with a grin.

'And you came all this way just to ask me that?' Zack led the way inside. 'I don't believe you.'

46

'Quite right,' said Libby, sitting down at a table near the bar. 'I wanted to ask you about the Crooked Horse.'

Zack turned back, looking serious.

'Doing the police's work for them again?' he said.

'Why does everyone say that?' Libby asked.

'Because you are,' said Ben. 'Yes, Zack, she is. And no, she isn't getting paid.'

'I'm known for my way with publicans.' Libby smiled winningly.

Zack laughed. 'All right. What do you want to know and what do you want to drink?'

'I don't suppose you do tea?' said Libby. 'Bit early for alcohol.'

'I'll make you a tea,' said Zack. 'How do you take it?'

'Dash of milk, no sugar, please.' Libby beamed at him.

'I'll have one too, please, Zack,' said Ben. 'Save boiling the kettle for one.'

'Come on then,' said Zack five minutes later, having placed two thick white mugs full of dark brown tea on the table between them. 'What do you want to know about the Horse?'

'Well,' began Libby, 'we know it was a Marsham's house, and it was going to be sold. We don't know if it was part of the great sale of last year, and we don't know who bought it, but we'd like to.'

Zack stared thoughtfully at the table. 'I can only go on gossip,' he said slowly. 'You realise that?'

'And possibly from your friend at the Shipwright's Arms?' suggested Libby.

'You remembered,' said Zack with a grin.

The Shipwright's Arms was a former pub, also in Felling, used by Marsham's Brewery, which stood on the creek in the town, as a sort of club-cum-conference-room. It was also used by the Felling Business Community Group, or FBCG, as a meeting place.

'The story is that the old Horse was losing money, so Marsham's sold it off, very quietly, earlier this year. They didn't want to rake up the scandal again.'

'Which had hardly died down by then, I would have thought,' said Libby.

'Exactly, so they kept the sale below the radar. Especially as there was a lot of ill feeling about it. Regulars were very unhappy.'

'How come it didn't get into the media?' asked Ben. 'Or social media, at least.'

'It did, but it was stamped on from a great height.' Zack shook his head sadly. 'Everyone thought there was something funny about it. And everyone at Marsham's denied knowing anything about it.'

'And the pub's near a nature reserve – is that right?' asked Libby.

'Do you know the Dunton estate?' Zack looked from Ben to Libby. 'You know it leads down to the cliffs?'

'Yes, and we know the Willoughby Oak, too,' said Libby.

'Right.' Zack nodded. 'Where there was all that black magic stuff a few years back?' He narrowed his eyes at her. 'You were involved in that, weren't you?'

She nodded. 'Don't remind me.'

'Well, the lane the Oak is on leads up parallel to the creek. Then there's the woods, and the marshes.'

'And a wire fence between the two,' said Ben.

'That's it. And then there's nothing. Except the Crooked Horse.' Zack smiled. 'Perfect for the antiques boys.'

Chapter Seven

'Yes, we wanted to know about these antiques boys,' said Libby. 'You heard Malcolm Hodges was found murdered in his barn at Shittenden?'

'Yes.' Zack nodded. 'Funny business.'

'What do you know about them?' asked Ben. 'As far as we're aware, they trade in low-end antiques – collectibles – and they bring a lot of them in from the Continent.'

'That's it. Come in here, a lot of them. But they all used to meet at the Horse. A bit of buying and selling, info exchanged – you know the sort of thing. But then Marsham's closed it down. No warning. Just put a notice up.'

'Blimey!' said Libby. 'And how long was that before the fire?'

'Dunno. Not long, anyway. Course, after the fire, there was an outcry. People wanted it restored – built back exactly as it was.' Zack pulled a face. 'But then the bloody digger arrived!'

'Yes, we heard, but it was stopped, wasn't it?' said Ben.

'Yeah. No one had permission, and no one admitted to giving the order. Someone said the police were looking at the developers. Don't know whether it was – whatjercallit – listed, but there was an order slapped on 'em. Police even came round here.'

'So is the digger still there?' asked Libby.

Zack shook his head. 'No. Police tape all round the building – what's left of it – but no police. Just a lot of notices.'

'And what do people think? The new owners were going to sell it on to developers, weren't they?' said Libby.

'That's the word. My mate at the Shipwright's says the Marsham's lot are furious.'

'They think it'll reflect on them,' said Ben. 'And it probably will. No sign of them selling out, I suppose? Marsham's, I mean.'

'Not so far as I've heard. Anyway, that's about it. Oh, except the developers. They were planning an estate of posh houses and trying to get permission to build on the nature reserve.' Zack laughed. 'As if! So what everybody reckons is they were going to knock down the old Horse and get permission to build there instead. There was quite a bit of land attached.'

Libby nodded. 'Makes sense. Are the new owners being prosecuted? And do you know who they are?'

Zack shrugged. 'Dunno. It wasn't them who sent in the digger, see – they said it was the developers. And the sale hadn't even gone through. I think they're being looked into.' He put his head on one side and frowned at Libby. 'So what's your interest?'

'We – er – just wanted to know . . .' she began, and tailed off.

'The police did, you mean?'

'In a way. Our friend wanted to know if there was a connection with Malcolm Hodges.' Ben patted Libby's hand. 'She gets dragged into these things.'

Zack laughed. 'Good job you know a lot of pubs, then. To be honest, I can't see that. We all reckon it was the new owners and the developers behind the fire and the digger. The antiques boys might be fed up because they've lost their meeting place, but that's all.'

Libby sat back in her seat and gazed into space.

'Uh-oh,' said Ben. 'I know that look.'

Zack cast him an enquiring glance. 'What?'

'She's thought of something,' said Ben. 'Lib?'

Libby looked at him and smiled. 'It's all right – I'm not plotting. I just wondered . . .'

'Wondered what?' asked Ben after a moment.

'Why did the antiques boys meet at the Horse in the first place? As we've established, there's nothing there. And it's all very well saying it's perfect for them coming up from the coast, but how? The creek up to Felling is unnavigable, and there's only that lane where the Willoughby Oak is. Does that carry on?'

Zack looked interested. 'That's a point. I've never thought about it before. It's just what people said – stuff was coming in from the Continent, being landed at the St Aldeberge Cut. But you're right – why?'

'And if that was what was happening and everyone knew about it, why hadn't the police, or customs or someone, raided them?' said Ben. He looked at his best beloved with admiration. 'You're right, Lib. Why?'

Libby gave them both a smug grin. 'And if that was the story going round and the antiques boys knew it, they were obviously happy to let it carry on. And are they always called that?'

'Yeah – I've never thought about that either!' Zack looked surprised. 'Do you want me to ask around? Some of the regulars might know a bit more.'

'Don't make it too obvious,' warned Ben.

'Nah! Just pub gossip, you know?' Zack tapped the side of his nose. 'Now, do you want to know how to get to the old Horse?'

'And the nature reserve,' said Libby. 'Yes, please.'

'Useful?' asked Ben as he drove back through the Sand Gate to the ring road and paused. 'Nethergate or back home?'

'Back home,' said Libby. 'And as we're going via Bishop's Bottom, we could—'

'No, we're not going to call in on either the Stewarts or your cousin,' said Ben. 'Neither of them will know anything about antiques dealers or demolished pubs.'

'I thought Cass and Mike might know about the nature reserve,' said Libby sheepishly.

Libby's cousin Cassandra lived with her partner, Mike, owner of Farthing's Plants, at Shott, near Bishop's Bottom.

'Why would they?' asked Ben reasonably. 'They don't get plants from a nature reserve.'

51

'OK,' said Libby with a sigh. 'So we're not going to go and look today, then?'

'I thought you would want to go with Fran. And I really have got to get back. I told them at the brewery I'd only be away for the morning.'

'You said last night there was nothing pressing.'

'I know, but . . .' Ben left the sentence hanging and grinned.

'You can't leave your precious brewery alone. I know.' Libby heaved another sigh.

Back at Allhallow's Lane, Libby was surprised to find a message on the landline from Hetty saying she had taken a booking for two of the Hoppers' Huts from Saturday for a week. This meant that this afternoon and tomorrow morning would be devoted to cleaning, airing and making sure there was enough bed linen available, and not, as she had hoped, an expedition to look at the remains of the Crooked Horse.

'Anyway, you wouldn't have been able to come with me, would you?' she said to Fran on the phone as she ate her lunch.

'No, Libby – I'll be somewhat busy! The tourists arrive earlier every year.'

'Actually, you know, the Nethergate tourists aren't bound by the school holidays any more. People take their children abroad these days.'

Fran sighed. 'Yes, I know. But as *you* know, there are still a lot of people who bring their pre-school children here. Because they like the old-fashioned – er – vibe, I think they call it.'

Libby chuckled. 'Hark at you! No, I know. And actually, I might come down to Nethergate myself tomorrow afternoon. Do a bit of browsing in the antique shops.'

There was a short silence.

'What are you up to?' asked Fran eventually.

'Nothing. I just want to look. I thought I might go and have a beer at Wally Mayberry's place.'

'You'll be driving.'

'I'll have a non-alcoholic beer, then.'

'All right. I'll join you there. If Guy can let me off at lunchtime.'

'It'll be a late lunch so you can cover the rush,' said Libby, grinning to herself.

'And when are you going to go and look at the pub?' asked Fran. 'I'm surprised you didn't ask me to take the whole of Saturday off.'

'As I said, I know you're busy on Saturdays. I might go over on my own.' Libby pushed her plate away. 'You know, I was thinking.'

'Be careful!'

'Yes, all right, all right. But seriously, St Eldreda's is over that way, isn't it?'

'The abbey? Yes, I suppose it is,' said Fran.

Some years ago, the Oast Theatre Company had performed a specially written play by Peter in the grounds of a ruined monastery attached to St Eldreda's Abbey.

'Well, I just wondered if they'd been affected by the slippage.'

'Undermined by the mine, you mean?' Fran chuckled. 'Would they be near enough, do you think? Anyway, if they had been, the ruins would have collapsed, surely?'

'Maybe. I just thought . . . well, I might go and see if Sister Catherine knows anything about all this.'

'You can't just pop in and talk to her, Lib. Ask Patti first. But quite honestly, what is an Anglican nun going to know about dodgy antiques and illegal demolition?'

'Hmm,' said Libby. 'That's a point. I'll call Patti.'

'She'll be busy in the community shop,' said Fran. 'Don't bother her.'

'I'll leave her a message. Meanwhile, I'd better go and make sure I've got everything ready for sprucing up the Hoppers' Huts. I'll see you tomorrow.'

Despite Fran's warning, Libby next called Patti, who, to her surprise, answered immediately.

'Oh – aren't you in the shop?'

'No, I did my shift early today. What can I do for you?'

'I was wondering,' began Libby, 'if you were still in touch with Sister Catherine.'

'Cathy?' Patti sounded surprised. 'Yes, of course. Why?'

'Well, I was thinking – St Eldreda's must be roughly in the same area as the Dunton estate and the nature reserve.'

'And the Crooked Horse, yes. Roughly.' Patti now sounded amused. 'And you want to know what she might know about it?'

'I just wondered . . .'

'Well,' she said thoughtfully, 'you know Cathy. She keeps up to date with things, and I expect the alongsiders will have kept her informed.'

Alongsiders, as they were often referred to, were women who lived in the religious house but were not as bound by the religious life as the nuns themselves, and often worked and even lived outside.

'So you think she might know something about it?' asked Libby.

'She might, but I doubt if it would be any more than anyone else in the area. Although there aren't many people *in* the area, are there? Anyway, do you want me to ask?'

'Oh, would you? Fran said I couldn't just pop round, and of course I know that,' said Libby. 'I've got the Hoppers' Huts to sort out ready for some holidaymakers this afternoon and tomorrow morning, and then I'm going over to Nethergate in the afternoon. I expect you're marrying someone, aren't you?'

'And if I'm not?' said Patti with a chuckle.

'After I've seen Fran, I could drive over to you. If you're not busy,' Libby added hastily.

Now Patti laughed out loud. 'I'll see you tomorrow afternoon, then,' she said. 'Somehow, not so many people want to get married in church these days, so I do get the odd Saturday off. Send me a text when you're on your way.'

'Result!' said Libby to Sidney as she ended the call. 'Now I'm getting somewhere.'

54

Chapter Eight

Libby handed the keys over to Hetty after making sure the Hoppers' Huts were in a fit state for visitors, then had a quick shower and set off for Nethergate at just after one o'clock on Saturday.

The town was busier than she had expected, and both Harbour Street and the car park behind the Blue Anchor were full, which meant parking in the small car park at the end of Victoria Place. She wandered back towards the high street, crossed over and found Beer and Bargains on the corner of Marine Parade. At first it looked like a typical antiques and collectibles shop, at the lower end of the market, but then Libby spotted a counter at the back and a door that appeared to lead out to a garden. She went inside.

'Mrs S!' A jovial Wallace Mayberry greeted her from behind the counter. 'And what can we do for you this fine afternoon?'

'Hello, Wally.' Libby smiled back and looked round at the artefacts adorning the walls. 'My friend and I thought we'd come and have a look at your shop.'

'Great! Well, everything here's for sale except me.' He laughed at his own joke. 'Can I get you a drink?'

'Non-alcoholic lager?' suggested Libby. 'I'm driving. I'll just send my friend a text to let her know I've arrived.'

Wallace poured a very pale lager into a straight glass and handed it over. 'On the house,' he said. 'Want to sit outside? We've got a very nice little garden.'

The little garden was indeed very nice. The few tables were all full, and under a canopy next to the back door a large television was attached to the wall, currently showing some kind of sport. Libby sat on a bench and waited for Fran, who arrived ten minutes later.

'Well, this is a bit different,' she said, sitting down next to Libby with a large glass of red wine.

'I quite like it,' said Libby, eyeing the wine with envy.

'Yes, so do I.' Fran glanced round at the other customers. 'Looks as though he's doing better as a bar than a shop.' She turned back to Libby. 'And what are you going to ask him?'

Libby stared down into her glass. 'What does he know about the Crooked Horse, I suppose.'

'Won't he think that's a bit odd?'

'Why?'

'Because you're supposed to be looking into Hodges' death.'

'Not really,' said Libby. 'We were asked to look into his disappearance. Then you found his body. I don't remember saying we'd look any further.'

'OK.' Fran sighed and sipped her wine. 'Not bad, this.'

After another few minutes, Wallace came out with a tray to collect glasses.

'All right, ladies?' He beamed down at them. 'Nice little place, isn't it?'

'It is, Wally,' Libby agreed. 'Great idea, combining the two. Has it increased trade on the antiques side?'

'Not as much as I'd've liked. But we'll see. Not been open that long.'

'Right.' Libby nodded. 'Oh, I was going to ask – what do you know about the old Crooked Horse?'

Wallace's smile froze on his face. 'The . . . Horse?' he repeated eventually.

'Yes. We heard it was used by a lot of . . .' Libby managed a strangled laugh, 'the antiques boys, as I think you're called.'

'Ah!' Wallace cleared his throat. 'Yes, of course. A lot of us used to

56

drink over there. Sort of unofficial meeting place, you know? We used to swap leads, that sort of thing.'

'Ah, I see. Such a shame, wasn't it? And they haven't found out who did it?'

'Er – no.' Wallace looked over his shoulder. 'Look, I'd better get on. There's no one behind the bar, and the customers will be getting thirsty.' With that, he vanished rapidly back inside.

'There isn't anybody waiting,' said Fran. 'And he didn't collect any glasses.'

'And he was definitely nervous.' Libby finished her lager. 'I'm going over to see Patti now. See if she's found anything out from Sister Cathy.'

Fran raised her eyebrows. 'You got in touch, then.'

'Yes, and she said people don't want to get married any more, so she gets Saturdays off.'

'I don't suppose she said that exactly,' said Fran. 'And really, this visit was hardly worth it, was it?'

'I suppose not.' Libby sighed. 'Except it confirms what we thought.'

'What *you* thought, you mean. Which is?'

'There was some kind of dodgy dealing going on at the old Horse.' Libby stood up. 'You did too – don't deny it. You thought it was dangerous.' She eyed Fran quizzically. 'Ready?'

Fran followed her inside, where Libby put her glass on the counter and thanked Wallace, who was now busy with customers.

'Let's just have a look at some of the stuff, Lib,' Fran said quietly, moving over to where a couple of stone ornaments stood either side of a rather battered display case. Libby joined her, peering in through the slightly dusty glass.

Inside, resting on a bed of ancient velvet, lay the usual collection of small articles. A couple of items of possibly Victorian jewellery, a clay pipe, a bowl that could have been bronze and a china cup and saucer that could, just possibly, have been Spode.

'I rather like this,' said Fran, bending down to examine what looked like a polished wooden side table.

'What is it?' Libby frowned.

'A Victorian coal box,' said Fran. 'Wonder how much he wants for it?' She straightened up and had another look in the display case. Libby shook her head and turned towards the door.

'Look at this, Lib.' Fran's voice stopped her.

'What.'

'That brooch. See – the one at the top.'

Libby looked at it. 'Yes? Victorian, is it?'

'Shh!' said Fran. 'No, I don't think so. It looks Anglo-Saxon to me.'

'But how would Wally Mayberry have got hold of an Anglo-Saxon brooch?' panted Libby, struggling to keep up with her friend, who was putting as much distance between herself and Beer and Bargains as possible.

'I don't know,' muttered Fran, slowing down as they reached the square opposite the Swan Inn. 'And to be honest, if it is Anglo-Saxon, I'm not sure why he's got it on display.'

'Eh? Why?'

'Those sort of artefacts go for huge prices, usually on the black market. If they're found legitimately and reported to the coroner and the finds liaison officer—'

'The who?'

'For the Portable Antiquities Scheme,' said Fran. 'You know – you used to watch *Time Team*.'

'Oh yes.' Libby frowned. 'Perhaps it isn't Anglo-Saxon, then.'

'Hmm.' Fran stood still, staring out to sea. 'I was just thinking – St Eldreda was Anglo-Saxon, wasn't she?'

'That period, yes.'

'Maybe you're right to ask Sister Catherine, then.' Fran looked at her friend and smiled. 'Something could be going on.'

What, though? Libby asked herself as she drove along the coast road towards St Aldeberge, past the old caravan site and Temptation House. If the so-called antiques boys used to meet at the Crooked Horse to discuss their possibly nefarious deeds, where did Anglo-Saxon brooches come into it? Yes, she could see that there might well be a profitable trade in smuggling artefacts – but which way? Into or out of England? And where would St Eldreda's monastery come into it?

St Eldreda came from what was then the Welsh Marches back in the seventh century and married a Kentish nobleman. When he died, Egbert, then the king of Kent, left her some land on which she built a house of prayer, which became famous after her death because miracle cures began occurring after pilgrims had visited her tomb. But then the first chapel was destroyed by fire, after which the stone monastery was built, the ruins of which were still standing, next to what was now St Eldreda's Abbey, home of Sister Catherine and her fellow Anglican nuns.

Perhaps, thought Libby, some small items had been abandoned in the old monastery and Wallace Mayberry, or one of his cohorts, had found them. Not that she could imagine Wally grubbing about in the old ruins – and what would decorative items be doing there? Nuns didn't wear brooches. As far as her limited knowledge went, those sort of items were usually grave goods, buried with their former owner after death.

She was still pondering the question when she pulled up on the forecourt of the vicarage, a slightly down-at-heel Victorian edifice, far too big for Patti on her own. Patti stuck her head out of the window to Libby's right.

'Come round the side,' she called. 'Door's open.'

Doors to vicarages, Libby found, were frequently open. It was astonishing they weren't burgled more frequently.

Patti was in the kitchen, boiling the kettle.

'Tea?' she asked.

'Please. I just had a half of non-alcoholic lager at Beer and Bargains, and I need a restorative.'

'Beer and Bargains?'

Libby explained. 'And what we were thinking, Fran and me, was . . .' she took a breath, 'St Eldreda was an Anglo-Saxon, wasn't she?'

Patti laughed. 'I don't suppose she'd have called herself that, but yes, she was. But she isn't buried at the monastery – remember? The bones were removed to Canterbury.'

'Except the finger.'

'The reliquary, yes.'

'Where did that end up in the end? Did the family get it?'

'Yes. St Eldreda's finger went home to Herefordshire. So I can't imagine there would be any Anglo-Saxon treasures left lying about in the monastery.'

'No,' sighed Libby. 'Anyway, I want to have a look at the Horse. It's near the Dunton estate, but I didn't know there was a nature reserve there.'

'Drink your tea, and we'll go over and have a look,' said Patti. 'Do you remember, way back when, when I first showed you the monastery? When we were out for a walk?'

'Yes. And on the way home in the car I wanted to stop at a pub . . . Oh!' Libby sat back on her stool, mouth open in surprise. '*That* was the Horse? And I said it looked nice!'

Patti grinned. 'That's it.'

Libby frowned. 'So it's near the Willoughby Oak?'

'You've driven along it loads of times. From here it runs alongside the canal, and then it joins the Bishop's Bottom road at Felling one way, and branches off towards the abbey the other. And there's a lane that turns off *that* leading to the pub and the nature reserve.'

'And that's what the developers want to develop?' said Libby. 'No wonder people were up in arms. It's completely unspoiled round there. And completely unsuitable. The whole area's marsh, isn't it? And what with the slippage . . .'

'Ah, yes. It didn't seem to strike the developers that if the pub had slipped, so could all their posh new houses.' Patti shook her head. 'Come on, drink up.'

Patti drove them in her comparatively new little Seat. 'Easier to nego-tiate the lanes,' she said, 'rather than your great big four-by-four.'

'It's Ben's, not mine.' Libby patted the dashboard. 'Nice little car, though.'

'I thought we'd go down by the Willoughby Oak and cut across,' said Patti. 'It's a nicer drive.'

Libby shuddered. 'Not such nice memories, though.'

The rutted lane ran alongside the Dunton estate to an empty field, where the huge old tree still stood, creaking in the slight wind.

'Look!' said Libby, sitting up straight. 'There are leaves!'

Patti slowed to a stop. 'Yes. For some very strange reason, after a couple of years it suddenly came back to life. No one knows why, and none of the experts could understand it.'

'Because the evil had stopped,' said Libby firmly. The Willoughby Oak had been the site of many somewhat esoteric and, frankly, illegal, goings-on for centuries.

Patti nodded and drove on.

'And here we are,' she said, turning down an even narrower lane towards what looked like an empty marsh. It turned sharply left at the bottom and Libby found herself staring at the blackened, half-ruined remains of what had once been the Crooked Horse.

Chapter Nine

They sat in the car, silent, for several minutes, before Libby turned to Patti with a look of horror on her face.

'Thank God no one was inside.'

Patti nodded. 'Indeed. And had it been only a few weeks earlier, there would have been.'

'Can we get out? I want to take a closer look.'

'We can get out, but you can't get too close, for obvious reasons. But we can look at the nature reserve if you like.'

They climbed out, and Libby went up to the fluttering blue and white crime tape and followed it right round to the end, where it disappeared behind the building. When she came back to Patti, she was frowning.

'The damage is almost superficial once you really look,' she said. 'The fire engines obviously got here quickly.'

'They did.' Patti nodded. 'And that's why they think the digger was sent in.' She indicated the large vehicle standing silent and almost mournful on the forecourt.

'Because the fire didn't do the job? So I heard. How dreadful.' Libby shook her head. 'Do *you* know if they've decided it was the developers who caused it? No one else seems to.'

'I'm not sure,' said Patti. 'It's being looked into. But the developers – look, that's their board over there – had the most obvious reason.'

Libby peered at the board. *Speedwell Homes*, it read, in large blue letters.

'But I thought they hadn't actually bought the pub yet?'

'No, they hadn't, but apparently the couple who bought it from Marsham's always intended to sell it on.'

'Yes, I heard, but Marsham's had put a stop on the sale because of that. So I doubt it would have been them.'

'They wouldn't have had access to a digger, anyway,' said Patti. 'Look, Lib, it's all very well investigating murders, but crimes involving big business are a different matter. Come on, let's look at the nature reserve.'

She led the way along a track past the pub to where a white, slightly sooty five-bar gate stood open.

'No fence?' said Libby. 'Just a gate?'

'I think it's meant to be symbolic,' said Patti, walking through. 'You're supposed to keep to the track, which they used to keep fairly tidy. I don't know what's happening now.'

'It hasn't been sold, though, has it? Who does the reserve belong to?'

'Felling Town Council. It's called the Felling Nature Reserve.' Patti stopped and pointed to her right. 'See – over there? There's Felling.'

'But it butts right up to the Dunton estate – I'm surprised it doesn't belong to them,' said Libby.

Patti shrugged. 'It may have done at one time. Don't forget, I haven't been here that long, so I don't know the history.'

'You've been here years!' said Libby in surprise.

'When we met because of the murder in my church, I hadn't been here more than a few months, remember? I was still winning over the congregation.'

'So you were.' Libby swivelled on her heel and surveyed the marshy reserve. 'It's a little bit like Heronsbourne Flats, isn't it? I bet there are species of insects or something that can only be found here.'

'Like that moth you heard about.' Patti nodded. 'Funny how these things just seem to settle in one small corner of the world, isn't it?'

'Mmm.' Libby looked round again. 'Can we go and see where St Eldreda's is from here?'

Patti laughed. 'Had enough of this, have you?'

'Well, frankly, I can't see what attraction this pub held for our antiques boys. It's on the road to nowhere, and there's nothing else around here. It's not even as if they could bring their boats up the creek to Felling, and anyway, that's a way off itself.'

'Do you actually think the fire could be to do with the antiques business?' Patti led the way back through the gate.

'Oh, I don't know,' said Libby. 'It's just because we found out that the antiques boys used to use it, and Malcolm Hodges was murdered . . .'

'You put two and two together and came up with two hundred,' said Patti. 'Come on, get in the car.'

'It wasn't just me,' Libby protested. 'Ian said the police were working on the same assumption. I keep telling people that.'

With a last look back at the sad Crooked Horse, she climbed in and they set off.

The land was still bare and marshy, but began to change as they drove further inland, until there were a lot more trees and slightly undulating ground. And then the ruined monastery loomed up before them.

'We're not going into the abbey, are we?' Libby looked worried. 'I'd hate to disturb them. They're probably doing one of their complines or matins or something.'

'No, Libby. You just wanted to have a look at the ruins. Cathy said we're welcome to go in. The gates are open.'

'Oh, great! That'll bring back memories.' Libby got out of the car.

'Not necessarily good ones,' said Patti.

As they walked up to the ruins, past the abbey on their left, no other members of the public could be seen.

'Too far off the beaten track and not spectacular enough,' said Patti. 'Not like Whitby or Tintern.'

'Oh, I don't know.' Libby looked up at the huge stone walls. 'I think it's impressive. But you're right — it's a bit in the back of beyond. And the nuns wouldn't like people wandering around all the time.'

'No, but they do leave the gates open if anyone wants to come and have a look.' Patti grinned at Libby. 'Like us.'

Libby looked thoughtful. 'So those antiques people could actually have wandered in here?'

'Well, yes, but if they were going to take anything from the site, they'd do it at night, wouldn't they? And the gates are locked then.'

'I don't suppose that would deter them. And I don't suppose there's a security camera, either.'

'That's where you're wrong,' said Patti. 'After the last unpleasantness –'

'Don't remind me,' interrupted Libby.

'– they had a complete security health check.' Patti continued. 'Cameras everywhere.'

'Shutting the stable door,' said Libby.

'Better safe than sorry,' countered Patti.

Libby wandered off through the ruins, peering at the ground.

'Find anything?' called Patti after a moment.

'No.' Libby straightened up. 'Wouldn't there have been a burial site near the monastery. Where the nuns were buried? And come to think of it, why isn't it called a nunnery?'

'Search me! And as for the burial site – I've not heard of one. There may have been. I know there've been archaeological digs in the area from time to time. I'll ask Cathy. She's bound to call me to find out if we came. I think she'd like to see you again.'

'I'd like to see her, too. Perhaps during the week sometime?'

'Good idea.' Patti looked at her watch. 'Do you want to see any more? Only I've got a parish thing this evening, and I ought to get back and change.'

'Put your dog collar back on,' grinned Libby.

'That's the idea.' Patti grinned back, and they made their way to the car.

*

'Of course,' said Libby to Ben later that day over dinner, 'if that brooch at Wally's actually *is* Anglo-Saxon and it *was* pinched from a proper site, it wouldn't be smuggling, would it?'

'No, just plain old theft.' Ben forked up Libby's version of chicken korma. 'And what's it got to do with anything anyway?'

'I just thought it was another possibly illegal area of activity worth exploring.'

'Why, though? Malcolm Hodges didn't have a clutch of Anglo-Saxon goodies in his barn.'

'No, but . . .'

Ben put down his fork and pushed his empty plate away. 'It's absolutely nothing to do with you, Libby. You don't even know if the brooch was genuine. It could be Victorian made to look medieval. They used to do that, apparently. And, as you so rightly said, it's nothing to do with smuggling.'

Libby regarded him with a frown. 'And can I only investigate if it's to do with smuggling?'

Ben sighed. 'Frankly, I'm beginning to feel I would rather you didn't investigate after all, despite what I said, but as I was the one who introduced you to Wally, I can hardly object.'

'No,' said Libby 'and Ian really only wanted me to see what the word on the street was about the Horse. But it isn't your fault. I told you before.'

'So what next?' Ben stood up and took his plate to the dishwasher. 'Will you tell Ian about the brooch?'

'I think I have to.' Libby collected up more dishes. 'Although how helpful it'll be in terms of evidence to link the Horse with Hodges' death, I've no idea.'

Saturday evenings had become the regular time for Libby and Ben to visit the Hop Pocket. It usually ended up with Ben helping his manager, Simon, behind the bar, whether he was needed or not. Luckily for Libby, several friends were usually there too, not least Bethany Cole, the Steeple Martin vicar, and her husband John. When the

Pocket had first opened, Beth had donated an old upright piano from the church hall, which now was John's particular province, although anyone was free to play. The regulars were delighted, especially those old enough to remember when the pub pianist was a feature of everyday life.

Tonight, Dan, a member of the Steeple Martin Morris dancers, his wife Moira and dog Colley, who, confusingly, was a Labrador, and old Brandon, who, like Dan and Moira, lived down Cuckoo Lane, were already ensconced round a table. Libby sat at a small table next to them, assuming that Beth would soon appear and take over Ben's seat when he went behind the bar.

'Brandon tells us you found another body, Libby,' said Dan. 'I'm not sure it's good for our health, being friends with you!'

Moira gave him a dig in the ribs. 'Shut up, you!'

'Oh, it's all right, Moira,' said Libby. 'I'm used to it now.'

'Found out any more about it?' asked Brandon. 'We're all waiting to help the investigation.' He beamed at her. ''Lo, Ben.'

'Evening all,' said Ben, sitting down and handing Libby her lager.

'We were just wondering about this body Libby found,' said Dan, leaning back comfortably. 'Antiques shop, was it?'

'No, an antiques barn,' said Libby. 'And it wasn't me actually, it was Fran.'

'Anyway,' said Ben, 'she's more interested in who tried to demolish the Crooked Horse.'

'Oh, I heard about that!' said Dan. 'Nice old place. Near the nature reserve, wasn't it?'

'Still is,' said Libby. 'Whoever it was didn't manage to destroy it, thankfully, although nothing can be done about it until the police have finished their investigation.'

'I went on a dig over there a while ago,' said Moira, frowning in concentration. 'When was it now?'

'A dig?' Libby sat up straight. 'An archaeological dig?'

'Yes. Didn't you know? I used to be a volunteer with the

Nethergate and District Archaeological Society.' She gave a rather self-satisfied smile. 'I'm still a member. Haven't done anything since lockdown, though.'

'Where was the dig? What was it? Roman?' asked Libby, leaning forward.

Moira looked startled. 'I don't remember. Why?'

Libby sighed and sat back. 'It doesn't matter. Just something we were looking into.'

'Oh. Well, I expect I could find out.' Moira looked hopeful.

'Don't worry about it,' said Libby. 'Really. It's not important.'

'Hi, Beth!' There was relief in Ben's voice as he stood up. Libby grinned down at the table. He was glad to get away from a potentially awkward conversation.

'Come and sit down,' she said. 'Ben's going behind the bar, aren't you?'

He gave her a wink. 'And John's already gone to the piano. See you later.'

'Evening!' said Beth, smiling round the table. 'Am I interrupting anything?'

'No!' said Libby and Dan together.

'We were just talking about the archaeological dig Moira went on,' said Brandon. 'Sounds interesting. *Time Team* sort of thing, eh?'

'Oh!' Beth turned to Moira and Libby cursed inwardly. 'I didn't know you did that! Where was it?'

'Over near the Dunton estate,' said Moira, animated once more. 'Quite near that pub that burnt down.'

'It didn't—' began Libby.

'Oh, I know.' Beth nodded and picked up her glass. 'They thought there might be an Anglo-Saxon burial site there, didn't they?'

Chapter Ten

Libby almost choked on her beer.

'Oh yes!' Moira's face lit up, enlightened. 'That was it, Libby! A burial site.'

'It wasn't, though, was it?' Beth frowned. 'Just a couple of items, as far as I remember.'

Moira was looking blank, and Brandon and Dan had started talking about something else.

'I wonder how the items got there?' said Libby, now in charge of her voice. 'It's nowhere near St Eldreda's, is it?'

'Who?' said Moira.

Beth smiled. 'It's an abbey, Moira.'

'And a ruined monastery,' added Libby.

'But the whole area has Anglo-Saxon connections, doesn't it?' said Beth. 'Eastry's not far away, and that's where Egbert lived.' She turned to Moira. 'He was the king of Kent back in the seventh century. And Lyminge, of course.'

Libby forbore to wonder aloud why Moira didn't know this, if she had been a member of an archaeological society.

'Patti and I went over there this afternoon,' she said. 'We're going to see Sister Catherine next week.'

'Anything to do with the Crooked Horse?' asked Beth.

'How did you guess?' Libby grinned at her.

Beth laughed. 'Actually, the dig site was almost next to it – and the nature reserve, of course. I gather they had a bit of trouble getting permission at the time.'

'Oh yes – I remember that,' said Moira brightly. 'And we weren't there for long. They closed it down after a week or so.'

'Actually,' said Libby, 'I said to Patti that there ought to be a burial site in the area for the nuns.'

'Yes, you would have thought so.' Beth nodded and lifted her glass. 'Cheers.'

'I see John's collected his usual group of fans.' Libby looked over to the piano, hoping to change the subject. She really didn't want Moira asking any more questions.

'Of course he has.' Beth smiled fondly. 'I don't think the regulars can quite believe they've suddenly got an old-fashioned pub pianist in their local.'

'And it brings people in from out of the village, too,' said Libby. 'Ben's delighted. Although he has been wondering if he should get a music licence. And if he should pay John.'

'Oh no!' Beth looked shocked. 'Don't do that. That would stop it being something he does for fun.'

Moira had lost interest.

Brandon stood up.

'Judy, dear!' he boomed. 'And Cyd, darling!'

Libby turned to see Judy Dale and Cyd Russell approaching the table.

'He's like a caricature of himself, isn't he?' she said in an amused undertone to Beth, who nodded.

'Hi!' she said out loud. 'Joining us?'

'Yes, please.' Judy pulled out a chair and beamed round at the company. 'How are we all?'

When they were settled, Cyd turned to Libby. 'What happened to you the other day? When the rehearsal was cancelled?'

Judy and Cyd, both professional singers, were, like Brandon, recent inhabitants of Steeple Martin, lured down to do last winter's pantomime and deciding to stay. They were currently renting Steeple Farm from Peter, whose mother, Milly, technically owned it but was a resident in a very upmarket home for the bewildered. They both now formed part of the cast of *Contraband*, again like Brandon.

Libby sighed and explained.

'So now I'm hoping to have a clear run at rehearsals,' she finished, 'or we'll never get on the stage.'

'Ah, yes.' Judy looked down into her wine. 'I need to speak to you about that.'

'What?' Libby narrowed her eyes. 'You're not baling out, are you?'

Judy gave her an embarrassed smile. 'No, no, of course not.'

Cyd shook her head. 'Honestly, Libby, she is *such* a wuss. I've been on at her to tell you about this for weeks!'

'Not weeks,' protested Judy. 'Just *a* week.'

'What?' said Libby. 'Come on, tell me!'

'Well.' Judy took a deep breath. 'You remember that cancelled concert?'

'Of course.'

'You remember I lost all that money when the Raincliffe Rep was closed?'

'Yes, yes. Of course I do. What about it? The Raincliffe's reopened now, hasn't it?'

'Well,' said Judy again, going a pretty shade of pink, 'Ray McCloud . . .'

'Your pianist?'

'That's him. He's set it up again!'

Libby was well aware of the circumstances of the cancelled concert, as it was part of the reason that Judy and Cyd were in Steeple Martin.

'That's wonderful, Judy! And Cyd? You're doing it too?'

'Oh yes.' Cyd patted her partner's hand. 'She's been so nervous, though. Ray's doing it to raise funds jointly for the Raincliffe and the Furnough. We can't say no.'

'Of course you can't!' said Libby. 'What a wonderful idea.'

The Raincliffe Rep, an old theatre in London, and the Furnough School, a dramatic academy for aspiring actors who couldn't afford the more traditional schools, had both been ruined by an avaricious and unpleasant acquaintance of them all. Both had been rescued thanks to some very clever work by a whole raft of solicitors, and now it seemed they were to benefit further.

'When is it?' asked Dan, who had tuned in to the conversation.

'We're doing it twice,' said Judy. 'Once at the Raincliffe next Saturday and then the following Saturday at your Alexandria!' She let out a breathless giggle. 'I'm so sorry, Libby. I hope you don't mind!'

'Will you still be able to do *Contraband*?' Libby frowned.

'Yes.' Cyd was definite. 'We'll rehearse with you whenever we can, and we'll be down here before the Alexandria concert, so we'll be there for the tech the next day.'

'It sounds like a lot of work,' said Libby, 'but you're professionals. I'm sure you'll manage it.'

'How exciting!' Moira clapped her hands. 'We'll go, won't we, Dan?'

'Of course.' Dan beamed at Judy and patted her on the back.

'And I'm sure we'll all be there too,' said Libby. 'Even all the oldies who went to the last one.'

'But we'll have to go up to London to rehearse next week, Lib.' Judy looked anxious. 'We'll miss *Contraband* rehearsals then.'

'I'll sort out read-ins,' said Libby. 'Don't worry. It's not as if you need the rehearsal. It's more for the resident amateurs.'

Cyd and Judy both relaxed with relief, and Dan offered everyone another drink.

'So is this new murder all about antiques smuggling?' asked Cyd. 'Or have I got that wrong?'

'It might be,' said Libby. 'Everyone keeps talking about the "antiques boys" as if they're a particular sort of gang, and we know now that they all used to meet up at the Crooked Horse.'

Judy looked puzzled.

'That pub that someone set fire to,' Cyd told her. 'It was on the news.'

'Oh yes. And this person who was murdered was connected to it?' Judy asked.

'He used to go there, yes. At least we think so.'

'That's like *Contraband*, then, isn't it?' said Judy. 'They met in a pub.'

'And they were avoiding the revenue men, too,' agreed Libby. 'Actually, my friend Lewis remarked on the coincidence, too.'

'Oh, he's the television handyman, isn't he?' said Moira. 'Who your son works for.'

'Is that another son?' asked Cyd. 'Your Adam works for Harry in the restaurant, I thought.'

'Same one,' said Libby. 'He works for Lewis during the day and part-time for Harry some evenings. Mainly as he lives in the flat upstairs for a very reduced rent!'

'Does your friend know about the smugglers, then?' Judy looked as though she was struggling to keep track of the conversation.

'He's the one who told me about the Crooked Horse being fired,' explained Libby. 'One of our publican friends had told him I ought to look into it.'

'So you are,' said Judy.

'Sort of. It was a nice old pub,' said Libby vaguely.

'And quite near an Anglo-Saxon burial site,' put in Moira. 'The artefacts could be smuggled.'

'The burial site was disproved, though,' said Beth. 'Remember?'

'Was it, though?' said Moira. 'They said it wasn't there, but some-one could have been keeping quiet about it, couldn't they?'

Libby and Beth stared at her as though Colley the dog had suddenly started spouting Shakespeare.

'She's right.' Beth turned a surprised look on Libby.

'Yes.' Libby didn't have the heart to say she and Fran had been won-dering the same thing.

'You do live an exciting life,' said Cyd admiringly. 'Burial sites and burnt pubs and murdered antiques dealers.' She shook her head. 'Is it safe to be your friend?'

'We've often wondered,' said Dan. 'But we're still here.'

Libby felt hot colour creeping up her neck. 'I don't mean it, you know.'

'Don't be silly.' Beth, surprisingly, leant over and gave her a kiss. 'We wouldn't know what to talk about if it wasn't for your adventures.'

Libby was quiet on the walk home.

'What's up?' asked Ben, after trying several topics of conversation and being ignored. 'Did someone upset you this evening?'

Libby sighed. 'It was something Cyd said. And Dan.'

Ben raised surprised eyebrows. 'But they're your friends! What can they have said?'

Libby told him.

He laughed. 'Oh, that's just normal banter. Pulling your leg – you ought to be used to it.'

'But what if I do come over as this incredibly annoying old biddy? What if they're all rolling their eyes inside and saying, "Here she goes again"?'

'That'd be a neat trick – rolling their eyes inside!'

'I'm serious, Ben.' Libby stopped dead in the middle of Allhallow's Lane. 'I'm a nuisance.'

'Don't be daft!' Ben took her arm and pulled her towards number 17. 'You're always having these crises. If it isn't this, it's that you should have a proper job. How many more times?' He took his key out of his pocket. 'We all love you as you are. Now come along, and I'll let you have a nice nightcap.'

Libby came along.

Chapter Eleven

'You know,' said Ben over breakfast on Sunday morning, 'it's not you you should be worrying about, it's Fran.'

'Eh?' Libby looked up from her scrambled egg. 'Fran? What do you mean?'

'Well, she often seems to be the one who causes your crises of confidence. She's always telling you to leave things alone.'

'Pot, kettle!' Libby sang.

'Yes, all right, but she does get a bit holier than thou, doesn't she? She doesn't seem to have as much . . . oh, I don't know.' Ben sat back in his chair and looked at the ceiling. 'What's the word I want?'

Libby watched him shrewdly. 'Empathy?' she suggested.

'Exactly!' He grinned at her. 'When she first arrived, it was different.'

'Well,' said Libby, getting up and fetching the simmering kettle to the table, 'she was more used to using her psychic powers then, wasn't she?' She poured water into the Brown Betty teapot. 'Hark at me! Psychic powers indeed.'

'That's what they were, though, even if she didn't like using them,' said Ben. 'And now she almost refuses to admit it if she's had one of her moments.'

'Yes, she does!' Libby sat down and rested her chin on her hands. 'I can understand her not liking them – and sometimes it's terribly difficult to interpret them – but you're right. She tries to pretend they aren't there.'

'Because it makes her a freak, do you think?' asked Ben.

Libby nodded. 'I think she just wants to be ordinary. A wife and mother – well, maybe not that, she doesn't get on that well with her kids – helping in the shop and living in her nice middle-class cottage in a nice middle-class town. For years she was a psychic consultant, professional actor and single mother. She wants to put it all behind her.' She picked up the teapot and poured tea into large Oast Theatre mugs. 'Do you know, I've never really thought about it before. It's always been about me.' She pulled a face. 'I told you. I'm being annoying again.'

'Shut up,' said Ben, adding milk to his tea. 'Forget Fran, and forget your own lack of confidence, and tell me what you're going to do next about murdered antiques dealers and burnt pubs.'

Libby regarded him with affection across the kitchen table.

'I do love you, Ben,' she said.

Libby's phone rang just as she was trying to decide what to wear for lunch at the Manor, given that the weather had turned changeable.

'I've been invited for lunch,' said Ian. 'Is there anything you've got to tell me that you can't say in front of the others?'

Ben's mother cooked an enormous traditional roast dinner on Sundays and invited anybody who was free to come and help her eat it.

'I haven't found out much,' said Libby, 'except Fran and I saw what we thought was an Anglo-Saxon brooch in Wally Mayberry's shop.'

Ian was silent for what seemed to Libby at least a minute.

'Well, say something!' she said at last.

'Did you ask him about it?'

'No. We weren't sure—'

'Good.' Ian sounded brisk. 'And you thought this linked up how?'

'I wondered if there was an Anglo-Saxon burial site anywhere near the Crooked Horse. You know – there could have been nighthawks around, and they could be offloading whatever they picked up to the antiques boys.' Libby waited to see how this would go down.

'And is there?'

'Is there what?'

'A burial site?'

'Oh! Well, apparently there was supposed to be, but Beth – you know Beth? – said it was disproved. One of the Pocket's regulars was a volunteer on a dig there.'

Ian burst out laughing. 'You see?' he said. 'I'd never pick all of that up!'

'I expect you would,' said Libby, feeling embarrassed. 'If you'd spotted the Anglo-Saxon brooch.'

'Well, maybe.' Ian let out a sigh of frustration. 'But it still doesn't give me any evidence, does it?'

'Not unless we can prove my theory,' admitted Libby. 'And you haven't really got the resources to do that, have you?'

'No – especially as Clare Stone has just been sent off on her Hydra course.'

'Eh? Hydra? Isn't that a monster?'

'It's also a course for training SIOs. Her promotion to DI will follow.'

'Oh. So she wasn't actually SIO when we met her at the barn?'

'Acting SIO, the same as she was acting DI.'

'Do you all have to do it?' Libby was intrigued.

'These days, yes. Ask your friend Rachel about it. Anyway, as there isn't another DI available, I'm having to take up the reins, so to speak. Today is likely to be my last day off.' Ian sighed again. 'I'll see you in about an hour.'

Libby relayed the conversation to Ben as they walked across the field past the Hoppers' Huts to the Manor.

'I thought he liked being out on the ground, so to speak,' said Ben. 'Now he doesn't have to skulk around in the office.'

'Not that he ever does that,' said Libby. 'But at least he'll be in the thick of it and be able to tell us things.'

'He's not supposed to tell you anything,' said Ben.

'But he does. Especially if he wants something.' Libby looked over at the Huts. 'Do you think I ought to go and ask them if they need anything?'

'Who?' Ben, momentarily confused at the abrupt change of subject, stopped dead.

'The people in the Huts,' said Libby. 'I just wondered.'

'No, then. They're fine. They'll come and ask Hetty if they need anything.' He resumed a leisurely pace. 'And you've got enough to do being a civilian investigator.' He gave her a conspiratorial grin.

'Yes.' Libby gazed into the distance. 'They actually have them, you know.'

'Civilian investigators? Yes, I know. I've been waiting for Ian to suggest it for the last couple of years.'

'Have you?' Libby looked at him in surprise.

'Ever since the murder of that girl Jackie,' said Ben. 'And actually since all that business when we met Colin. You and Fran were brought in over that, too, weren't you?'

'It wasn't really me,' said Libby. 'But the last two – yes, he's used us quite shamelessly, hasn't he?' She grinned. 'And he did say that if he could pay me, he would.'

They arrived in front of the Manor in time to meet Flo Carpenter and Hetty's brother Lenny emerging from the drive.

''Lo, gal,' said Flo. 'Wotcha, Ben.'

Lenny grinned. 'Mornin'.'

Flo and Hetty had originally come to Steeple Martin from London for the annual hop picking, and both ended up marrying local men – Hetty married Greg, the owner of the Manor estate, and Flo married Frank Carpenter, who bought Home Farm. She and her first love, Lenny had finally got together and now lived in Maltby Close near the church.

'Just us today, then?' asked Flo.

'Ian's coming,' said Libby.

'What about that Edward?' asked Lenny.

'No, he'll be down with his girlfriend in Heronsbourne,' said Ben, ushering them all through the big oak door. 'Hello, Mum.'

They fell into their usual routine. Ben went to fetch wine to add to Flo's contribution, Lenny fetched glasses and Libby set out the cutlery.

'Heard you're lookin' into the old Horse, gal,' said Hetty, accepting a glass of wine from her son.

'Did you?' Libby looked startled. 'How?'

'Edie.'

'Oh, of course.' Lewis's mother and Hetty had become friends after Libby's involvement in some unpleasantness at Creekmarsh. 'Have you seen her recently?'

'Went down to see that Chloe,' explained Hetty.

'Ah. How is she?'

'Enjoying 'erself,' said Flo. 'I went too.'

'Oh good.' Libby looked at Ben and shrugged. 'They have a better social life than I do.'

'Don't talk rubbish,' said Hetty. 'Come and put these spuds out.'

Ian appeared as the various dishes were being brought to the table, kissed his hostess and sat down heavily next to Lenny.

'Tired?' said Ben.

Ian nodded. 'I'll be fine after this, though.' He smiled up at Hetty. 'Cure for all ills.'

Libby managed to contain her soul in patience until everyone was served before asking if Ian had thought any more about their earlier conversation.

'This about the old Horse?' asked Flo.

Ian lifted an eyebrow. 'You know about that?'

'Course we do. Common knowledge.' Flo looked smug. 'Old Jenny Richards' pub.'

Libby, Ben and Ian stared at her.

'You know the publican?' said Ian eventually, swallowing a chunk of beef whole.

'Jenny and her old man,' said Flo. 'What was his name, Het? He died years ago.'

'Fred.'

79

'Oh yeah. Fred and Jenny Richards. Had it for years.'

'They were tenants, were they?' asked Libby.

'Yeah. Then Marsham's sold it.' Flo turned to her. 'Prob'ly all part of that business you was lookin' into.'

'Yes, I know about that,' said Ian. 'Did you ever go there?'

'Course we did,' said Lenny. 'Flo and me used to take a drive out there sometimes. Wasn't posh like the Coach here. And me and old Joe Wilson went too. Pity they closed it.'

'What happened to Jenny?' asked Libby.

'In a home.' Hetty pulled a face. 'Nowhere else to go.'

The table fell silent.

'Be fair, Het,' said Flo after a moment. 'She was gettin' on. Couldn't'a carried on any longer anyway.' She forked up a Brussels sprout. 'No central heating.'

Libby spluttered through a mouthful of wine.

'Wouldn't'a put it in, gal,' said Lenny. 'They was goin' to knock it down, wasn't they?'

'That definitely wasn't common knowledge,' said Ian, putting down his knife and fork. 'How did you hear that, Len?'

'I dunno,' said Lenny cautiously. 'Just heard, y'know.'

'Come on, Len. Who told you?' said Ben firmly.

Lenny darted a look at Flo. 'It were Wally Mayberry.'

Chapter Twelve

Once again, Libby, Ben and Ian were silenced.

'What?' said Lenny, looking injured. 'Weren't my fault, was it?'

Ben cleared his throat. 'When did you see Wally Mayberry, Len?' he asked. 'I didn't know you knew him.'

'Course I do. He used to drink in the old Horse, too. Him and his mates.'

'This was after you came down here from London, was it?' asked Ian.

Lenny had been living in a very nice retirement home until he moved down to join Flo several years ago.

'Well, course it was. Told yer. Used to drive over there.' He smiled reminiscently. 'Used to pick up some nice little bits and pieces, didn't we, Flo?'

This time it was Ben who choked.

Ian sat back in his chair and looked at the ceiling. 'I don't believe this.'

Lenny looked indignant.

'What have I done? What did I say? Wasn't my fault, Wally told me!'

'When did you see him, Lenny? You didn't say,' said Libby.

'Went down with Flo and Het the other day.'

'When they went to Temptation House?' said Libby. 'You went to Beer and Bargains – is that it?'

'Yeah, that's it!' Lenny smiled gratefully. 'Nice little place. You bin there?'

81

'Yes, I went yesterday.' Libby smiled back. 'It *is* a nice little place.'

'Got our Ben's beer on too, he has.' Lenny, now restored to cheerfulness, winked at Ben.

'So, Lenny,' said Ian, after refusing more beef from Hetty, 'what bits and pieces did you used to pick up over at the Horse?'

Lenny's mouth dropped open.

'Oh, you know.' Flo stepped into the breach. 'Bits o' china. That sorta thing.'

'Right. And did Wally sell them to you?'

Now Flo was looking shifty. 'Mighta done.'

Hetty stood up. 'Apple and blackberry pie,' she announced. 'And no more questions.'

After lunch, Hetty retired to her private sitting room, Flo and Lenny went home and Ben and Libby loaded the dishwasher. Ian excused himself, saying he had better check on the progress of the investigation into Malcolm Hodges' murder.

'I thought you said you had today off?' Libby flapped a tea towel at him.

'You don't get complete days off on a murder investigation,' said Ian. 'You know that.'

'Where are you up to?' asked Ben. 'All the technical stuff done?'

'Post-mortem, yes. Crime-scene analysis, partial.' Ian frowned. 'That barn is a nightmare.' He gave them a mock salute and left.

They finished loading the dishwasher and left to walk down the drive to spend the rest of the afternoon with Peter and Harry in their cottage, their normal routine on a Sunday afternoon.

Harry, still in his chef's whites, was stretched out on the sofa, while Peter was assembling bottles and glasses in the kitchen. Libby settled into her favourite shabby chintz-covered armchair.

'I see Ian was with you this lunchtime,' said Peter, bringing the drinks out.

'How did you know?' Libby accepted a whisky.

'Saw him drive past as we were closing up,' said Harry. 'So come on, dear heart, spill.'

'Nothing to tell, really.' Libby glanced at Ben. 'He just said his investigation's ongoing. And I haven't found out anything except that there might have been an archaeological dig over near the Crooked Horse.'

'That reminds me.' Harry held up a finger. 'I have a message for you.'

'For me? Who from?' Libby frowned.

'From whom, petal, from whom.' He wagged the finger at her. 'From the dreaded Moira. Apparently you were talking to her last night.'

'Sort of,' said Libby.

'Well, she said her mate Tara would like to speak to you.' Harry raised an eyebrow. 'An archaeologist, she is. What *have* you been digging up?'

'Oh, for goodness' sake!' Libby shook her head. 'What's *she* been digging up, more like!'

Ben chuckled. 'As far as I could make out, she was getting very excited about the whole Crooked Horse business because she'd been on a dig over there some years ago.'

'Moira?' Peter spluttered over his brandy. 'On a *dig*?'

'Apparently she was a member of the Nethergate and District Archaeological Society,' explained Libby. 'I assume this Tara is also a member.'

'So not a proper archaeologist, then?' said Harry, as Peter sat down on the sofa next to him. He lifted his feet into their usual position on Peter's lap.

'I don't know. I can't honestly see Moira being friends with an archaeologist, can you?'

'You never know,' said Peter. 'Look at all the odd friends you've got.'

'What does Moira want Libby to do, then?' asked Ben. 'Are we supposed to ring this person?'

'Moira said to let her know and she'll give this Tara your number.' Harry sighed theatrically. 'I'm just your lackey, aren't I? Nothing but a messenger service.'

Libby glowered. 'Tell her to give her my email.'

'I'm not telling her anything, petal. You can do your own dirty work.' Harry sniffed.

'I'll call Dan,' said Ben peaceably. 'Then neither of you has to do anything.' He got up and wandered out to the kitchen.

'So how did you find out about this dig?' asked Peter. 'Who told you?'

'Moira, actually.' Libby gave him a shamefaced grin. 'I mentioned that there might have been an Anglo-Saxon burial over there, you see, and Moira said there was. But Beth said it was disproved.'

'How did Beth know?' asked Harry.

'I expect she's interested because of St Eldreda's.'

'She wasn't around when we did the play over there, was she?' said Peter.

'No, but she'll know about the monastery. After all, it's Anglican.' Libby looked up as Ben came back into the room.

'All sorted,' he said with a grin. 'Dan's giving Moira your email, with strict instructions *not* to give out your number. Either of them.'

'Good.' Libby took a healthy sip of whisky and coughed. 'I wonder what the woman wants?'

'She could just be nosy,' said Harry, looking innocent.

Libby threw a cushion at him.

On Monday morning, Libby started on a revised rehearsal schedule for *Contraband*, to allow for the absence of Judy and Cyd. She'd just got to the stage of formulating a round-robin email to the rest of the cast – and the rehearsal pianist – when a new email pinged into her inbox.

Hello, Libby,

I hope you don't mind Moira Cruikshank giving me your email address. I work occasionally with the Nethergate and

District Archaeological Society, and just before lockdown we began a dig on what was thought could be an Anglo-Saxon burial site fairly near St Eldreda's monastery, which Moira tells me you know well. We found nothing in the first week, and then lockdown forced us to stop, and the site was shut down. I was never convinced that there was nothing there, and I wondered if you had any more information?

Thank you in advance,

Tara Nichols FSA

Libby stared wide-eyed at her screen. So Tara was a proper archaeologist after all. She picked up her phone and called Ben.

'We did Moira a disservice,' he said. 'You'll have to buy her a drink.'

'As long as she doesn't start trying to muscle in,' said Libby.

'On what? You aren't doing anything.'

'But we might.' She sighed. 'I'd better call Fran.'

'If I were you,' said Ben, 'I'd send this Tara a reply and wait to hear from her. Then you can tell Fran what she says. And Patti too, I should.'

'You're right.' Libby thought for a moment. 'What shall I say?'

'Just tell her what you've been up to over the past week and leave it with her. Look, I'm in the middle of something – I'd better go.'

Libby stared at the screen for a little longer, then decided to finish her *Contraband* email first to give her time to think. Then, to give herself even more time, she made a cup of tea. Finally she wrote a brief reply to Tara Nichols and included her mobile number. Then, unable to contain herself any longer, she called Fran.

'So there we are,' she concluded. 'What do you think?'

'What do you mean, what do I think?' Fran sounded irritated, and Libby remembered what Ben had said yesterday. Fran often sounded irritated.

'Well, is it worth looking into this Anglo-Saxon business any further?' Libby hesitated. 'And . . . into the murder.'

Fran's gusty sigh made her cringe.

'All right, all right. I'll leave you alone,' she said hastily. 'I just thought you'd want to know – after we saw that brooch . . .'

'Let me know if it really is Anglo-Saxon,' said Fran. 'Otherwise I'm a bit busy right now. Oh – and we thought we might come up for a drink on Wednesday, if that's all right?'

Was that an olive branch? wondered Libby. 'Of course,' she said out loud. 'You going to stay over?'

Fran's voice softened. 'If that's OK.'

'Course it is,' said Libby. 'Ben'll be pleased.'

And he would, she reflected after ending the call. He always liked to see Guy.

Tara Nichols called just as Libby arrived back from a quick shopping trip to the village.

'It's very nice of you to speak to me,' said a young-sounding voice. 'I thought you might think it was a cheek!'

'Why would I think that?' asked Libby, sliding sausages into the fridge.

'Well, you working with the police . . .'

'Oh-oh! Hang on – what's Moira been telling you?'

'Well, she said you were a sort of investigator and you worked with the police. And I know you helped with that murder at St Eldreda's, didn't you?'

'Oh.' Libby tucked the phone under her chin while she filled the kettle. 'How did you know that?'

'I read about it when I was doing research on the monastery. It came up in some news reports.'

'I see.' Libby put a teabag into a mug. 'You know I'm not a proper investigator, don't you?'

Tara laughed. 'You certainly sound like it!'

'Hmm.' Libby scowled at Sidney, who had jumped up beside the bread bin.

'Anyway, I just wondered what you knew about the site,' Tara continued. 'I'm still certain there's something over there.'

'Actually,' said Libby, 'I don't know very much. I don't know what Moira told you, but this is what the situation is.' She poured water into her mug and sat down. 'It all started because someone disappeared . . .'

It took her some time to explain the events of the last week, and apart from the odd request for clarification, Tara listened attentively.

'Well,' she said, when Libby had finally run out of steam, 'I think you're right. I'm pretty sure there is a burial site over there. It makes sense, doesn't it? It's right in the thick of the Anglo-Saxon territory, and King Egbert gave Eldreda that land for her house of prayer.'

'That's what I thought,' agreed Libby. 'I want to go over and talk to Sister Catherine at the abbey and see what she knows – or have you already done that?'

'Oh, we spoke to them before we started the dig,' said Tara. 'They weren't sure about a burial site – they had nothing in their records – but they agreed it was a possibility.' She paused. 'Do you think I could go and look at this brooch you saw? In Nethergate, you said?'

'We-ell,' said Libby, 'I'm not sure that's a good idea. The police know about it now, and if we show too much interest it might disappear before they can investigate.'

'Oh yes, I hadn't thought of that.' Tara sounded disappointed. 'But you think this man's death is connected to the pub burning down?'

'We don't know. It's a theory. I don't know what other theories the police have, other than a disagreement between antiques dealers.'

'Nighthawks,' Tara said. 'That links the dealers with a possible site.'

'But there isn't a site. Not officially,' said Libby.

'No. But the pub was being removed in order to build houses.' Tara was sharp. 'To cover up a site?'

'But the dealers and the nighthawks wouldn't have wanted that,' Libby demurred. 'They would have been against the development, wouldn't they?'

Tara heaved a gusty sigh. 'Well, it's made me even more certain that there is a site over there,' she said. 'I'm going to go and have a look. Want to come with me?'

87

Chapter Thirteen

It took Libby about ten seconds to recover from her surprise. 'When?' she said.

'When are you free?'

'Whenever you like.' She passed a mental calendar under review. 'As long as it's not evenings.'

Tara laughed. 'Bit difficult searching the ground in the dark. What about tomorrow morning? I can get down there by about half ten.'

'Where are you coming from?' asked Libby.

'Canterbury. And you're in the same village as Moira, aren't you?'

'Steeple Martin, yes. Are you at the university?'

'How did you guess?' Tara laughed again. 'Visiting only at the moment. So I'll see you down there tomorrow? Where shall we meet?'

'By the Crooked Horse,' said Libby. 'You said you heard about the attempt to burn the pub down?'

'Yes, I did. Awful. And quite close to where we were. Is there still room to park?'

'Oh yes,' said Libby, 'as long as we avoid the police tape.'

'So there we are,' Libby reported to Fran, 'I'm going on an archaeological recce. Sure you don't want to come?'

'No thanks – I've had enough of going on expeditions with you. Just be careful.'

Libby sighed and called Ben.

'You were right,' she said. 'Fran's getting more irritable all the time.

And yet she was quite interested in finding out about Hodges' boat the other day – after we'd seen that brooch. But now she says she doesn't want to go anywhere with me.'

'Well, to be fair, the last time she did find a body,' said Ben.

'Hmm,' said Libby.

'Anyway, you be careful, poking about on the marshes. Last time you did that, someone hit you over the head.'

'I shall be with a pillar of the community,' said Libby. 'I'll be fine.'

'Well if I were you, I'd tell Ian what you're going to do. Just in case.'

'He'll tell me not to do it.'

'And will you take any notice?'

'I'm not going anywhere near the Horse,' said Libby. 'Not really. Only to park. He can't stop me poking around on the marsh, as you put it.'

Ben sighed. 'All right. But I'd still tell him.'

So Libby left a text message on Ian's work phone. Just in case.

Ian called the following morning as Libby was negotiating the road from Bishop's Bottom to the lane Patti had told her about. She realised she did know it, she just hadn't realised this was where it led.

'Why are you going there?' he asked.

'I'm driving.'

'Pull over.'

'I can't. There isn't anywhere.' Libby threw the mobile onto the passenger seat and ignored the voice still talking.

Arriving at the Crooked Horse, she saw a rather muddy Land Rover parked outside, and a small, dark-haired woman leaning against it looking at a map.

She picked up the phone and rang Ian back.

'Right, I'm parked outside the pub,' she said. 'It being the only place we *can* park round here. And no, we aren't going anywhere near it.'

'All right. Just keep your eyes open, and if you see anyone lurking about, tell me.'

'We won't be near here, I told you. Now I'm going to say hello to Tara. I'll let you know what happens.'

She ended the call and climbed out of the car.

'Hello!' Tara was waving and walking towards her. 'Libby?'

'Yes! Tara?' They shook hands, and Libby was delighted to find that Tara was as short as she was herself. Not so delighted that she was at least twenty years younger and very pretty.

'Where are we going, then?' she asked.

'Along that way,' said Tara, pointing left. 'Towards St Eldreda's. The couple of finds that identified the site were found by field walkers on that little rise – can you see?'

Libby nodded. 'It's quite a long way from the monastery, though, isn't it?'

'It is, but burial sites often were a fair distance away. And of course,' Tara fixed earnest brown eyes on Libby's own, 'there were other buildings as well as the remains that you can see now.'

'Were there?' They were walking now, across rough grassland that looked boggy in places.

'Oh yes. If you think of all the other monasteries that are still standing, the buildings are spread over quite a wide area.'

'Oh,' said Libby, trying to picture some of the other ruins she knew about. 'And why was it called a monastery when it was for women?'

'Oh, it wasn't only for women by the time it was built,' explained Tara. 'Didn't you know? It was what's known as a double monastery, for men *and* women. Occasionally, as in the case of St Eldreda, the abbess was the head. Quite rare.' She was looking excited. 'And it was obviously quite a big site, which is why I was absolutely positive there would be a burial ground. I wanted permission to excavate the rest of the site, and I thought if I could find evidence of burials, I'd get it.'

'Hasn't it been excavated before, then?' Libby was hurrying to keep up now. Tara was practically sprinting over the difficult ground.

'No, permission was sought a couple of times, but it was never granted. Mainly because no one was really sure who owned the site.

But the present lot are, as you know, Anglican Benedictines, and since the interest aroused by the Tredega Relic . . .' Tara paused and looked back at Libby. 'That was you, wasn't it? I looked you up.'

'Yes,' sighed Libby. 'It was.'

'Well, after that, they rather changed their tune.'

'I wonder why.' Libby stopped and rubbed her back. 'I would have thought they'd have become more protective of the site. They increased security, apparently. More cameras and so on.'

'I don't know.' Tara shrugged. 'I was just pleased to have been allowed to dig. But then there was the pandemic and we were shut down.'

'I heard the theory about the burial site was disproved?'

'Yes, I heard that too,' said Tara with a grin. 'And no one ever found out who set the rumour going. I'm guessing it's someone who didn't want us poking around.'

They continued walking until Tara came to a halt beside a rusting metal pole leaning at a drunken angle.

'Here we are!' she said.

'What's that?' Libby pointed at the pole.

'One of my markers. I left it here deliberately in case I was able to come back.' Tara took off her rucksack and pulled out a pair of nitrile gloves. 'I thought we'd do a bit of field walking first.'

'Right.' Libby looked dubiously at the slightly scrubby field in front of them. 'Are you not going to tell St Eldreda's what we're doing?'

Tara looked surprised. 'Why?'

'Well, it is their land. You said yourself . . .'

'They gave me permission!' She sound belligerent.

'For the original dig, but not this time. It's only polite to tell them you're looking at the site.'

Tara stood staring at her feet and then turned her back on Libby. 'Well, you can do what you like. I thought you wanted to come.'

Now Libby was getting annoyed.'I did, but Sister Catherine is a friend of mine.' Stretching it a bit, but never mind. 'I don't want to upset her. It was bad enough when we brought murder down on their heads.'

Tara was several yards away now, bending over as she walked to peer at the ground. She waved a hand airily over her shoulder. 'OK,' she called back.

Libby frowned. Tara was behaving like a spoilt child, and she didn't know whether she ought to stay and keep an eye on her or call Patti to ask her to let Sister Catherine know what was going on. She sighed and pulled out her phone.

'Libby!' Tara's voice stopped her.

'What?' Libby looked up and saw her waving.

'Someone's been here!'

She put her phone away.

'Could be anybody,' she said. 'The nuns may have come to have a look.'

Tara was running back to her now. 'No – they've been digging!' She was wild-eyed and panting. 'Someone's been raiding the site!'

Libby's thoughts went immediately to the Anglo-Saxon brooch. 'How can you tell?'

'I'm a bloody archaeologist! Of course I can tell.' Tara took a deep breath. 'We must notify the police.'

Libby smiled. 'Actually, yes. We must.'

Tara looked faintly surprised. 'You agree?'

'Remember what Moira told you?' Libby pulled out her phone again. 'I work with the police.' She tapped Ian's number and turned away.

'I'm at the dig site,' she said when he answered. 'And Tara – the archaeologist, remember? – says someone's been raiding it.'

'Raiding it? How?'

'Digging, I assume.' Libby raised an eyebrow at Tara, who nodded. 'Nighthawks, probably.'

'Or rogue antiques dealers,' said Ian grimly. 'What evidence has she got?'

'Any evidence?' Libby asked. Tara shook her head. 'No – just

92

what she could see on the ground, I think.' Tara nodded. 'What shall we do?'

'I'll get on to the abbey,' said Ian, 'and someone will meet you – where? By the pub?'

'Yes. That's where we parked. We'll have to leave the site.'

'I don't suppose it'll run away,' said Ian, 'and I hardly think anyone's been watching you stomp all over it.'

'I didn't,' Libby snapped.

'All right, all right.' Ian sighed. 'And by the way, Clare got hauled over the coals for not taking your fingerprints last week.'

'She what?' Libby was appalled. 'Who by? I thought you were her senior officer in MIT?'

'She's actually not part of MIT,' said Ian, 'so it wasn't me. I did, however, stand up for her. But we have got to take your fingerprints. And Fran's, of course.'

'Oh bugger. So we've got to come in to Canterbury, have we?'

'Sorry.'

'All right. I'll speak to Fran. Now, how long have we got to wait here?'

'Local patrol already alerted,' said Ian. 'Multitasking. It shouldn't be long.'

'How did you manage that?'

'They already knew you were going over there. I shall now contact them and tell them the situation.' The line went dead.

'Police are coming,' said Libby. 'We're to wait by the pub.'

'I can't leave the site.' Tara planted her feet firmly and set her mouth in a thin line.

'Why not? It's been sitting here unattended for years.'

'Someone could be watching.'

'And if they are,' said Libby, 'they'll see me going off and leaving you on your own.'

'Oh.' Tara looked doubtful. 'You could wait with me.'

'We're to meet the police and show them where the site is,' said Libby in a tired voice. 'Wake up, Tara. This is not an adventure movie.'

93

She turned and began to trudge back towards the Crooked Horse.

After a few minutes' silence, Tara spoke from behind her.

'What's MIT? I heard you saying . . .'

'Major investigation team.'

'Oh. Is that what this is? A major investigation?'

'No. That's another investigation entirely.'

By now they were in sight of the pub and their two vehicles, and just in time to see a liveried police car draw up alongside. As Libby approached, with Tara trailing behind, two uniformed officers climbed out.

'Mrs Sarjeant?' said one, a stocky individual with fox-coloured hair and a broad smile. 'PC Ford. We've met before.'

'We have?' Libby stopped. 'When was that?'

'I came to your house to take away an unwanted visitor. Last autumn, it would have been.'

'Oh yes!' Libby smiled back. Not that she remembered him, but she certainly remembered the incident.

'And this is PC Reynolds.' Ford indicated the tall, dark-haired woman coming from the driver's side.

'Ma'am,' said Reynolds.

'Oh, Libby, please.' Libby waved a hand towards Tara. 'And this is Tara Nichols, who discovered that the site had been – er – tampered with.'

Chapter Fourteen

Tara looked as if she'd like to run away. The two officers converged on her and Libby stood back as her phone began to buzz in her pocket.

'Yes, they're here,' she said. 'They're questioning Tara and I'm staying out of the way.'

'What exactly happened?' asked Ian. 'Could you see any disturbance?'

'No – she said simply that someone had been raiding the site. I couldn't see because I hadn't gone onto the field, but she seemed certain of it.'

'Hmm. I'm assuming this would be the site the Anglo-Saxon brooch came from. Is that your thinking?'

'It sort of links up, doesn't it? But how does it link up with Malcolm Hodges?'

'I don't know,' said Ian, 'but I'm going to see Mr Mayberry and ask to see the brooch. Perhaps he'll tell me.'

'And perhaps he won't,' said Libby. 'And he'll know I told you about it.'

'I shall merely say I heard via a CHIS.' Libby could hear the smile in Ian's voice.

'What the hell's a CHIS?'

'Covert human intelligence source,' said Ian. 'That's what you are. And actually, there is a budget for them. You know I said I'd pay you if I could?'

'Oh, stop it, Ian! This is posh speak for a snout, isn't it?'

'In layman's terms, yes.'

'Well, I don't want to be one,' said Libby firmly.

Ian laughed. 'We'll talk about it when you come into the station. Meanwhile, I'd leave your pet archaeologist and my officers to sort things out between them and go home.'

After ending the call, Libby joined Tara and the officers.

'Sorry to interrupt,' she said, 'but I've just spoken to DCI Connell and he's told me to go home. Is that all right with you, or would you rather I stayed?'

'That's fine, Mrs Sarjeant,' said the unsmiling PC Reynolds. 'Miss Nichols will take us to see the site.'

'Great,' said Libby, avoiding Tara's frantic eyebrow signalling. 'And if a statement's needed, I'm going in to the station tomorrow.' She turned to Tara. 'I'll call you later, Tara – or you can call me.' She smiled all round and made smartly for her car.

She drove back to the lane that ran past the Willoughby Oak to St Aldeberge and on from there to Nethergate. It occurred to her that perhaps she should have warned Fran she was on her way, but that would give Fran a chance to put her off, and right now, she needed tea and sympathy.

'Why?' asked Fran, as she installed Libby on the customer's stool by the counter in Guy's shop. 'I'll give you tea, but why do you need sympathy?'

Libby looked over her shoulder at the couple perusing the shelves of artwork, including some of her own, on the other side of the shop. 'Because I feel embarrassed and a bit ashamed,' she said in a stage whisper.

Fran made a disbelieving face and went through a door to put the kettle on. Libby fidgeted.

'Come on then,' said Fran. 'Tell me what happened.'

Libby began on the saga of Moira, the dig and the archaeologist.

'Hold it there,' said Fran when she reached the moment Tara and Libby met at the Crooked Horse. 'The kettle's boiled.'

Libby resumed when Fran came back with mugs. 'And then,' she finished, 'Ian told me to go home. Oh – and we've got to go and have our fingerprints taken.'

'I wondered why they hadn't done that,' muttered Fran. 'So why are you embarrassed and ashamed?'

Libby heaved a sigh. 'Because I was all excited to be going and looking at a dig site and then I ran away.'

'Hardly,' said Fran. 'Ian told you to go home. And you were quite right that Tara should have got permission from St Eldreda's. She sounds rather selfish, this Miss Nichols.'

'I think she's just completely oblivious to anything other than what she wants to do – or thinks *should* be done.'

'Sounds familiar.' Fran raised her eyebrows at Libby.

Libby scowled back and took a sip of tea.

'Look, Fran,' she said after a minute, 'if you no longer want to get involved with anything in the investigation line, just say so. It strikes me' – and Ben, she added mentally – 'that you disapprove of most of what I do these days, so if that's the case, I won't bother you any more.'

The silence that followed this unequivocal statement was broken by the couple who had been looking at the items for sale approaching the counter holding out a small, unframed painting.

'Thank you,' said Fran. 'It is rather nice, isn't it? And this just happens to be the artist.'

Libby slid off the stool, going rather pink, and accepted the couple's enthusiastic praise. By the time the painting was wrapped and paid for, both she and Fran had recovered their equilibrium.

'I'm sorry,' said Libby.

'No.' Fran put a hand on her arm. '*I'm* the one who should be sorry.' She came round the end of the counter and gave Libby an unaccustomed hug. 'I've been a crabby old bitch.'

Libby laughed. 'I wouldn't say that. And you're entitled to feel a bit discombobulated after finding a body.'

Fran sighed and reached for her own tea. 'It isn't that. I think it's because I don't feel I contribute anything.'

'To what?' Libby frowned.

'To the investigations. I mean, they're nearly all because of you, aren't they?'

'Sometimes. But the homeless man – when we met Ricky – that was you. Ian rang you in the first place.'

'Yes, but I didn't exactly go looking for anything, did I?'

'Neither do I!' said Libby. 'I stumble over things.'

'And then follow them up. I tend to avoid them these days.'

'Because, as I said to Ben the other day, you're enjoying being married, living in a nice cottage in a nice town, with your raffish acting career behind you.' Libby grinned at her friend.

'You were talking to Ben about me?' Fran sounded offended.

'Only saying just what I've said!' said Libby, inwardly cursing. 'And how nice it was for you.'

'Oh.' Fran subsided. 'I suppose so.'

'And what about your moments?' Libby crossed her fingers. This was delicate territory. 'You don't seem to want to acknowledge them any more.'

Fran smiled. 'I know. And we've discussed this, haven't we? They aren't as frequent these days, and I'm pretty sure it's because of what you just said – I've settled into comfortable middle-class life. My brain has settled down too.'

They smiled fondly at each other.

'Shall I pick you up on the way to Canterbury tomorrow?' asked Fran. 'We can have our fingerprints done and then go and have some lunch.'

Libby beamed. 'In our favourite pub?'

'Where else?' said Fran.

Libby's phone buzzed on and off all the way home to Steeple Martin. She ignored it, assuming it was either Tara or Ian or both. The answerphone light winking from the landline when she got home confirmed that one of the calls at least was from Ian. Once she had a comforting bowl of soup in front of her, she returned it.

'Where have you been?' He was peremptory.

'Having tea with Fran, driving home and making lunch. Where have *you* been?'

'Wha—' Libby heard her inquisitor take a deep breath. 'I'm sorry, Libby. I was going to tell you that you needn't come into the station tomorrow – someone will come to you.'

'Oh.' Libby swallowed a mouthful of leek and potato soup. 'That's a pity. Fran and I were going to come in and then go to lunch.'

Ian gave a snort of laughter, quickly suppressed. 'If that's what you'd prefer, of course. I was trying to be helpful.'

'And duck out of being asked questions,' added Libby.

'I would not necessarily be present while your prints were taken.'

'Of course not,' said Libby. 'So can you answer a couple of questions now?'

'It depends on the questions,' said Ian warily.

'Don't you tell your covert human intelligence sources anything, then?'

'All right, go on.'

'What I was wondering,' said Libby, 'was whether you were now certain that Malcolm Hodges' death had something to do with the attack on the Crooked Horse. And if so, why?'

After a moment, during which Libby could swear she heard the cogs turning, Ian replied.

'I thought we talked about this?'

'You just said you needed some firm evidence connecting the two events so you could get a warrant – or permission – to investigate the pub. But you weren't particularly pleased when I told you I was going over there this morning.'

There was another silence.

'Well, say something,' grumbled Libby. 'At least tell me why you were ringing me – apart from telling me not to come into the station tomorrow.'

'Very well.' Ian suddenly sounded tired. 'I was going to tell you that the Anglo-Saxon brooch has disappeared from Wallace Mayberry's shop.'

'Oh.' Libby sat back, stunned. 'But nobody said anything!'

'What do you mean?'

'I thought that if anyone showed any interest – which we didn't, by the way – it would disappear. That's why I told Tara not to go. So surely . . .' She stopped. 'Tara didn't go there, did she?'

'Of course she bloody did!' Ian exploded. 'What did you have to tell her for?'

'She's an archaeologist! She ran the dig at a presumed Anglo-Saxon site, for heaven's sake! Of course I told her.' Libby pushed her soup bowl away. 'I'm very sorry if something I said inadvertently caused you to lose a vital lead. But when you ask me to do things for you, you should give me a full briefing, the same as you do with your officers. Then maybe I wouldn't make mistakes. So I'm sorry, and I hope you find whoever killed Hodges, and I hope somebody finds out who wanted the pub destroyed. Bye, Ian.' And Libby switched off her phone.

Feeling distinctly upset, she also deleted all the texts from Tara that had appeared on her mobile, put her bowl and saucepan in the dishwasher and left the cottage.

'And where are you going?' she asked herself, as she stood in the middle of Allhallow's Lane. The Manor to see Hetty? The brewery to see Ben? She turned left towards the high street.

'What ho, petal!' Harry greeted her from the kitchen doorway of the Pink Geranium. 'Lunch?'

'No thanks.' Libby looked round at the customers occupying the tables and recognised none of them.

'Garden?' suggested Harry.

She nodded and followed him through the kitchen into the little yard at the back, where a couple of white iron tables occasionally accommodated the few smokers left in the world. These no longer included Libby, who had finally eschewed the demon weed, to the delight of her friends.

100

'So what's up, chuck?' asked Harry, leaning against the stairway that led up to Adam's flat. 'You look in need of pastoral care.'

'I've had a row with Ian.' Libby slumped onto one of the spindly chairs.

'Makes a change from Fran or Ben,' observed Harry. 'Wine?'

She gave him a lopsided smile. 'Why not.'

Harry went back into the kitchen and returned immediately with an opened bottle.

'Might as well use this up,' he said, putting two glasses on the table. 'Won't keep. And now,' he continued, once they both had full glasses, 'what's it all about? Horrible Hodges or Perilous Pubs?'

'Both, really. And I'm not sure the Crooked Horse is actually perilous.'

'It would be if you were inside when someone set fire to it,' said Harry.

'Yes, OK. But as I said, it's about both. I think Ian was fobbing me off again.'

Harry sighed. 'I doubt it. Go on.'

Libby told him what had happened since he had informed her of Moira's request.

'So I think,' she concluded, 'he was sending me off to look into the pub to keep me away from Hodges.'

Harry put his head on one side and gave her a searching look. 'How many times have you thought something like that? I've lost count. And he never is, you know. What was it he called you?'

'A covert human intelligence source – CHIS.'

'Chiz, chiz!' quoted Harry with a grin. 'Molesworth rules.'

'I know, I know.' Libby reluctantly grinned back. 'It's a posh name for a snout. And he could actually pay me, apparently.'

'What a good idea!' Harry clapped his hands. 'Then you might stop bellyaching about not having a proper job.'

'Sorry if I'm a nuisance.' Libby picked up her glass and scowled.

'Yes, you are, petal, but never mind. Look,' he sat forward on his chair, 'Ian doesn't magic up situations for you to go and investigate, he asks you to look into things the powers-that-be haven't got the resources for.' He sat back and picked up his own glass. 'He probably gets fed up with you taking umbrage about things.'

Libby opened her mouth and closed it again. Harry was quite possibly right.

'OK,' she said. 'I'm being an idiot.'

'Yes, dear,' said Harry. 'And I bet you your little expedition this morning will turn up something, or . . .' he paused for effect, 'make those powers-that-be find some resources to do some proper investigating. So for goodness' sake stop doing the "poor little me" act.' He took a sip of wine. 'Tell me – why hasn't there been a proper investigation into the cause of the fire already?'

Chapter Fifteen

Libby stared. 'Well,' she said eventually, 'I don't really know.'

'Sounds very dodgy to me.' Harry nodded wisely.

'Yes, it does, doesn't it?' Libby frowned. 'What I know so far is that Marsham's were selling the pub – although no one seems to know if it was part of the great clearance of last year – and a London couple had agreed to buy it. Then it came out that they were going to sell it on to the developers, Speedwell, I think they're called, who wanted to knock it down and build luxury houses.'

Harry nodded. 'Because they'd been told they couldn't build on the nature reserve.'

'Oh, you know that?'

'Everybody does, dear.'

'Right. So then Marsham's withdrew from the sale, and the next thing was the digger or bulldozer, whatever it was, turned up to demolish the building. As far as I can gather, no one will admit to sending it in.'

'Didn't they ask the driver?'

'I expect it was hired and the hire company didn't actually know who by.'

'You'd have thought they would have asked if all the relevant permissions were in place, wouldn't you?' Harry stared thoughtfully at the kitchen door.

'You would. And there must have been a search for the new owners – or prospective owners.' Libby tapped impatient fingers on the table. 'Oh, I wish Ian had told me more.'

'Didn't he tell you another team were looking into it?'

'Did he? I don't know who, though. And there's still police tape up. Makes you wonder, doesn't it?'

'If someone doesn't want it looked into?' said Harry. 'Yes, it does, but who? Who would have that sort of clout with the police to stop an investigation?'

'And why did Ian need some actual evidence to look into it?' Libby shook her head.

'We-ell,' said Harry, 'I suppose if Marsham's said don't bother, the only thing the police could do would be to find out who hired the digger, and they've got no further with that, so it's stalemate.'

'I'm still not sure why Ian linked Hodges' death to the Horse, though. I know why I did, but that's different.'

'Too true,' said Harry. 'More wine?'

Somewhat comforted, Libby went home. Tonight was a *Contraband* rehearsal with Susannah, the Oast Theatre's regular pianist, so she took her script and iPad into the garden and sat down underneath the cherry tree.

She was woken some time later by her mobile chirruping insistently from inside the conservatory. She struggled up and went to answer it.

'Mrs Sarjeant?' asked an unfamiliar voice. 'DS Boyd here.'

'Oh, yes?' said Libby. 'Are you coming to take my fingerprints?'

There was a short silence. 'Er, no.' DS Boyd cleared his throat. 'Um – DCI Connell asked me to call you.'

'Oh.' Libby was surprised.

'He asked if it would be convenient to come and take a statement from you later today.'

'He did? Oh – well, of course, but if it could be before seven thirty? I have an appointment.'

Now it was DS Boyd's turn to be surprised. 'Oh. I can't confirm the time, but thank you.'

Libby rang off, frowning. Obviously Ian hadn't wanted to speak to

104

her again himself in case he got his head bitten off. She went into the kitchen and filled the kettle, feeling once more ashamed and embarrassed. Why had she flown off the handle like that? Ian had, perfectly nicely, told her why he had linked the two events, and here was she accusing him of fobbing her off. It was no wonder people got fed up with her. 'Including,' she told Sidney, 'Fran. I really can be a pain in the arse.'

No word had come from Ian by the time the *Contraband* rehearsal was due to start, so, having made sure the cast knew about Judy and Cyd's absence, she set them to a chorus rehearsal. The songs had been written for the piece and were therefore not well known, so Susannah had her work cut out. Cyd had been acting as chorus master, which made life even more difficult, and by just after nine o'clock they were all ready to call it a day.

'Sorry, Susannah,' said Libby as the cast collected belongings and drifted out. 'But it's a great opportunity for the girls.'

'Of course it is,' said Susannah. 'And by the time they come back, the rest of the cast will be note-perfect.'

'Let's hope so.' Libby sighed and took out her phone. 'Oh no,' she said as it buzzed into frantic life.

'Important?' Susannah raised an eyebrow.

'I think so,' said Libby gloomily, and opened the latest text from Ian.

I'm in the bar, it read.

'Bloody hell,' she muttered. 'Sorry, Susannah.'

She made her way to the auditorium doors, took a deep breath and pushed them open.

'Evening.' Ian greeted her with a grin from his seat by the bar, where Ben was busy pouring drinks.

'Hello.' Libby went slowly towards him.

Ben handed her a glass of wine. 'I didn't know what you'd want, so I took a guess,' he said. 'Go and sit down. Ian wants to talk to you.'

Ian followed her to one of the little tables.

'I'm sorry,' she blurted out, before he could say anything. 'I shouldn't—'

He leant over and patted her hand. 'Don't, Lib. It's quite all right. I don't tell you everything I need to if I'm wanting information. So here's the latest update.'

'Oh!' Libby sat back and relaxed. 'Did they find anything at the dig site? Was Tara able to show them?'

'Well, yes. And I got on to the abbey, as I said I would, and the upshot is they are allowing her to reopen the dig. So she's extremely pleased.'

'Oh, that *is* good,' said Libby. 'And did you speak to Wally Mayberry about the brooch?'

'No, we don't want to alert him, do we?' Ian grinned again. 'But that wasn't the update I was going to give you.'

'Oh?'

'I spent a happy half-hour talking to my superintendent after I'd spoken to you, and got permission to search the pub, as there is a strong possibility that it was being used for the sale – or at least the distribution – of illegally sourced artefacts.'

'So that's why you need a statement from me?' asked Libby. 'Because I was there this morning?'

'Exactly. And because, when we go in tomorrow morning, I want you there to see if anything looks different to how it looked today.'

'Oh, I see.' Libby gazed at him. 'You actually want me? Really? This isn't a – a sop to my *amour propre*?'

'Nor to your vanity,' said Ian with a laugh. 'Come on, Lib, you can see why it would be important.'

'Yes, I can. But surely you need someone who saw it last week as well? I mean, I did see it on Saturday when I went to have a look with Patti, but . . .'

'We have a representative of Marsham's and the excavator driver coming as well.' Ian frowned. 'We can't trace the couple who were supposed to be buying the place.'

'What have the developers said?' asked Libby.

'They know nothing. They took the offer of sale on trust, which seems highly unlikely to me.'

'Hmm. And did *they* send in the excavator?'

'They say not, and the plant hire company have already provided the paperwork they received along with an assurance that there was nothing preventing the demolition. It's fake, as you would expect, which is more than enough reason for a warrant, but I gather it wasn't thought important enough last week.' Ian smiled and raised his glass. 'Which is why I asked you to get me some evidence. Which you have.'

'Well, I didn't really,' mumbled Libby. 'I sort of fell over it.'

'Drink up, then,' said Ian, 'and we'll go and have one at the Pocket. I'm staying with Hetty tonight, so I can give you a lift to the site in the morning if you like.'

'You'll have to be there really early, though, won't you? I'll come down on my own.' Libby stood up.

'Eight o'clock – and we would need you there before we actually go in.'

'Oh, all right, but I'll still drive myself, or I won't be able to get home, will I?' Libby smiled at him. 'Friends again?'

Libby, woken at 6.30 the following morning by a phone call from Ian reminding her of her appointment at the Crooked Horse, made it there by shortly after 8 a.m. Various official-looking vehicles were parked on the forecourt.

'Good morning.' Ian came over with a grin. 'This is DC Farrell. He'll record our conversation, if that's all right?'

A large young man in a crime-scene suit beamed at her and waved a tablet.

'Fine.' Libby smiled nervously and looked round the sad-looking site. 'It doesn't look any different to when I was here. Except the excavator's all taped up.'

'Yes, we did that. It's being collected later – although how the lorry will get here I have no idea. We may have to drive it away.' Ian frowned. 'Still . . . otherwise it's all the same?'

107

'Yes. It was only yesterday, after all.' Libby stared up at the blackened pub sign. 'What a shame. Such a lovely old place.'

Ian gave her an amused look. 'A lot of people seem to think so.'

'What's going to happen to it?'

'After we've finished with it, Marsham's are sending in a team of surveyors to see if it can be restored.' He shrugged. 'No idea if that'll be possible.'

'So they've definitely taken back ownership?'

'It seems so. Now,' he went on, 'can you walk me through what else you did yesterday?'

Libby led him and DC Farrell along the track to the nature reserve gate and waved a hand at the surroundings. 'We looked at this on Saturday when I came with Patti,' she said.

'That's the Reverend Patti Pearson,' Ian told Farrell.

'But I didn't come here yesterday.' Libby turned and walked back to the pub. 'We went down here' – she pointed – 'to the dig site. Your officers know where that is, because they came and met us here.'

'Right.' Ian turned back to the pub. 'Can you look at the doors, please? Is there anything different about them?'

'Different how?' Libby asked.

'Are there any marks that weren't there yesterday.'

'I've no idea,' said Libby. 'I didn't look that closely.' She began to walk along the police tape as she had on Saturday, right round to where it went behind the building. She turned back to Ian. 'Now that *is* different,' she said.

'What is?'

'The tape's been torn away from the doorpost.'

Stockport Libraries
and Information Service

You should retain this receipt.

Items that you have returned

Title: Flags on the Bayou
ID: C2000003281518

Title: The unexpected guest
ID: C2000003176578

Title: Waiting for sunrise
ID: C2000001905126

Total items: 3
Account balance: £4.20
Borrowed: 3
Overdue: 0
Reservation requests: 0
Ready for collection: 0
17/12/2024 15:24

Ask staff how to sign up for our Libraries
newsletter
www.stockport.gov.uk/libraries
libraries@stockport.gov.uk
@SMBC_Libraries
Facebook: Stockport Libraries

Stockport Libraries
and Information Service

You should retain this receipt.

**Customer ID: **********8561

Items that you have renewed

Title: Murder at the Crooked Horse
ID: C2000003290974
Due: 07 January 2025

Title: The history of England. Volume III,
Civil war
ID: C2000002052485
Due: 07 January 2025

Title: To kill a king
ID: C2000003289362
Due: 07 January 2025

Total items: 3
Account balance: £4.20
Borrowed: 3
Overdue: 0
Reservation requests: 0
Ready for collection: 0
17/12/2024 15:25

Ask staff how to sign up for our Libraries
newsletter
www.stockport.gov.uk/libraries
libraries@stockport.gov.uk
@SMBC_Libraries
Facebook: Stockport Libraries

Chapter Sixteen

Ian narrowed his eyes. 'Are you sure?'

'Positive.' Libby nodded. 'I walked down here, and the tape was tied to the doorpost and the door was hanging open.' She looked at him. 'It isn't now. It's closed.'

'Get that?' Ian snapped at Farrell. 'Right. Let's get the team in.'

The next ten minutes were a positive maelstrom of activity. Libby was sent to sit in a patrol car, while a team of white-suited individuals poured into and around the outside of the building. Eventually Ian came back to her.

'Sorry to keep you waiting.' He sighed. 'But you see how essential it was for you to be here? We'd never have known about that door.' He smiled down at her. 'You can go home now. I'll get someone to come and take your fingerprints later.'

'And Fran's? We were going to come into Canterbury today.'

'Yes, you said. I'm sorry if I spoiled your day out. Go on, off you go. If I can, I'll see you at the pub this evening and let you know what's happened.'

Libby climbed out of the car. 'I can stay if you want me to?'

'No, thank you, Libby. We'll be fine now. Go and tell your network of invaluable help.'

'Don't be sarky,' said Libby, and set off for her own car.

Having been warned of the change of plan, Fran was unsurprised to find Libby once more in the shop. Guy appeared from the rear, wiping his hands on a paint-stained rag.

'Go on, go home,' he said. 'It's not busy this morning, and believe it or not, my beloved daughter has deigned to come home for a few days and is upstairs.'

'Is she all right?' asked Libby. Guy's daughter, Sophie, had for some years been in a relationship with her own son, Adam.

'I think the nice man from the museum might be history,' said Fran with a sigh. 'I told you about him, didn't I?'

Libby nodded. 'That's a shame.'

'Hmm,' said Guy.

Libby and Fran left the shop.

'Guy not a fan of the nice man from the museum, then?' said Libby, as they walked back along Harbour Street to Coastguard Cottage.

'Not noticeably,' Fran admitted. 'He preferred it when she and Adam were a couple.' She unlocked her front door. 'How's his love life these days? I haven't seen much of him this year.'

'Oh, he was going out with one of Harry's "apprentices" at the caff for a few months. PhD student at Christchurch. But that's over, as far as I know.'

Fran went into the kitchen to put the kettle on. 'So they might get back together, do you think? Adam and Sophie?'

Libby shrugged. 'No idea. Now, do you want to know what happened this morning?'

They took their tea out into Fran's small courtyard, where Balzac uncurled himself from the big plant pot to greet them.

'Were you of any use?' Fran folded her arms and put her head on one side.

'You look as though you don't think I would have been.'

'No – I think you were. What happened?'

Libby told her.

'So does Ian think this proves a connection between Hodges' death and the burning of the pub?'

'I don't know. All I know is that for some reason, the fact that someone has been trying to get into the pub during the last week has given him a reason to get inside and investigate. That and the mystery of the disappearing brooch.' Libby sipped her tea. 'And he said he's sending someone to take my fingerprints later today.' She shook her head. 'It worries me that he's still sharing so much with us. And that's my fault, because I had a go at him. He's going to get suspended again.'

'If Ian isn't worried, why should you be?' asked Fran.

Libby looked shocked. 'Aren't you?'

Fran smiled into her mug. 'I think Ian can take care of himself.'

'Hmm.' Libby hunched a shoulder. 'Well, I want to know what we think we ought to be doing now. I mean, we haven't got any connections—'

Fran looked up. 'Don't start that again. We were actually asked to look into Fay's husband's disappearance, remember? And George at the Red Lion and Lewis thought you ought to look into the fire at the Crooked Horse. So those are the connections. And now Ian's asked for more help.'

Libby grinned. 'That's more like the Fran I used to know.'

Fran laughed. 'I thought so!'

'OK,' said Libby. 'What do we think, then? Are we going to bother to work things out, or are we going to leave it to the police?'

'It won't hurt to try and work things out,' said Fran. 'And then you can drop it into conversation when you see Ian.'

'He said he'd be at the pub tonight,' said Libby slowly. 'It *wouldn't* hurt, would it?'

'No. And it'll keep us amused.' Fran stood up. 'More tea?'

Libby shook her head. 'I just need to think. And you said the other day that you and Guy would come up this evening. Is that still on?'

'If you don't mind, I think we'll stay here. I'm sure I'll be seeing a lot more of you in the next few days.'

'All right.' Libby screwed her eyes shut. 'Now, working things out.'

Fran sat down again. 'Start at the beginning, then. When Lewis told you about the Crooked Horse.'

'Right.' Libby cleared her throat. 'George told Lewis I ought to look into the Horse because it might be linked to all the pubs Marsham's sold off last year. And Lewis said jokingly that because I was

111

directing a play about smugglers it would be appropriate because it used to be a smugglers' pub.'

'*Used* to be?'

'That's what he said. So anyway, the next thing was Wally Mayberry wanting us to look into his mate Fay's husband's disappearance, as you said.' She looked up at Fran. 'Why did we link the two together?'

'Because the antiques fraternity had started smuggling stuff in to avoid all the Brexit nonsense,' said Fran. 'Go on.'

'Well, then we – or rather you – found Hodges' body. And I mentioned the Horse to Ian. And I talked to George. And then you' – she squinted at Fran – 'told me to go and talk to Zack and warned me it could be dangerous.'

'Oh, yes.' Fran smiled sheepishly. 'Well, I thought it might be.'

'So,' continued Libby, 'Zack confirmed the pub was used by the antiques boys. And then we went to Beer and Bargains and found the brooch, and Patti took me to see the Horse. And,' she took a deep breath, 'linking everything up has been, as the police say, purely circumstantial.'

'Which is why Ian wanted proper evidence.'

'Yes, but all he got from me this morning was the fact that someone might possibly have been in there.'

'Probably, I would have thought,' said Fran. 'And that gave him all he needed to go in and search. Remember he wondered whether it was fired to conceal something like a body?'

'And if he finds nothing, all that effort will have been wasted,' said Libby with a sigh.

'No, it won't, because your friend Tara has got permission to reopen the dig, which is a result, and the police can start investigating the possible theft of artefacts.'

Libby stared at her friend thoughtfully. 'But he still won't have anything to link Hodges' death to the pub. He wasn't found there, after all.'

They sat looking at one another.

'Well, that didn't get us very far, did it?' said Libby at last. 'And there isn't anything else for us to do.'

'No.' Fran sighed. 'Except have out fingerprints taken.'

Libby stood up. 'And that being the case, I'd better go home, in case a police officer is hopping up and down on my doorstep with his kit.'

'All right.' Fran stood up and collected their cups. 'Ring me as soon as you hear anything.'

They went back into the cottage and Libby collected her basket.

'Do you realise it's exactly a week ago that we found Hodges' body?' she said as she opened the door.

'I know.' Fran made a face. 'And that's still a puzzle. I mean, we don't know why Fay thought he was out on his boat.'

'Presumably she checked and found the boat wasn't where it should be?' suggested Libby. 'We never asked.'

'And his car!' added Fran. 'He must have had a car. If he did go out on the boat, he had to have driven down to the creek.'

'Unless his car was still at home and he used to take a taxi to the creek,' said Libby.

'But why?' asked Fran. 'When he came back, he'd need the car to get back to Shittenden.'

'Oh, it's all so complicated.' Libby frowned. 'And we don't know the half of it, do we?'

Fran smiled at her. 'Same old, same old,' she said.

Chapter Seventeen

'It could still be a simple insurance job,' said Ben, when Libby told him about the morning's activities.

'That's what I said when Lewis first told me about it,' said Libby, selecting a sandwich from the plate Hetty had brought in to the estate office. 'But it doesn't work now we know that Marsham's put a stop on the sale. They certainly wouldn't have tried to burn it down, and neither would the couple who were trying to buy it – it would be of no benefit to them. They didn't own it. Same goes for Speedwell.'

'Who's Speedwell?'

'Speedwell Developers,' explained Libby.

'Hmm.' Ben sat back and gazed at the ceiling. 'Who *would* have done it, then?'

'I don't know.' Libby shook her head. 'I can't see any of the antiques fraternity doing it – there's no reason. Unless they stored loads of smuggled stuff there.'

'But they'd have cleared everything out when the pub closed,' said Ben. 'And why would they have stored stuff there anyway? It's a real puzzle, isn't it?'

'The real puzzle,' said Libby, 'is why the excavator was sent in. Because if it hadn't been, I think the fire would have been written off as an accident.'

'So who sent it in?' asked Ben.

'Perhaps the developers didn't know Marsham's had pulled out?'

'No reputable business would do that without checking,' said Ben.

'But they hadn't checked on the planning issues,' Libby pointed out. 'There was some kind of preservation order on the pub itself, and they'd never have been allowed to build on the nature reserve.'

'I thought they'd bought part of the Dunton estate?' Ben was frowning.

'That's what I was told, but it borders the reserve.' Libby sighed and sat back. 'I don't know all the ins and outs. As I said to Fran, we don't know the half of it.'

Ben smiled. 'Ian'll get to the bottom of it, you'll see. And you'll help, of course.'

By the time Libby and Ben left for the Coach and Horses that evening, no one had turned up to take Libby's fingerprints, and given that Ian was having to be an on-the-ground officer in the current investigations, Libby had decided not to call and ask.

'No one else here yet?' Ben asked Tim at the bar.

The landlord shook his head. 'Could be just you and the girls this evening.'

'I suppose he means Patti and Anne,' said Libby with a grin. 'Must tell them he calls them the girls.'

Shortly afterwards, a familiar whoop of laughter heralded the arrival of Anne's wheelchair getting stuck in the doorway. Ben got up to help and a flustered Patti emerged hanging onto the handles.

'I swear she only does it for the entertainment value,' she said to Libby as she sank down in the chair next to her.

'What – gets stuck?' Libby laughed. 'Could well be.'

'So,' said Anne, when the four of them were seated at the large round table. 'Where is everybody? Is Ian off solving your murder?'

'We think he must be,' said Ben. 'He had Libby down at the Crooked Horse this morning.'

'Really?' Anne's face lit up. 'What's happened?'

Libby gave them a precis of events since she and Patti had gone to see the pub on Saturday.

'I'm glad your friend's got permission to reopen the dig,' said Patti.

'She's not my friend, actually,' corrected Libby. 'She's an acquaint-ance of Moira, who's one of the Pocket's regulars.'

'Whoever she is, it's good that it's going to happen,' said Patti. 'When I spoke to Cathy about it, she said she'd always been disap-pointed that it was closed down before.'

'Yes.' Libby frowned. 'I wonder who did that. I assumed it was the nuns. But if Cathy was disappointed . . .'

'No, it wasn't them.' Patti shook her head. 'They were all for it. It would have brought them more income with visitors to the old mon-astery, wouldn't it? And they're always broke.'

At this point, the door swung open to reveal a very tired-looking Ian, followed by Peter. Patti and Libby both nudged Anne to keep her quiet, while Ben and Peter went to the bar and Ian more or less col-lapsed into a chair.

'No questions?' he said with a rather pained smile.

Anne opened her mouth and Libby said, 'No!' very loudly.

Ian laughed. 'It's all right. You deserve to know, and none of you will say anything outside these four walls, will you?

Peter and Ben returned to the table.

'We're quite safe,' said Ben, 'but only tell us if you're allowed to. Libby's been worried that you're telling her too much.'

Ian looked slightly disbelieving.

'Well,' he said, after a restorative sip of Ben's Best Bitter, 'as far as we can tell, someone definitely had been into the Crooked Horse since Libby and Patti had been there. But worse than that . . .' he looked round at the interested faces, 'it's also a crime scene.'

He allowed the shocked exclamations to subside before going on.

'I shan't go into details, but it would appear that it is the scene of some kind of violent attack.'

'Last week's body?' breathed Anne, eyes alight.

'We don't know,' said Ian. 'And that's all I'm going to tell you for the time being.'

Libby kept uncharacteristically silent, while Peter asked after Edward.

'Spring term's finished, so he's spending more time with Alice,' said Ian. 'Wouldn't surprise me if we're looking for a new owner for our downstairs apartment soon.'

'You've said that before,' said Ben. 'Do you really think he'll move in with her?'

'It's a long way from his campus,' said Peter.

'He had rooms there before he bought Grove House,' said Libby. 'Perhaps he'll go back to them.'

'So we won't see as much of him,' said Anne, her face falling. 'Shame.'

The door burst open once more: Harry, still in his whites as usual, followed unexpectedly by Philip Jacobs, looking every inch the country solicitor and beaming at them all.

'Hello, Philip!' Libby smiled and stood up. 'We don't usually see you here on a Wednesday.'

He gave her a kiss on the cheek. 'I wanted a word,' he said, looking briefly at Ian. 'With both of you.'

After a certain amount of rearranging, Philip, Ian and Libby shunted themselves away from the table.

'Come on then,' said Ian. 'Tell me the worst.'

Philip, smiled at them both. 'It's about Marsham's,' he said.

Ian's eyebrows went up. 'Why are they talking to you? They've got their own legal department.'

'I'm a barrister, remember?' Philip held his glass up to the light, admiring the golden glow of the beer. 'They seem to think they might be in trouble.'

'So should you be speaking to me?'

'This is entirely off the record,' said Philip, 'or I wouldn't be including Libby.' He tweaked the crease in his trousers and crossed his legs.

'Go on.' Libby glanced briefly at Ian and frowned.

'As you know, there is no longer a member of the Marsham family on the board of the brewery,' Philip began, 'and they are now somewhat concerned that there may be something wrong about the sale of the Crooked Horse near Felling.'

'I thought they'd put a stop on the sale,' said Libby.

'They did. You know the story?' He raised his eyebrows at her.

'They closed the pub and were selling it to a London couple, I thought,' said Libby.

'And then they found out that the couple were planning to sell it to developers,' added Ian.

Philip nodded. 'So they pulled out of the sale. And as you're aware, the pub was fired.'

'And then an excavator was sent in,' said Ian. 'Yes, we know all that – I've been down there today.'

'So I understand,' said Philip. 'I gather there's more to the situation than meets the eye.'

'Probably,' said Ian, giving nothing away.

'The current board has been trying to get in touch with the prospective buyers since last week,' said Philip, 'but they seem to have disappeared.'

Ian nodded slowly. 'We've been trying ourselves.'

'You didn't tell me that!' said Libby.

'No, I didn't.' Ian twirled his almost empty glass in his fingers. 'But now it has become rather more urgent that we find this couple. What have Marsham's said, Philip?'

Philip grinned. 'They want Libby to look into it!'

Ian spilt what was left in his glass and Libby choked.

''Ere!' Harry was on his feet. 'What's going on? Are you upsetting everybody, Jacobs?'

Philip burst out laughing. 'No, Hal, I'm really not!'

'He waltzes into the caff asking if everyone's around as usual and gets me to bring him in here,' griped Harry, 'and now look.' He sat down again. 'Come on. You'll have to tell us now.'

'Don't you dare, Philip!' warned Ian. 'It's nothing really, Hal. Don't worry about it.'

'Oh, fine.' Harry threw himself back in his chair. 'And we're all supposed to just forget about it, are we?'

'What's to forget?' asked Peter. 'Come on, Harry. Don't be difficult.'

Harry turned a cold shoulder on his partner and spoke to Anne. 'Locking us out, they are,' he complained. 'Always the same, isn't it?'

Everyone was laughing by now, and Harry sent Libby a surreptitious wink.

'Can you both come into the station tomorrow?' Ian asked under cover of the general hilarity.

Philip nodded. 'I'll bring Libby. What time?'

'Could you make it early?'

Libby groaned.

'What do you think?' Ben asked as they walked home later. Ian had gone off to stay with Hetty again, and no more had been said about antiques, pubs or bodies.

'I honestly don't know.' Libby slipped her arm through his. 'What exactly do Marsham's want? I can't see why they'd want me anywhere near their business. I can't have endeared myself to them back in the winter.'

'I don't know,' said Ben thoughtfully. 'You were instrumental in finding the bad apples, and getting the Fox and Hounds reopened.'

'That was Debbie pouring money into it,' said Libby. 'Anyway, I'm not sure I want to get involved. I was thinking, you know. I'm not enjoying this investigating lark as much as I used to.'

'Is this because of Fran?' Ben fished in his pocket for his key as they arrived at number 17.

'No.' Libby stepped inside the cottage, managing to avoid Sidney. 'It's because it isn't directly to do with me any more. Or us.'

'That sounds a bit . . .' Ben paused and looked at her. 'Self-centred. Not like you.'

Libby felt the colour creeping up her neck. 'I know. And I'm sorry. But it's because I haven't got a legitimate reason for interfering.'

'We've been through this already,' said Ben tiredly. 'And you've talked about it to Fran and Harry. You've been asked. Isn't that enough?'

Libby regarded him pensively. 'I'm doing it again, aren't I?' she said.

119

'Being annoying?' replied Ben. 'Yes, you are. Now, do you want a nightcap, or shall we go straight to bed?'

Philip picked Libby up at 8.30 on Thursday morning, looking far brighter than Libby felt.

'What do you suppose this is about?' she asked as they drove up the Canterbury road. 'I'm supposed to have had my fingerprints taken, but that can't be it.'

'Fingerprints?' Philip gave her a quick look.

Libby explained. 'Although they'd already have them on the system, I'd have thought.'

'Maybe they were deleted, as you were never a suspect. They're usually there for elimination purposes, as they would be this time,' said Philip. 'Anyway, no, you're quite right. This isn't about fingerprints. I think Ian's going to set out his stall and warn us both off.'

'He can't warn *you* off, surely?' Libby shot him a horrified look. 'You're the law!'

Philip smiled grimly. 'Oh, he can. And under the circumstances, if Marsham's are under investigation, we should definitely not be talking to each other.'

'Oh.' Libby sat silent, digesting this.

'What I told you last night was strictly off the record. And Ian will want to lay out the lines you must not cross if you agree to Marsham's request.'

'I'm not sure I want to,' said Libby. 'And why me?'

'If you agree, they'll tell you,' said Philip. 'And now stop speculating and enjoy this wonderful midsummer scenery. Tell me, when are you hosting our friends' production of the *Dream*?'

For the rest of the journey, they discussed the forthcoming production of *A Midsummer Night's Dream*, and Libby arrived at the police station a lot more cheerful than she had been at the start of the journey.

'Thanks for coming,' said Ian, looking even more tired this morning as he ushered them into his office. 'I won't keep you long. But I just wanted to warn you both.' He shook his head. 'And I can't believe I'm doing this. If anyone finds out . . .'

'Nobody will hear it from us,' said Philip. 'Now, what is it?'

Ian sat down in his chair and sighed. 'I told you, Libby – the Crooked Horse is now a crime scene.'

Libby nodded. 'You didn't find a body, though, did you? We'd have heard by now.'

'No, we didn't. What we did find, though, was definite proof that Malcolm Hodges was killed there.'

Chapter Eighteen

After a shocked silence, Philip said, 'Ah.'

'Exactly.' Ian gave him a humourless smile.

Libby looked from one to the other. 'What does that mean? You both obviously know.'

'It means, Lib, that Marsham's are now in the frame,' said Ian.

'And *that* means,' said Philip, 'that you really *shouldn't* be looking into anything for them.'

'But,' said Libby, frowning, 'you can't arrest a whole company.'

'No, but we can look at all the members of the board, and everyone who had anything to do with selling the pub,' said Ian.

'Why couldn't you tell us this last night?' asked Libby. 'Or on the phone?'

Both men looked at her, astonished.

'This is part of a murder investigation, Libby. You can't chat about it in a pub!' Ian threw himself back in his chair.

'You usually do.' Libby lifted her chin.

'I don't reveal sensitive information pertaining to a suspect or suspects,' said Ian formally.

Libby slid a sideways look at Philip, who nodded.

'If it came to court, it would be thrown out,' he said. 'Prejudicial.'

'Right,' said Libby with a sigh. 'So what do I do?'

'Nothing?' suggested Ian. 'Go and help your friendly archaeologist with her dig?'

'Hmm.' Libby stared down at her hands. 'And what about the antiques boys? Are they suspects?'

'We shall be looking into Hodges' background and associates, obviously,' said Ian. 'And by the way, we'll take your fingerprints while you're here.'

'What about Fran's?'

'Someone will go and see her.' He smiled. 'I'm sorry, Lib.' He looked at Philip. 'And I'm sorry about dragging you in here, but I didn't know what else to do.'

'You didn't have a choice,' said Philip. 'What do you want me to tell Marsham's?'

'Don't say anything until we've spoken to them,' said Ian. 'I'm sorry to mess things up, but you'll see—'

'You had no option,' said Libby. 'OK. So where do I go to have my fingerprints done?'

Ian took her out into a large open-plan office and delivered her to a plain-clothes officer, who escorted her to another part of the building and then ushered her back to Ian's office, where he and Philip were now drinking coffee.

'There's tea for you,' said Ian, and handed her a mug. 'Not from a machine.'

'Thank you.' Libby sat down. 'What's happening now?'

'You can go home – or in Philip's case, back to work.'

'Right.' Libby sipped at the tea. 'And I'm not to say anything to anybody, I take it?'

'I expect you'll tell Ben and Fran,' said Ian. 'But try not to let too many people know.'

Libby was indignant. 'You know I wouldn't.'

'Well, I must get on.' Ian stood up. 'Finish your tea, Lib, and I'll be in touch when I can. Possibly not this week.'

'OK.' Libby looked up at him. 'Try and get some sleep, eh?'

'I look that bad, do I?' He grinned.

'Yes,' said Libby.

'Right.' He opened the door. 'I meant what I said about the

123

archaeologist. And you'll obviously see some of those "antiques boys", as you call them, won't you?' He smiled down at her. 'See you.'

Libby was left with her mouth open.

Philip laughed. 'There you are! Not quite so out in the cold as you thought, are you?'

'I don't understand!' wailed Libby. 'What does he want?'

'I think,' said Philip, 'he assumes, quite rightly, that you will go about your normal business and carry on asking questions. As long as you don't get in the way of his official murder investigation. Now come on. As we're here, I thought we might pop into Waitrose. What do you think?'

By the time Philip dropped Libby back at Allhallow's Lane with a bagful of Waitrose shopping, she had recovered her equilibrium and it was lunchtime. Before she descended on Harry, she called Fran on speakerphone while she put the shopping away.

'So what are you going to do?' asked Fran.

'Philip thinks I should speak to Marsham's and see exactly what they want. Apparently he told them he would ask me, but warned them that I might not be able to do anything because of the police investigation.'

'But they still wanted to talk to you?'

'Yes. There's a whole new board of directors now, as you would expect.'

'Of course. What was it? A buyout?'

'I suppose it must have been. As far as I know, it wasn't sold to one of the big boys.'

'No. And the remaining directors would probably have been there for years. What a shock for them all.'

'I bet some of them have been there all their working lives,' agreed Libby. 'Horrible for them.'

'Have you got a name?' asked Fran.

'Yes, a – hang on – a weird one.' Libby fished out the piece of paper she had written it on. 'Portia Havilland.'

'Good heavens!' Fran laughed. 'Doesn't sound like a brewery executive.'

'No. She's something to do with the estates department. That's a poisoned chalice if ever there was one.'

'Makes sense, though. It was the estates department that sold off the pubs last year, so she'll know all about the proposed sale of the Horse.'

'Yes, of course she will. Anyway, I said I'd give her a ring. And if I happen to come across any of the antiques boys, I think Ian's given me permission to talk to them. Oh – and Tara, of course.'

'The self-absorbed archaeologist?'

'Yes, her. And she can't be too mad at me, because in a way it's me she's got to thank for reopening her dig.'

'True. Well, you'd better get on with it then.'

'Yes.' Libby cast a rueful eye on the *Contraband* folder lying on the table. 'And I've got another rehearsal tonight.'

'Oh yes. When's the concert at the Alexandria?'

'Saturday week. They're at the Raincliffe this Saturday – it's all been pulled together very quickly, but I suppose they'd rehearsed it pretty well before. I haven't done anything about getting tickets – I'd better ask Hetty.'

'Yes, you had. Anyway, I'm on duty at the shop, so I'd better go. Let me know what happens.' And Fran rang off.

'Well,' Libby said to Sidney, who was sitting hopefully by the bread bin, 'she sounds a lot more like the old Fran, doesn't she?'

Sidney didn't answer.

Harry waved from the counter as Libby pushed open the door of the Pink Geranium, and to her surprise, Donna, his former right-hand woman, came forward to show her to a table.

'You're not back, surely?' said Libby, greeting her with a kiss. 'What about the baby?'

'Who is now at preschool, Libby,' said Donna. 'I just came down to deliver and collect accounts. So I'm not officially here.'

'Oh, right. So how are things?' Libby sat down at one of the little tables near the counter.

'Oi!' Harry loomed over her. 'Keeping the staff gossiping?'

Donna excused herself and Libby ordered soup.

'Are we in need of a heart-to-heart again, petal?' Harry put his head on one side interrogatively.

'Not really.' Libby smiled up at him. 'Feeling a bit better today, thank you.'

'Oh good. My services are not required, then.' He patted her on the head and went back to the kitchen.

She was halfway through her bowl of soup when he rejoined her with two glasses of wine.

'So why are we feeling better?' he asked. 'Is this a result of your little chat with Philip and Ian last night?'

'Partly.' Libby told him as much as she felt she could, including the fact that Fran had perked up, as she put it.

'So you're going to become an amateur archaeologist?'

'I'll offer to help, but to be perfectly honest, it all seems a bit too much like hard labour.'

'And what about Dodgy Hodgy? That's Ian's official baby, so you can't get involved?'

'Yes, but he has said I can talk to any of the other antiques boys, as long as I don't give anything away.'

'You don't know any,' said Harry. 'Except Wally Mayberry, I suppose.'

'Yes,' said Libby thoughtfully. 'And I suppose I could go and talk to him, couldn't I?'

'I thought you went down to see him last Saturday?'

'I did. That's when we saw the brooch.'

'Hang on – back up a bit. Brooch?'

Libby explained. 'That's why we've started getting interested in a possible Anglo-Saxon burial site.'

'Ah. And if it was right next door to the Crooked Horse, perhaps . . .' Harry stopped and frowned. 'Perhaps what? They were selling these illegal goodies there?'

'That's the only thing I can think of. And it's what Ian thinks too. Possibly.'

'And is that why the place was fired? No, can't be.'

'No idea. But I shall go and talk to Wally again, I think. And I want to find out about Hodges' boat, and how he got to the mooring and—'

'Hold on – that's the stuff you *aren't* supposed to be getting into.'

Libby grinned. 'Oh, I'll just be chatting,' she said.

The *Contraband* rehearsal went as well as it could without Judy and Cyd, who, Libby was relieved to find out, were going to make two of the rehearsals next week after all. She was also relieved to hear that one of the enterprising cast members had booked a minibus to take anyone who wanted to go to the Alexandria the following Saturday.

'Hetty's coming with us and will meet up with Joe Wilson down there,' said Ben as they walked home. 'He's coming with some of his old boys. Flo and Lenny have opted out. They said they've already seen it.'

'True, they have.' Libby tucked her arm into his. 'So have we.'

Ben sighed. 'The things we do for our friends,' he said.

Libby dug him in the ribs.

The next morning, after calling on the outgoing holidaymakers in the Hoppers' Huts and relieving them of their keys, she called Tara's mobile.

'Libby! Have you heard?' Tara sounded excited.

'That you can reopen the dig? Yes. I was going to offer my help, if you needed it.'

'That's very kind of you, but I think I've got enough help. We don't want to overcrowd the site – it isn't very big. And your friend Moira's coming.'

'Oh good. I can come and have a look, though, can't I?'

'Oh yes! After all, it's down to you we've got permission to go back.'

'Thank you,' said Libby, 'but I didn't really do anything.'

'But you know that policeman – and you know the nuns.'

'Sort of,' said Libby. 'Anyway, when are you going to start?'

'I'm going down over the weekend to recce, and then we'll start properly on Monday.' Tara took a deep breath. 'I know it's childish of me, but I'm so excited!'

Next Libby called Patti and told her of the latest development, and finally Fran.

'So I'm going to come down to have a drink in Beer and Bargains again tomorrow,' she said, 'and hope to have a chat with Wally.'

'Hmm.' Fran sounded thoughtful. 'You know what? I was wondering – suppose we went over to the Fox and Hounds this afternoon? Weren't we told that Hodges used to drink in there? And didn't Mayberry say he popped in too? Don't you think a visit there might be worthwhile? Now that we know a bit more about everything?'

Chapter Nineteen

'Who are we going to talk to?' Libby asked as Fran drove out of Canterbury towards Shittenden. 'I'd have said Trisha, but she'll be at work.'

'Stan, of course.' Fran turned left just past the oast houses that were now flats and a community centre.

'And what are we going to ask him?'

Fran tutted, exasperated. 'What he knows about the whole business, of course.'

'Oh. OK.' Libby turned to look out of her window. The countryside was looking perfect in its June apparel, as if nothing evil could ever exist under the surface. Then, ahead, the Fox and Hounds appeared, hanging baskets as usual overflowing with colour.

'I recognise that car,' said Libby, as Fran pulled up alongside. 'It's Debbie's.'

'I suppose we shouldn't be surprised at that,' said Fran. 'I wonder how long it'll last.'

'What, with both their children disapproving, you mean?' Libby chuckled. 'Not to mention Linda.'

'Does she disapprove?' Fran looked surprised.

'She thinks Debbie has terrible choice in men. I don't think she's given Stan a chance.' Libby stepped inside the cool interior and made for the bar.

'Libby!' Stan appeared, wiping his hands on a tea towel. 'How lovely to see you! And Fran. What'll you have?'

'Could I have coffee, Stan?' asked Fran. 'I'm driving.'

'And I'll have half a lager, please.' Libby looked round the room at the few customers. 'Not many in this afternoon.'

'Not until the after-work crowd,' said Stan from the shiny new coffee machine. 'Still can't get used to this thing.'

Libby took out her wallet, which was waved away. 'Have you seen anything of the antiques boys since . . . you know?' she asked.

Stan looked serious. 'Oh, that was awful, wasn't it? I feel so guilty.'

'Guilty? Why?' Fran accepted her coffee cup.

'I introduced you to Fay. Well, I suggested she ask you about Malc. And you found him, didn't you?' He shook his head at Fran. 'All my fault.'

'Don't be daft,' said Libby. 'You were just trying to be helpful. And it's a good job we did go and look at the barn – Fay never went in there, apparently.'

'No. She'd already refused to let some of the other dealers in before you went over.'

'Did many of them use the barn? Did he let them store stuff there?' asked Libby.

'Oh yes. They used to drop in here – I think I told you?'

'Wally Mayberry said he did.'

'Ah, yes.' Stan shook his head. 'I reckon there was something going on between him and Fay, to be honest. Malc was always going away, see.'

Fran and Libby looked at one another.

'Makes sense,' said Fran.

'Oh, but he wouldn't . . . I mean, they wouldn't . . .' Stan looked horrified.

'No, no, of course not. They'd hardly have asked us to look into it if one of them had done away with him, would they?' Libby sipped her lager. 'Mmm, nice.'

'Not one of your Ben's, I'm afraid,' said Stan.

'I know what I wanted to ask you.' Libby put her glass down.

130

'Hodges moored his boat near Creekmarsh, didn't he? Did he always drive down there?'

Stan looked surprised. 'Yes. Bit far to walk! But he was found at the barn – the boat didn't have anything to do with it.'

'But the boat was missing, surely, because that's where Fay thought he was. On the boat.'

Stan frowned. 'Oh yes. I never thought of that.'

'So have any of the other antiques dealers dropped in since Hodges was found?' Fran tried to get back to the point.

'Yes, more than usual, actually. They've been in here moaning about Malc and the old Horse. I told you that, didn't I?' He turned to Libby.

'About them using the Horse? Yes. But it's a long way inland if they were bringing things in from the coast. You can't get up the Felling creek.'

Stan shrugged. 'I dunno. Would have thought they'd come in down at Creekmarsh, wouldn't you? Perhaps the old Horse is a bit more isolated, if you know what I mean!' He tapped his nose with a finger and grinned.

'That's true,' said Fran. She gave Stan a speculative look. 'Stan, I don't suppose you could keep an ear out for us, could you?'

Stan's eyebrows shot up to his hairline. 'Eh?'

'Well, we are looking into Hodges' death a little bit,' said Libby, 'for Fay, you know. The police are too, of course, but . . . well, you know we sometimes hear things . . .'

'Ah!' Stan beamed, understanding. 'Course! Look what it did for me!'

'Oh, we didn't do much,' said Fran. 'But if you hear anything. Not,' she added hastily, 'that we want you to spy on your friends and customers.'

'No, I get it,' said Stan. 'And if I do hear anything, I'll pass it straight on.' He looked over his shoulder and leant forward. 'And I won't say anything to anybody else.' He nodded. 'You know?'

'Thank you, Stan,' said Libby. 'You're a mate. And how *is* Debbie? We don't see her round Steeple Martin much these days.'

'Oh, she's fine.' Stan looked over his shoulder again. 'In the kitchen, I think. Shall I call her?'

'No, it's all right,' said Libby. 'Just wondered.'

'Yes.' Stan gave them an awkward smile. 'She – er – well, she helped get this place up and running.'

'Yes.' Fran smiled back.

'So it's a bit difficult, sometimes.' He picked up the tea towel and began polishing a glass unnecessarily hard.

'I thought you and she were getting on well?' said Libby. 'When we were here last week . . .'

'Oh yes.' Stan nodded vigorously. 'Great.'

Fran gave Libby a sharp nudge that nearly knocked her off her bar stool.

'Well, that's good,' said Libby, glaring at her friend. 'Say hello for me.'

'Young Ricky comes over sometimes.' Stan put the glass down. 'Nice lad. Learning to drive, did you know?'

'Is he? No, I didn't.' Libby finished her lager. 'His term's finished now, hasn't it? I suppose he's got more time.'

'Yes. Our Trisha's teaching him.' Stan smiled with fatherly pride. 'They get on so well.'

'That's nice.' Fran pushed her coffee cup away and stood up. 'We ought to get going, Lib.'

'Yes, we should.' Libby held out her hand to Stan. 'Lovely to see you, Stan. We'll come over for a meal sometime soon.'

Stan laughed. 'Now why would you do that? With young Harry's Pink Geranium and Tim turning the Coach into a gastro pub!'

'Always nice to go somewhere different,' said Libby. 'And have you got my number, in case you hear anything?'

'Here.' Fran handed over one of the gallery's cards. 'That's our shop.'

'Oh, right – Guy, isn't it?' Stan peered at the card. 'And I think I've still got your number somewhere, Libby.'

★

'Path of true love not running smooth by the sound of it,' said Libby, once they were outside.

'And you were all ready to poke your nose in,' said Fran, opening the car door.

'I wasn't!' Libby was indignant.

'Yes, you were.' Fran turned the car round and pulled out into the lane. 'But otherwise – helpful, do you think?'

'Yes. Not that Stan actually knew anything, but he can listen in. And interesting that more of the antiques lot have been in since Hodges was found. Or did he mean since the Horse was closed?'

'Could be both,' said Fran. 'But it certainly means that they've been upset by it all.'

'Well, it's natural to be upset when a friend dies. Especially when he's murdered,' said Libby. 'But it sounded to me as though they're bothered because they've lost their place of business.'

'I think you're reading a lot into it,' said Fran. 'Now, are we going home?'

'Did you know,' said Libby on the phone to Lewis later, 'that the bloke we found dead up near the Fox and Hounds moored his boat down on your creek?'

'Yes, course I did,' said Lewis. 'And it isn't my creek. It just runs along my property.'

'You can drive down there, can't you?'

'Yeah, not easy, but there is a track. The boat's not there now.'

'Is his car there?'

'There's *a* car there. Dunno if it's his. Why?'

'He was reported missing in his boat. We were wondering why the boat is still missing when he was actually found in his own barn.'

'Was he? Bit of a mystery, then.' Lewis was grinning, Libby could hear it.

'And I *am* looking into the fire at the Crooked Horse, as you suggested,' she said. 'Sort of.'

'So they're linked?'

'No idea,' lied Libby. 'Have you heard any more about smuggling over there?'

'No – why? Was it still going on?'

'Might have been.' She sighed. 'Well, keep your ear to the ground, just in case.'

'I don't hear anything here,' said Lewis. 'The only gossip I get is from George at the Red Lion and Bren at the Fox.'

'It's very confusing having two pubs called the Fox in the area,' complained Libby.

'The other one is the Fox *and Hounds*,' clarified Lewis. 'Perfectly easy to know which is which.'

'Yes, dear,' said Libby. 'And Bren at your Fox does a smashing sausage bake.'

Lewis laughed. 'Is that a hint?'

'Might be.'

'Come over Monday.' he suggested. 'I've got a wedding tomorrow and the bridal party are staying over for Sunday.'

Creekmarsh was run as a hotel and conference centre, and Lewis, as a popular television personality, was a great draw and had ensured its success from the beginning.

'I'm going somewhere in the morning,' said Libby. 'I'll come over after that. Will Edie mind if we go out to lunch? Or will she come too?'

'No, she'll be at Temptation House again. They do something on Mondays. Can't remember what – tatting or something.'

'Crafts, I expect. Right, I'll see you Monday.'

So Lewis didn't really know anything, she thought after ringing off. But perhaps Bren at the Fox might. Perhaps Malcolm Hodges went in there on his way back from a boat trip? And meanwhile, she'd try and talk to Wally Mayberry.

'Yer mate not coming this week?' asked Wally on Saturday lunchtime, handing over an alcohol-free lager.

134

'She might pop up,' said Libby. 'She's busy in the gallery at weekends.'

'Oh, ah,' said Wally, leaning his elbows on the counter. 'Tourists. They love a bit of art, don't they? I'd do a lot better down there on Harbour Street than up here.'

'Don't they come up here, then?' Libby looked round the empty shop. As before, the garden was full, but with drinkers not antiques buyers.

'Nah.' Wally looked gloomy. 'Mind, the business isn't what it was.'

'Not with the old Crooked Horse closing, I suppose not,' said Libby artlessly.

Wally reared back as if stung. 'Eh?'

Libby put on an innocent face. 'I thought that was where you antiques people did a lot of business?'

'Where d'you hear that?' Wally sounded suddenly short of breath. Libby decided she'd better be careful.

'Oh, here and there,' she said with a shrug. 'In the pubs, mostly.' She wondered whether a mention of Anglo-Saxon artefacts would be a step too far, and thought it probably would. 'You had some nice little pieces in your display cabinet last week, we saw. And my neighbours, Lenny and Flo, said they used to go over there to buy the odd piece.'

Wally relaxed. 'Oh, them! Yes – I forgot you'd know them. Isn't old Lenny your Ben's uncle or something?'

'That's right! We're family.' Crisis averted, thought Libby. 'So you all used to do business over there? Pity it closed, then.'

'Yeah.' Wally nodded. 'And burning it down like that . . .'

'Well, it wasn't actually burnt down,' said Libby. 'And the police are looking into it now. They've been over there since Thursday morning.'

'Oh, ah?' Wally looked slightly shifty. 'I thought they were looking into Malc's murder.'

'They can do both, you know!' Libby laughed. 'Have you heard any rumours about Malcolm, Wally? No one seems to know much. I heard he moored his boat up at Creekmarsh.'

'Yeah – that's where it should be.' Wally frowned. 'That's how Fay knew he was missing, see? The boat was gone and his car was still there.' He looked up at Libby. 'You going to look into it then? For Fay?'

Chapter Twenty

Libby gazed at him across the bar counter.

'Yes,' she said eventually. 'Although the police won't like it.'

Wally made a scoffing noise. 'Couldn't do it without you, that's what Stan says.'

'That's not strictly true,' said Libby with a smile. 'My mate and I just help occasionally, that's all.'

'I reckon you should have a proper office. You know, like proper detectives. You could have it here, couldn't you?' He crossed his arms on the bar and leant forward confidentially. 'Always something going on in Nethergate.' He winked.

Yes, thought Libby, there is.

'I don't think we'd have time, Wally,' she said out loud. 'Fran works in the gallery, and I've got the theatre and our holiday business at home.'

'Shame.' Wally shook his head. 'Anyway, you're going to look into Malc's murder. Good enough for now.'

'Let's start with where he might have been going in his boat.' Libby took another fortifying sip of her lager. 'And how he would have got to the Crooked Horse if he'd moored up at the St Aldeberge Cut.'

'Oh, you know about that?' Wally looked nervous.

'Of course. If some of you were bringing stuff in across the Channel – avoided the migrant boats, did you? – you had to land somewhere, and George and Bert down at the harbour said you'd never do it here.'

'Right.' Wally looked up as two customers arrived at the bar. 'Hang on, Libby.'

Libby took her glass and moved over to have a look at the display cabinet again. Sure enough, the Anglo-Saxon brooch was conspicuous by its absence, but there were some very pretty small pieces there, including a rather strange little figurine in what looked like bronze. She was still staring at it when Wally appeared at her elbow.

'Ready for a top-up?' he asked, his eyes ranging swiftly over the display case.

'No, I'm fine, thanks.' Libby looked at him curiously. He gave her a sickly smile and turned pointedly back to the counter.

'You were asking about the – ah – the guys and their boats.' He cleared his throat. Libby gave in and followed him.

'Yes. You don't have a boat?'

'No. Got enough to do with this place. And I hate boats. The others – see, it got difficult. Bloody Brexit.'

'Yes, I can see that.'

'So the boys used to go across, do the markets, see?'

'And bring stuff back? Well, it's not as if any of it's worth a huge amount, is it?'

'No, that's it. Cost us more than what it's worth, all that paperwork.'

'And people took it up to the Horse to sell?'

'That's about the size of it, yeah.' Wally looked relieved.

'Who are the other boys, then?' Libby tried to look only mildly interested.

Wally gave her a sharp look. 'Only a few guys from here, couple from Canterbury, Felling. You know.'

And that was all he was going to say, thought Libby.

'OK, Wally. And none of them knew where Malcolm was going when he went off in his boat?'

'No.' Now Wally looked worried. 'And I meantersay, where is the bugger now? It's not at the cut, or the creek.'

'Hmm.' Libby looked at the remnants of her drink. 'Well, the coastguard are keeping an eye out for it, so let's hope it turns up. It might tell us a lot.' She drank her last mouthful. 'Now I'd better get on. Oh – before I go – where do you all meet up now? At the Fox and Hounds?'

Wally looked shocked. 'Well, maybe – sometimes.'

Libby smiled. 'I might see you there, then,' she said. 'Bye for now, Wally.'

She wandered back down the high street to Victoria Place and the little car park at the end. Had she learnt anything new? Or merely confirmed what she and Fran had suspected? One thing was certain: according to her recent research online, that little bronze figurine was most definitely Anglo-Saxon.

So, she thought, as she stood leaning over the railings and looking down at the Alexandria, the concert hall she and Fran had helped bring back to life, Wally Mayberry wasn't telling her everything. Yes, he had been upfront about the illegal import of 'antiques' from the Continent, but no one – including, apparently, the police – was too worried about that. After all, they weren't talking about items of enormous value. If they had been, the Arts and Antiquities people from the Met would have been involved. As they certainly would be if the theft of Anglo-Saxon artefacts was proven. Although she could understand, she supposed, the finders-keepers feeling that anything found in the ground was fair game. However, the Portable Antiquities Scheme would not agree. Especially if the site the items came from proved to be on land owned by St Eldreda's Abbey.

Saturday afternoon was spent with the theatre's current wardrobe mistress making sure that all the eighteenth-century costumes assembled for *Contraband* were in a decent state of repair, hanging them on rails in the dressing rooms ready for the cast and putting in an order at Libby's favourite theatrical costumiers for lacking items. Judy and Cyd would only just be back in time, Libby thought, as the production opened at the end of the week following the Alexandria concert. Good job they were professionals.

'And then, of course,' she said to Ben over dinner, 'we've got the Glover's Men a week later.'

'Well, at least they do everything themselves,' said Ben, 'and they're no trouble.'

'They've already almost sold out,' said Libby. 'I wish we could say the same for *Contraband*.'

'Pity we can't link it to the modern smugglers.'

Libby laughed. 'That'd sell a few tickets!'

The Saturday evening visit to the Hop Pocket was enlivened by Moira's overexcitement about the reopening of the dig on Monday.

'And it's all due to you, Libby! If you hadn't been looking into it, it would never have happened!'

'It's more to do with the police, Moira.' Libby gave her a rueful smile. 'Not really anything to do with me.'

'Of course it is,' said Beth, belatedly joining the party. 'Patti was telling me all about it.'

Libby sighed. 'That's the trouble with knowing vicars. You can't keep anything secret.'

Beth gave her a shrewd look. 'Vicars and publicans. That's what you're good at. Although I'm not sure either have a beneficial effect on your spiritual health.'

Old Brandon reached across the table and patted Beth's arm. 'You're very good for the rest of us sinners, though.'

Dan, Libby and Ben laughed, while Moira merely looked confused. Noticing, Beth quickly changed the subject. 'No Cyd or Judy this evening?'

'They're up in London for their concert.' Libby sighed. 'Rehearsals are a bit difficult without them. They'll be fine; it's the local amateurs I'm worried about.'

'Don't worry,' said Brandon. 'Your local amateurs are better than a lot of the pros I've worked with over the years.'

Libby gave him a grateful smile. 'It's probably because they're so used to working with pros like you. We've been more or less pro-am since the beginning.'

'And very good you are too,' said Dan and stood up. 'Anyone for another drink? I'm going to put one in for your old man, Beth. He's working his socks off on the old Joanna.'

John Cole was accompanying an enthusiastic group of regulars in an apparently inexhaustible repertoire of old London songs, led by a new face in the pub.

'Who's that?' Libby asked Ben. 'I've not seen him before.'

'I'll find out,' said Ben, standing up to follow Dan to the bar.

'Don't make it obvious,' muttered Libby.

Beth was amused. 'You don't have to know who *everybody* is, Lib.'

'No, I know, but he's making sure he's noticed, isn't he? So I'd like to know why.'

'Probably, as we've said before, he's just delighted to find an old-fashioned pub with a piano and a pianist.'

'Yes, all right.' Libby sighed and turned to Moira. 'So who's going to be at the dig on Monday? Tara said she had plenty of help.'

'Everybody who can make it from the Archaeological Society. Everybody who's not working, that is.' Moira looked smug. 'I'm all right because I work from home.'

'Oh?' Beth looked interested. 'I didn't realise you worked . . .' She paused. 'From home,' she continued.

'Neither did I,' Libby muttered sotto voce.

'Oh yes.' Moira waved an airy hand. 'I make found art.'

Brandon frowned. 'Sorry, Moira – what's that?'

Beth stood on Libby's foot under the table.

Dan arrived back in time to hear Brandon's question.

'Things she picks up and makes into something else,' he explained helpfully.

'You must come and have a look, Brandon.' Moira turned to him enthusiastically. 'Pop in one morning.'

'I notice she didn't invite us,' Libby murmured to Beth, who unsuccessfully smothered a snort of laughter.

Luckily, Ben also returned to the table just at the right moment.

'Our chorus leader,' he said, sitting down, 'is – wait for it – an antiques dealer.'

'No!' Libby covered her mouth. 'Really? What's he doing here?'

'How do I know?' Ben shook his head at her. 'Simon said he introduced himself earlier on. He came in asking for food, and Simon sent him across the road. He also asked if there were any dealers – or shops, rather – in the village.'

Beth raised an eyebrow at Libby. 'This is suspicious, isn't it?'

'I think so,' said Libby, staring across the bar at the slim, dark man bellowing out the chorus of 'The Marrow Song'. 'I wonder if he went to the caff or the Coach to eat.'

'I've no doubt you'll find out,' said Ben. 'But it is a bit of a coincidence.'

'Ian doesn't like coincidences,' said Libby.

After another few songs, John shut the piano lid and got up, amid cries of 'Shame!' from his audience. The newcomer was borne off with some of the other regulars and John joined his wife.

'I shall ask before Libby does,' Beth said, passing him a fresh pint supplied by Dan. 'The antiques dealer. Did he say anything?'

John looked bewildered. 'Who?'

'The bloke leading the singing,' said Brandon. 'I was tempted to join in myself.'

'Oh, is he a dealer?' John sank at least a third of his pint in one go. 'I needed that.'

'Come on, darling,' said Beth. 'He must have said something.'

'He came over when I started playing and asked if I knew any cockney songs, so I started playing "Daisy, Daisy" – which isn't, of course. Why?'

'And he said nothing else?' persisted Libby.

'He said it seemed a nice little village, and wasn't Nethergate quite close.' John looked round the group. 'What's all this about?'

'They think he might have something to do with Libby's murder,' whispered Moira. 'Exciting, isn't it?'

Chapter Twenty-One

A charged silence settled over the table. Moira, gazed round, surprised. 'What? What's the matter?'

Dan shook his head and sighed. 'Sorry. I think we'd better go.'

Moira bridled. 'What for? Why should we go? I only said what everybody was thinking.'

'No you didn't, Moira,' said Beth gently. 'You said it was exciting. Murder is *not* exciting. In any degree at all.'

Moira turned to Libby, an ugly expression on her face. 'Oh, isn't it? Then why do you keep on "investigating" it?' The invisible quotation marks were clear to everybody.

Dan, his face now bright red, stood up, leaving his half-finished pint on the table. 'Come on, Moira.' He took hold of her arm and pulled her to her feet. She tossed her head.

'Well, I'm sure I'm not staying where I'm not wanted,' she snapped, and shaking herself free of Dan's grip, she strode out of the pub, leaving a horrified silence behind.

'Sorry,' muttered Dan, and followed her out.

'Well!' said Brandon eventually. 'That wasn't very nice, was it?'

That broke the mood, and everyone laughed.

Libby turned to Beth. 'Did we overreact, or did she?'

Beth smiled. 'I think we can safely say she did. It wasn't malicious, though. That's the trouble with having all these crime series on television and in books. People treat it as entertainment rather than reality.'

'I wish they could see how horrible it really is.' Libby stared down into her glass. 'You'd think Moira would, after the last year or so.'

'None of it's touched her personally,' said Beth. 'That's the problem.'

Libby nodded, just as Ben leant over to attract her attention.

'Look out,' he said. 'Here's trouble.'

She looked round to see Peter pushing his way towards them.

'Hello!' she said. 'What brings you here? Hal's not closed, has he?'

'Just a little heads-up,' said Peter, pulling Dan's chair towards him. 'The gentleman up at the bar.'

Everyone looked round.

'Don't look!' hissed Peter.

Everyone looked back.

'What?' whispered Libby.

'Has he spoken to you?' asked Peter.

Libby risked another look towards the bar, where the gentleman in question appeared to be deep in conversation with Simon.

'No.'

'He had dinner with us earlier.' Peter sent a casual look over his shoulder. 'He was asking questions.'

John nodded. 'He asked me about the village, and if Nethergate was close.'

'Not about Libby?'

Libby's mouth fell open.

John shook his head.

'He asked Adam if he knew a Mrs Sarjeant. Luckily, the boy's got his head screwed on and denied all knowledge and told me. So Hal took his order to him and got asked the same thing.' Peter grinned. 'Hal asked what you'd done.'

Ben snorted with laughter.

'What did he say?' asked Libby.

'Brushed it off. Said he'd just heard the name.' Peter looked towards the bar. 'Looks as though he's asking Simon the same thing.'

'He's been talking to Simon for quite a time now,' said Beth. 'He was singing songs with John earlier.'

'Just thought we'd warn you,' said Peter. 'I'd better go back to the washing-up.'

'Washing-up? You?' scoffed Libby. 'That'll be the day.' She leant over and kissed his cheek. 'Thanks, Pete.'

'See you tomorrow,' he said, patting her shoulder, and left.

'What do you think he wants?' muttered Libby.

'To find out what's going on, I should think,' said Beth. 'Isn't that obvious?'

'Yes, but if he's new to the area, how does he know Libby's name?' Ben scowled towards the bar. 'If there was something illegal going on around the Crooked Horse, yes, he'd know about that – but how would he know Libby had anything to do with it?'

'Wally Mayberry,' said Libby with a sigh. 'He definitely didn't like me being there this morning.'

'Well, he can't be here to cause any harm,' said Brandon, 'he's being too upfront about it. So does he just want to ask Libby questions?'

They were about to find out.

'Hi, John – sorry to interrupt.'

Close up, the man was smoother and smarter than Libby had thought. Altogether, the very epitome of the East End wide boy, she thought.

John looked up with a cautious smile.

'Just wondered if you were coming back to the piano? Such a treat – I shall have to bring some friends down here.' The man smiled at the wary faces around the table. 'Where is there to stay in the area?'

'Only the Coach and Horses,' supplied Beth in her best upper-class headmistress voice. 'They have two or three rooms, don't they?' She looked at Ben for confirmation.

Ben simply nodded.

'Right.' The smile was becoming forced. 'And I'm sure you can tell me – Libby Sarjeant. She lives here, I believe?'

There was a charged silence, until Libby sighed and gave in.

146

'That's me,' she said. 'Why do you want to know?'

She was conscious of Beth on one side and Ben on the other shifting their chairs slightly closer.

'Oh, I just wanted a word.' The smile was now a positive rictus. 'May I?'

'Go ahead.' She shrugged. 'How do you know my name?'

'A mutual friend.' He looked round – for a spare chair, Libby assumed. She was wrong. 'Perhaps we could go outside?'

'I don't think so.' Ben stood up. 'If you want to speak to Ms Sarjeant, you can do so here.'

'Jim Frost.' The man held out a hand. 'No offence, mate. Just wanted a word.'

Brandon suddenly surged to his feet. 'An' you c'n 'ave it, cock. Right 'ere.'

Jim Frost, confronted by Brandon-turned-Magwitch, stepped back.

'All right, all right!' He held out both hands, palms upwards. 'As I said – just a word.'

Brandon and Ben both remained standing.

'Well, what is it?' Libby's voice was sharp. 'And just who is this mutual friend?'

Jim Frost's mouth opened and closed again. He shook his head. 'Well, what a surprise. I was told you were a friendly bunch down 'ere.' His accent was slipping. 'This 'ow you usually treat strangers, eh?'

He was met with a hostile silence.

'All right.' He heaved a theatrical sigh. 'Wally Mayberry said you found a friend of mine. Murdered.' He fixed Libby with a steely blue stare. 'That right?'

'Yes.'

'An' you'd know what the cops were fu – doing about it?'

'No.'

'Oh?'

Libby gave a sigh even more theatrical than his own. 'I have no knowledge of the police investigation into Mr Hodges' death. Or even

147

his life. I never met the man.' She hitched a shoulder and turned away in dismissal.

'Oh.' Frost continued to stare at her, and Ben and Brandon moved slightly closer to him. He turned his head to look at them and laughed. 'What an overreaction, if you don't mind me sayin'. I'll be off then.'

'Have a safe journey,' said Beth politely.

With a final forced laugh, Frost moved away from the table towards the door, just as Dan came back in, preceded by an overenthusiastic Colley. Frost backed up and swore before forcing his way past and out of the door. Dan looked surprised.

'What was that all about?' He followed Colley to the table.

'Bloke wanted a word with Libby.' Brandon, returned to his usual teddy-bear persona, sat down. 'Needed sorting out.'

Ben laughed. 'And Brandon was superb.'

Libby, still a little shaken, frowned. 'Did we overreact, as he said? He didn't threaten me or anything.'

'He was asking questions about you – here and in the Geranium,' said Beth.

'Yes, but if somebody came to the village knowing I lived here, they would ask around, wouldn't they?' Libby looked at Ben. 'Are we all a bit oversensitive?'

Ben sighed. 'Maybe. And perhaps we were guilty of prejudging – he was such a stereotype.'

Libby cleared her throat and glanced up at Dan while stroking Colley's head, now placed adoringly on her knee. 'You came back, Dan. Everything all right?'

He looked down. 'I wanted to apologise. She doesn't mean it, you know. She doesn't think.'

Everyone immediately rushed to reassure him, and Brandon insisted on going to the bar for drinks all round.

By the time Dan had been filled in on the Jim Frost episode, they had all relaxed, and congratulated Brandon on his impromptu performance.

'Now that *was* stereotyping,' he admitted. 'I went straight into Dickens' cockney villain, didn't I?'

'I thought Magwitch,' said Libby with a grin.

Brandon beamed with pleasure. 'Still got it, then!"

Beth looked amused. 'Dickens next year at the theatre, then, Lib?'

'Or possibly at Christmas,' said Ben thoughtfully.

Libby clapped her hands delightedly. '*A Christmas Carol*!'

John held up a hand. 'And can we use the Muppets' score?'

The famous Muppets' *Christmas Carol* film was a perennial favourite.

Beth laughed. 'I think you've got a new recruit, Libby.'

The remainder of the evening passed in blessed normality, and at just after eleven o'clock, Libby and Ben walked slowly home along the high street.

'If you think about it,' said Libby, tucking her arm through Ben's, 'that's exactly what I do. Go to places and ask about people. Exactly the same.'

He looked at her in surprise. 'So you do! I never thought of that.'

'And sometimes people aren't happy about it. Again, exactly the same.'

'No wonder you get into trouble,' said Ben, with a sigh.

The following day, after a quiet Sunday lunch with Hetty at the Manor, Libby proposed this theory to Peter and Harry at their usual afternoon get-together.

'But you aren't a suspicious-looking character,' said Harry, and cocked his head on one side. 'Oh, I don't know, though.'

Libby threw a cushion at him.

'If he hadn't been,' said Peter, handing round their usual choices of alcoholic beverage, 'Adam would have automatically said, "Oh yes, that's my mum", wouldn't he?'

'I suppose he would,' said Libby, much struck.

'So by the time he was talking to Simon, we'd all formed an opinion of him,' said Ben.

'Despite the fact that he hadn't asked John anything while he was singing at the piano.' Libby took a thoughtful sip of her whisky. 'We'd already judged him on his appearance.'

'Not that he did anything to dispel that opinion when he spoke to us,' said Ben darkly.

'We didn't really give him the chance, did we?'

'So are you going to tell Ian?' asked Harry.

'To be honest, I don't quite know where Frost fits in to either the inquiry into the Crooked Horse or Hodges' death,' said Libby.

'We still don't know why either of them happened,' said Peter, sitting down next to Harry. 'Not that I'm completely up to speed, of course.'

'No,' said Libby, feeling unwarrantedly uncomfortable about agreeing. 'And I'm far too often guilty of making wild assumptions, so I must be careful.'

'Like linking the two events,' said Harry. 'Exactly.' He swung his feet up on to Peter's lap. 'Remind me – why did you do that in the first place?'

'It wasn't just me!' protested Libby. 'Ian linked them up too.'

'You did it first,' said Peter.

'All right – it was Lewis. When I went over to give Edie a lift to see Chloe.'

'And why did you do that? All the way from here to Creekmarsh, just to drive Edie to Temptation House!' Harry shook his head.

'I took Adam's work bag down to him, if you remember. And Edie needed a lift. I'm nice like that.'

'Oh yeah?' Harry scoffed.

'Never you mind,' said Ben, patting her arm. 'You're very nice. I've always said so.' He grinned at Peter and Harry.

Libby sniffed. 'Anyway, that's why I was there, and Lewis told me he'd been talking to George at the Red Lion, and they'd been discussing the Crooked Horse. That was the first I'd heard about it. And they wondered if it might be to do with the whole Marsham's Brewery business.'

'And where did Hodges come in?' asked Peter.

'That evening at the Fox and Hounds, Stan introduced us to Fay.' Libby frowned. 'And then I asked Stan if he knew anything about the Horse. That was all. And now . . .' She paused. 'Oh hell, you'll find out eventually. There's evidence of a violent attack at the Horse.'

'Ah.' Peter narrowed his eyes and Harry whistled.

'Is it Hodges?' Peter asked.

'Don't know,' Libby lied. 'And the other thing is,' she carried on hastily, 'Marsham's asked Philip to ask me to look into it.'

'Oh, bloody hell!' Harry exploded.

'I know. I'm not supposed to say anything. But I've got the name of the estates person at Marsham's to speak to. Except I really don't want to.' She looked up from her now empty glass. 'And tomorrow I've said I'll go and look at the revived dig site and then have lunch with Lewis.'

'You wouldn't be going looking for Malcolm Hodges' car, by any chance?' asked Ben, who was by now familiar with all the details of Hodges' disappearance. 'I'm pretty sure the police will have removed it by now.'

'I know.' Libby sighed. 'I'm just looking for clues, I think. Lewis said Bren at the Fox is good for gossip, so we're going to have one of her sausage bakes.'

'Heaven help us,' said Harry. 'More pubs.'

Chapter Twenty-Two

When Libby arrived at the dig site on Monday morning, it was obvious that Tara had been there for some time. Little flags and marker posts similar to the one Libby had already seen were dotted over the field, and hunched figures crouched on the ground wielding small trowels. Tara, in shorts, sleeveless vest and a very disreputable wide-brimmed hat, spotted her and came over, grinning.

'Look!' she said, waving a proprietorial hand. 'My site – and all down to you!'

'It really wasn't,' protested Libby again, feeling awkward. 'Is Moira here?'

'Yes, and she came with me yesterday, too, to begin setting up.' Tara pointed to the far corner of the field. 'There she is. Did you want a word?'

'No, no!' said Libby hastily. 'Just wondered. So are you still convinced about the site.'

'Oh yes.' Tara looked momentarily guilty. 'I got into trouble because I went to see that antiques dealer.'

'Yes. DCI Connell told me. And the brooch had disappeared.' She fixed Tara with a stern eye. 'I did warn you.'

'I know.' Tara sighed. 'I just got so excited.'

'I can see that.' Libby stood looking at the scene of hushed busyness. 'Nothing I can do, then?'

'No, but I'll let you know the minute we find anything, if you like?' Tara looked eager to please.

'That would be good.' Libby smiled at her. 'Are you going to do a dig diary – a video one, I mean?'

'Probably, but I'll see how things go for the first few days.' Tara looked round at her little empire and sighed happily. 'I promise I'll be in touch.'

Libby went back to her car, and stood looking at the Crooked Horse, still adorned with its blue and white tape, for a long moment. So Malcolm Hodges had been killed here presumably sometime before the fire had been set, and then transported somehow to his own barn. She shook her head and got into the car.

How had he got to the barn? And what had his boat got to do with it? And try as she might, she couldn't link the antiques boys and the possible theft of Anglo-Saxon artefacts with his murder. It just didn't add up. Why would they draw attention to themselves by dumping his body in his own barn? No, far more likely that was a distraction technique. Misdirection on a grand scale.

And what, she wondered, as she gained the Nethergate road, was she going to ask Bren at the Fox? Lewis had merely said he got gossip from her, but had added nothing more. Perhaps, she thought, it was simply an excuse to have a sausage bake for lunch.

Lewis was already at a table in the garden at the back of The Fox when Libby arrived.

'I drove here, as I shall have to go and collect Mum from Temptation later,' he said. 'I love the name of that house.'

'Typical Victorian. Like that other one we came across – Rogation House. Have you ordered?'

'Not yet. What do you want to drink?'

'Would Bren do me tea?' Libby asked.

'Two teas and two sausage bakes then,' said Lewis with a grin. 'Coming up.'

'What do you want to ask Bren?' he said, when he had provided them both with tea. 'She said she'll be out in a minute.'

'I don't really know,' admitted Libby. 'I was thinking about it on the way over here. Only if she'd heard anything about the Crooked

153

Horse, I suppose, although I think I've exhausted all the gossip about that. I've talked to George at the Red Lion, Zack at the Gate, Stan at the Fox and Hounds and even the odd antiques dealer.'

'So you don't think it was anything to do with the antiques boys?' Lewis leant back in his chair.

'Can't see it. It was their trading place, by all accounts,' said Libby. 'Did you know, even Lenny and Flo used to go over there? To pick up a few bits, Flo said.'

Lewis laughed. 'I can just imagine. Londoners, see?'

'I'm not sure what London's got to do with it,' said Libby.

Lewis looked disbelieving.

The back door to the pub opened and Bren, cheerful and red-cheeked as ever, emerged with a tray.

'Nice to see you again, Libby!' she said, depositing the tray on the table. 'Now.' She sat down next to Lewis and gave them each their fragrant dishes. 'You wanted to talk to me?'

'We-ell . . .' Libby put her head on one side. 'I don't know if you know, but—'

'You're looking into that business with the Crooked Horse, *and* that antiques dealer what got murdered.' Bren nodded. 'I know.'

'Oh,' said Libby. Lewis grinned.

'We used to see him,' said Bren. 'Used to pop in sometimes on his way down to the creek. He moored his boat there, I 'spect you know?'

'Yes, I heard. I don't suppose he ever said anything about his business?' Libby took a mouthful of sausage bake and burnt her mouth.

'Careful,' said Lewis, amused.

'No,' said Bren, looking thoughtful, 'but there was that bloke who came round asking if we knew him.'

'When was that?' Libby dropped her fork.

'Oh, before he went missing. At least, before you found him. Two or three weeks ago?'

'Really?' Libby frowned. 'What was he like?'

'What my mum would have called a "wide boy". You know, bit flashy. Londoner.'

154

'Tall and skinny? Dark hair?'

'Yes, sounds like him. Know him, do you?' Bren looked interested.

'I think we might have met,' said Libby. 'Jim Frost, his name was.'

'Never give us a name,' said Bren. 'Is he a suspect?'

Libby sighed. 'I've no idea, Bren,' she said.

Bren had no further useful information about antiques dealers or the Crooked Horse, and Libby and Lewis finished their sausage bakes in companionable silence.

'Has the car gone from Hodges' mooring spot?' Libby asked, as they relaxed with a second cup of tea each.

'Yes, the police came and took it away, so it obviously was Hodges' motor. Big old thing, it was.'

Libby nodded. 'It would be.'

'What do you reckon to this bloke Bren said came round asking questions? Same bloke you met?'

'Sounds like it.' Libby stared up at the trees surrounding the garden. 'What would he want with me, though? And how did he hear about me?'

'Asked for you, did he? You didn't mention that.' Lewis looked concerned.

'Oh, didn't I?' Libby told him about Jim Frost's visit to Steeple Martin. 'And I decided we'd all been overreacting,' she concluded. 'After all, it's what *I* do, isn't it? Go round pubs asking about people.'

'Yeah, but the point is – how did he get your name and *why* was he asking?'

'I know.' Libby gave him a worried smile. 'I keep thinking about it. I only came into the picture after Wally Mayberry and Fay Hodges asked Fran and me to look into his disappearance. So who knew my name?'

'Stan at the Fox and Hounds,' said Lewis, 'Fay, Mayberry, any of their friends.'

'OK, and Bren said he was round here asking about Hodges before we found his body.'

'But *after* he'd disappeared,' Lewis pointed out. 'Or at least, after his missus *thought* he'd disappeared.'

'Hmm.' Libby was quiet for a moment. 'I think I'd better tell Ian.'

'He might, o' course, have been missing for another reason. Another woman? A secret antiques trip?'

'That's what Wally and Fay thought,' said Libby. 'That he was on a buying trip to the Continong, as Harry put it.'

'P'raps he was,' said Lewis, 'and bringing back some tasty piece that he was keeping secret.'

'As in antique, rather than woman.' Libby smiled at him. 'Could be. Anyway, I'll send Ian a text.' She sighed. 'And I expect he'll tell me off, as usual.'

Lewis grinned. 'Do you good. I thought he asked you to find out the gossip, though.'

'He did – about the Horse. But we got ourselves mixed up in Hodges' death. I'm just curious.'

'Nosy,' said Lewis. 'That's what it is.'

Libby sent Ian a text to his personal mobile when she got in her car, which took some time, owing to a lack of thumb capability and not knowing quite what to say. By the time she reached Nethergate, he still hadn't replied, which was hardly surprising, so she parked behind the Blue Anchor and messaged Fran.

Why didn't you come to the shop? Fran replied.

Because you'd tell me off for not letting you know I was coming.

Correctly interpreting this as an invitation, Libby got out of the car and walked down Harbour Street.

'What's been going on, then?' asked Fran, as Libby climbed onto the stool by the counter. 'Where have you been?'

Libby told her.

'And this Jim Frost. You think he's important?' Fran placed a mug of tea on the counter.

'Well, I've sent Ian a text about him. He was a bit unnerving.'

Fran stared into space for a long moment. Libby began to fidget.

'No, it's no good.' Fran pulled a face. 'I hoped I'd get something – but I didn't.' She gave Libby a regretful smile. 'Although after thinking Ian might have put you in danger before, I should have known better.'

'It doesn't matter,' said Libby, feeling slightly uncomfortable. 'And how many times have you said you can't do it to order? Or even know where it comes from?' She patted Fran's arm. 'It's all down to good old ferreting now.'

'But what are we – you – supposed to be ferreting?'

'I'm not sure any more,' said Libby with a grin. 'I think I'll just have to wait for something to happen. And as I've got *Contraband* rehearsals all this week . . . Oh – I haven't asked Judy and Cyd how their Raincliffe concert went on Saturday. Must do that.'

Fran nodded. 'Yes, you must. Go home and – as you said – wait for something to happen.'

Chapter Twenty-Three

Libby was just setting out for the theatre that evening when her mobile rang.

'Who or what is Jim Frost?' asked Ian. 'Jack's little brother?'

'I'm on my way to rehearsal, Ian, can I call you back later?' Libby pulled the front door shut behind her.

'Not really. I'm still at work, and I don't know where I'll be later.'

Libby sighed and began her story.

'So what did he actually *do*?' Ian interrupted just as she'd got to Frost's departure.

'Well, nothing!' Libby said, surprised. 'As I said. And we all agreed it's exactly what I do when I'm looking for information – go into a pub and ask.'

'Indeed you do. And it often works. So why was he different?'

'I'm not sure.' Libby frowned at her feet. 'We all felt it, though.'

'And he asked for you by name?'

'Yes. And I think we were all guilty of stereotyping – he looked, as Bren said, like an old-fashioned wide boy.'

'Who's Bren?'

'Oh, I hadn't got that far. Yes, I had lunch at the Fox at Creekmarsh today, with Lewis, and Bren was talking about how Hodges used to pop in there sometimes on his way to and from his boat. She said this Frost came asking after him.'

Ian made a sound like steam escaping. 'Why didn't I know this?'

'Why would you?' Libby turned the corner into the Manor drive. 'Unless you had reason to question them at the Fox.'

'They should have been questioned,' muttered Ian.

'After the body was found?'

'Yes. Once we knew where his boat had been moored and found his car, it would have made sense.'

'I expect it got overlooked when you had to take over from Clare,' suggested Libby. 'No one's fault.'

'Don't be naive. It's my fault.' Ian let out an impatient breath. 'I'll get somebody over there.'

'It was very tentative,' protested Libby. 'That's why I was a bit worried about telling you. It might be nothing.'

There was a short silence. Then: 'What does Fran think?'

Libby sighed. 'Nothing. She tried, and couldn't see anything. She thinks that part of her brain's shut down.'

'Hmm.' Ian was quiet again.

'Actually, Ian,' said Libby, 'I'm just about at the theatre now, so I'm going to have to go. Anything else you want?'

'No, thank you, Libby. I'm sorry if I snapped.'

'Don't mention it,' said Libby, suppressing a chuckle.

'Oh – and have you heard anything about the builders on your travels? At the moment they're looking all wide-eyed and innocent and know absolutely nothing about anything.'

'All I've heard,' said Libby, struggling to find her keys one-handed, 'is people saying they think it must be the developers who fired the pub so they could build their luxury homes.'

'Yes, which is the obvious conclusion – but they claim no knowledge of either the fire or the excavator, and the plant hire company say they don't know exactly who hired them.' Ian groaned. 'What a bloody case.'

Cyd and Judy, fresh from their triumphant London concert, arrived early, and regaled the assembled cast with an account of the evening.

'It was fabulous,' Judy finished up. 'Absolutely full – and your lovely Sir Andrew gave a speech at the end. He says he's coming again to the Alexandria on Saturday.'

Sir Andrew McColl, a theatrical knight and great supporter of the Oast Theatre, was a favourite of Libby's.

'Excellent!' she said. 'And now, if you've come down to earth, perhaps we'd better get on with smuggling.'

By half past nine, everyone felt ready to call it a day, and Libby offered to buy Susannah a drink before she drove home.

'Non-alcoholic, of course!' said Susannah. 'Yes, that would be lovely. We don't get out as much as we used to, obviously, being parents.'

'So make the most of it, eh?' Libby laughed. 'I'll tell Ben we're going to the Coach.'

Several members of the cast joined them, and Libby was about to go into the big back bar with them when Tim leant over the counter and beckoned.

'Philip's in the little bar,' he said. 'He thought you might be in after rehearsal.'

Libby's heart sank. 'I was going to sit with the cast,' she said. 'And I'm buying Susannah a drink.'

'I'll give her a drink,' said Tim. 'You pop in and have a word with Philip, and you can come in here afterwards.'

Libby sighed and went through the door to find not only Philip, but Ben and Edward at the big round table.

'I'm supposed to be with the cast,' she warned them. 'Is this urgent?'

Philip stood up. 'I'm sorry, Libby. It's Marsham's. They've been on my back.'

Libby sighed and sat down. 'I guessed. I've been putting off that phone call.'

'What phone call?' asked Edward. 'Or aren't I allowed to ask?'

'To a Ms Portia Havilland,' said Libby. 'She's a Marsham's executive – I think.'

'Ah,' said Edward. 'The Crooked Horse.'

'Indeed.' Libby nodded. 'All right, Philip, I'll call in the morning.'

'If you would, Lib,' he said, 'only they're getting a bit twitchy. Apparently the police have been all over them.'

'Well, yes, they would be,' said Libby.

'Why?' asked Edward.

Libby looked at Philip, who shrugged. 'Edward's part of your Wednesday Murder Club, isn't he? He's safe.'

'Otherwise known as Libby's Loonies,' said Ben with a grin.

'The Horse is now a crime scene,' Libby explained. 'Forensics have confirmed it's where Malcolm Hodges was killed.'

'Oh.' Edward's eyebrows shot up. 'That's a bit of a facer.'

Philip gave him a wry smile. 'A facer indeed. And Marsham's — what's left of it — want Libby to look into it.'

'Well, the firing and attempted demolition,' said Libby. 'Not Hodges' death.'

'All part of the same thing now, surely?' said Edward.

'Possibly,' said Libby, standing up. 'Look, I promised Susannah a drink, and I've abandoned her. I'll come back in here when she leaves — if you're all hanging around for a bit?'

Back in the main bar, she found Susannah deep in conversation with Cyd and Judy.

'Tim poured you a half of lager,' said Susannah, pushing a glass towards her. 'And thank you for mine!' She raised her own glass.

Libby took a grateful swallow. 'Sorry about that,' she said. 'What were you all talking about?'

Twenty minutes later, Susannah finished her drink and stood up. 'I'd better go,' she said. 'It's such a bind having to drive back to Nethergate. I'm seriously thinking we ought to move here.'

Libby laughed. 'We'd love to have you, but I'd probably take advantage of you. See you tomorrow.'

She turned to Cyd and Judy. 'I'd better go and join them in the other bar.'

'Is it something to do with this murder?' asked Cyd. 'We've missed out a bit while we've been in London. Brandon told us something

161

about an archaeological dig and an antiques dealer who came looking for you?'

With an inner groan, Libby gave them a precis of the past week's events. 'So now I'd better go and talk to Philip about it,' she said. 'Sorry to leave you.'

'That's fine,' said Judy. 'We'll see you tomorrow.'

She found Edward, Philip and Ben immersed in a highly technical discussion about beer and went to buy a round from Tim.

'All sorted?' he asked as he put glasses on a tray. 'It's about poor old Marsham's, I suppose. I couldn't help overhearing a bit.'

'Yes, as if they hadn't had enough trouble.' Libby frowned. 'Tell me, Tim, do you know what's happening there? I mean, it's a family-run brewery, but there's no family left, is there? Who's in charge?'

'I think it's a buyout,' said Tim. 'Not sure how that works legally, but I heard they ended up with a lot of debt after that business back in the winter. Compensation and what have you.' He shook his head. 'I hope they don't go under. They were always a good company before the old boy died.'

'One of the big breweries might take them over,' said Libby.

'Bloody well hope not!' said Tim.

Libby carried her tray to the table.

'Thanks, Libby,' said Edward, looking surprised. 'It was my round.'

'Never mind, Edward. You're always buying me drinks. And it's nice to see you. You're more often down on the Flats these days.' Libby sat down.

'I know.' Edward's dark skin became a shade pinker. 'And it's not easy for Alice to get away, what with the farm and the children, so I can't bring her up here too often.'

Ben trod on Libby's foot.

'Shame,' was all she said.

'What exactly is it that Marsham's want Libby to look into?' asked Ben. 'I mean, the whole thing is now being investigated thoroughly by the police. What can she do?'

'I think it's something to do with Stan at the Fox and Hounds,' said Philip. 'He's convinced it was all down to Libby that he got his pub back, and he's not been shy about telling the brewery what he thinks.'

'How much does this Portia Havilland know about it?' asked Libby.

'I'm not sure.' Philip leant back in his chair, tweaked his trousers and crossed his legs. 'I should ask if I were you.'

'Yeah, yeah, all right.' Libby sent him a reproachful glare and picked up her glass. 'Cheers.'

Tuesday morning found Libby industriously cleaning the cottage, changing bed linen and even sorting clothes for the charity shop.

Ben, calling in on his way past, observed this phenomenon with interest.

'What are you putting off?' he asked, as she bustled past him with an armful of washing.

'Eh?'

'You're putting off doing something. Could it possibly be the phone call to Ms Havilland?'

'No.' Libby's voice was muffled.

Ben followed her into the kitchen. 'Yes it is. Come on, Lib. Why are you worried about it?'

She withdrew her head from the washing machine and pushed her hair back from her face.

'Because I'm not a proper investigator.' She blew a strand of hair away from her nose. 'I keep saying, people seem to think we are, Fran and me. And we're not.'

'Stage fright, then.' Ben went to the sink and filled the kettle. 'But people have asked you to look into things before – it's not exactly a new thing, is it?'

'But not big business,' protested Libby, with what sounded suspiciously like a whine. 'That's a whole different thing.'

'Worse than doing it unofficially for the police?'

'But that's *Ian*! He's a friend.'

'You'd never think it, the way you talk about him sometimes. Tea?'

'Yes please.' Libby sat down at the table. 'OK, I'm being a wuss. I suppose I see what she wants, and then, if I can't do it, I say so.'

'Exactly. Go on – do it now. I won't listen.' Ben turned his back and poured boiling water into mugs.

Libby chose to use the landline and punched in the number Philip had given her.

'Oh, Mrs Sarjeant!' Portia Havilland's voice was a pleasant contralto. 'I'm so pleased you called. I was beginning to think I'd overstepped the mark by asking Philip to ask you . . .'

'Not at all,' said Libby, striving for the most businesslike tone she could manage. 'You do understand I'm not an official investigator, though?'

'Yes, yes, Philip explained that, but you do work with the police, don't you?'

'Sometimes,' admitted Libby. 'But I don't have the resources they do.'

'No, I quite understand. But – well, you know all about the problems the company has had over the past year, don't you?'

'Yes.' She could hardly deny it.

'So you know the background. And we're rather concerned that the business of the Crooked Horse could link back to that. We wondered if you would do some investigating – unofficially, perhaps – on our behalf, to help us get to the bottom of it. We're very worried that the good name of the brewery is going to be damaged beyond repair, and it will mean the end of the company.'

Chapter Twenty-Four

'So no pressure, then?' said Ben, when she returned to the kitchen for her tea.

'Exactly.' Libby shook her head gloomily. 'It's even worse than I thought. The whole future of Marsham's is now on my puny shoulders.'

Ben passed her a mug. 'Not quite that bad, surely. She did say unofficial?'

'Yes. And she's suggested I go in and meet her.' Libby sighed. 'So I said I would. But I'm not going to be any use looking at facts and figures, if that's what she wants me to do.'

'I doubt it. Did she say Philip had told her about you?'

'Yes.'

'There you are then. He will have explained.'

'But there's an official investigation going on into the whole business now. What does she think I can do?'

'Probably just make sure Marsham's come out of it as clean as possible.'

'How am I supposed to do that?'

'I don't know, Lib! Go and see her and find out. When are you going?'

'This afternoon. I'd better tell Ian. There might be things he doesn't want me to say.' Libby drank some tea and frowned. 'I'll wait until the washing's finished.'

Ben laughed. 'Ring him now. He probably won't answer anyway, but at least you'll have told him.'

Having left a message for Ian, Libby made herself a sandwich for lunch, made herself look as presentable as possible and set off for Felling and Marsham's Brewery. Unsure of parking availability on site, she opted for the town square and walked across to the brewery, where, she was surprised to find, Portia Havilland was waiting for her in reception.

'I thought we might go and have a cup of tea,' said Portia after they had introduced themselves. 'There's a nice little café in the square.'

'The Tea Square, yes, I know it well,' said Libby, puzzled but willing.

'Good.' Portia gave her a tight little smile and almost pushed her out of the building.

Libby watched as Portia led the way into the cafe. Tall, slim and beautifully turned out, the estates manager wasn't as young as Libby had expected, but a woman in her fifties with ash-blond hair. She stopped at the counter and turned back to Libby.

'Tea? Or coffee?'

'Tea, please.'

Portia placed the order and then led Libby to a table in the window, where she sat down with a sigh of relief.

'I'm sorry if this seems a little odd,' she said, 'but some of the interim management board aren't too happy.'

'With you talking to me?' Libby's eyebrows rose.

'No, no. There's a split, you see.' Portia turned to look out of the window. 'I'd better explain.'

'Might be a good idea,' muttered Libby.

Portia turned and gave her a wry smile. 'I know. I must sound like a complete doofus.'

Libby, charmed by the unexpected use of 'doofus', laughed. 'A bit!'

'Well, it's like this.' Portia leant forward, elbows on the table. 'You know only too well what happened last winter. So after – well, after the family had – er – gone, we got the solicitors in and formed an interim board. Because there are debts – mostly as a result of . . . of . . .'

'Yes, yes, I understand. Go on.'

'There's a feeling that we should sell up. At the moment, it's more or less a fifty-fifty split, and the workforce is on our side – the ones who want to keep Marsham's as Marsham's. And when all this trouble with the Crooked Horse started – you can imagine!' Portia shook her head and sent her fair hair flying. 'That added fuel to the fire.' She stopped, looking shocked. 'Oh, sorry! I didn't mean that!'

Libby grinned. 'Very apt,' she said. 'So what's the position now?'

'Some of us still want to keep the brewery going, but we need to know what happened at the Horse. Some of us,' she leant forward confidentially, 'are wondering if it wasn't an inside job.'

At that moment, a young man arrived at the table with a tray and a smile, and unloaded a pot of tea, cups, milk jug, sugar and a plate of scones. When they'd served themselves, Portia continued.

'You see, there were a couple of people who said the whole episode proved that we should sell up.'

'Are they long-established employees? Shareholders?' asked Libby.

'Shareholders, and yes, a couple of the older ones just arrived the morning after the fire looking smug and saying "I told you so".' Portia shook her head again. 'And what's worse is that no one can find out who exactly decided to sell the place.'

Libby took a thoughtful bite of scone. 'It wasn't part of the wholesale selling-off last year?'

'We can't find records,' said Portia. 'The solicitor had paperwork – both ends, the buyers and our own – but no one seemed to know who had authorised it.'

'Sounds very unlikely,' said Libby. 'Do *you* think it could have been part of the sell-off?'

Portia looked uncomfortable. 'Well . . .'

'You do.' Libby took a sip of tea. 'I'm inclined to agree, but everyone connected to that fiasco is out of it now, aren't they? If not behind bars awaiting trial, then on bail.' She looked up at Portia and put her cup down. 'When exactly did the first indication of the sale come to light? I gather it wasn't that long ago that it was closed.'

'No.' Portia looked even more uncomfortable. 'We got the legals, and because of – well, everything – assumed it was on the level and had been overlooked in the – er – investigation. And then the buyers got in touch and asked why the sale hadn't been actioned.' She sighed. 'We rather thought it was our fault, so we set about trying to repair the damage. Which included closing the pub.' She shook her head. 'That meant Jenny . . .' She looked at Libby.

'The landlady, yes.' Libby nodded. 'She was suddenly homeless.'

'We found her a very nice residential home.' Portia was defensive.

'And if the Horse can be refurbished, will you let her back in, as you did with Stan at the Fox and Hounds?'

Now Portia was confused. 'I – er – I don't know.'

Libby leant back in her chair and gazed at the ceiling. 'It looks to me as if someone took advantage of the kerfuffle after the scandal and set you up. I doubt the buyers were genuine, and I would be very suspicious of their solicitors, too.' She sat forward and fixed Portia with a gimlet eye. 'Not to mention your own solicitors, who should have known better.'

Portia cleared her throat. 'They're new. The old ones – well, they closed down after . . . well, after. They had links to . . . to . . .'

'I get it.' Libby gave her a wry grin. 'You're in a right fix, aren't you?'

Portia tentatively returned the grin and relaxed. 'You see why I didn't want to talk to you at the office? Those of us who want the business to survive suspect there might still be someone on the inside behind it all.'

'Behind the sale, you mean?'

'Yes. I can't imagine anyone setting fire to the building.'

'Or murdering someone?' suggested Libby.

'Well, no.'

168

'You've talked to the developers who were going to buy it from your buyers?'

'We were advised not to.'

'Who by?'

'Our solici— Oh.' Portia closed her eyes and gave a small moan.

Libby let the silence between them stretch for a full minute. Then she leant forward again.

'I see why you wanted me to look into it,' she said. 'And I shall do my best. Can you give me the name of both sets of solicitors? And your buyers?'

Portia sat up straight and took a deep breath. 'I'll text you our solicitors and the buyers, but I can't remember the name of the buyers' solicitors. I'll look it up when I get back to the office. What's your number?'

Libby gave it, and watched while Portia, with enviable facility, sent the text.

'Now what?' she asked, putting her phone away.

Libby tapped her fingers on the table. 'To be honest, I don't know what I'll be able to find out, but I'll do my best. What happens if I discover that it was someone in the company who authorised the sale?'

'I suppose we take it from there. But we'd need proof.'

'Of course. Well, as I said, I'll do my best. Oh – and at some point someone mentioned a possible protection order on the building. I rather thought it would have been listed, given its age and history.' Libby raised her eyebrows interrogatively.

'It wasn't. We prepared an application to Historic England a couple of years ago, but it never got made.' Portia frowned. 'It is surprising, isn't it? Given its history, as you say.'

'Odd that the application was dropped,' said Libby. 'Makes me wonder if it was done on purpose.'

'But it was ages ago, as I said.' Portia shook her head. 'It's all beyond me, frankly.'

Me too, thought Libby. 'We'll try and find out,' she said aloud, trying to sound more confident than she felt.

Portia was looking uncomfortable again.

'Was there something else?' Libby paused in the act of putting her phone away.

'I know you said you weren't a proper investigator, but should I – I mean, we have a budget . . .'

'Oh, good Lord, no!' said Libby hastily. 'Please, don't even think about it.' She stood up. 'Thank you for the tea and scones, and I'll be in touch as soon as I have anything to tell you.'

Portia stood up too and smiled. 'I'm really grateful, Libby,' she said. 'You've already pointed out a couple of things we should have thought of ourselves. Thank you.'

Libby smiled back. 'Only too pleased to help. And I'll be in touch, as I said.'

Though when that'll be, goodness only knows, she said to herself as she walked across the square to retrieve her car.

Once in the driving seat, she took out her phone, thought about the information Portia had supplied and decided she needed to discuss it with Fran.

'You'd better come over,' said Fran with a sigh, when Libby had given her a precis of the conversation.

'I won't be long,' she promised. 'I'm rehearsing again this evening, so I've got to get back.'

The journey from Felling to Nethergate was more straightforward than from Steeple Martin to Felling, and Libby arrived at Harbour Street in just under fifteen minutes. Parking behind the Blue Anchor, she was surprised to find Fran already seated at one of the tables outside.

'I've just had tea and scones at the Tea Square in Felling,' said Libby, taking a seat opposite her friend. 'But I can always manage another cup. Why aren't we sitting in your house?'

'Because Guy's there with a crashing headache and Sophie's looking after the shop. So tell me all about Portia Havilland.'

Chapter Twenty-Five

'Let me get this straight,' said Fran, when Libby had finished her report. 'This woman wants you to find out what happened without providing you with any sort of concrete evidence – no paperwork, no nothing? And presumably doesn't want you poking your nose into the business in case some of the people who want to sell up find out?'

'She didn't actually say that, but it looks that way. She started off by saying we had to have the conversation away from Marsham's because of the dissenters.' Libby smiled up at Mavis, who had arrived with two large white mugs of tea. 'Thanks, Mavis.'

After Mavis had left, they sat in silence, both contemplating the enormity of Portia Havilland's request.

'Frankly,' said Fran eventually, 'I don't see what you can do. I don't even know quite what she wants.'

Libby frowned. 'No. I suppose what she wants is Marsham's exonerated from all blame so that it will be easier to persuade the board not to sell.'

'And you're supposed to do that?' Fran raised an eyebrow. 'Impossible, I would have thought.'

'Well, yes. Because they'll never be able to get away from the fact that it was the family itself who caused the scandal.' Libby took a reviving sip of tea. 'And I wonder – do you think the decision to sell the Horse was part of that?'

'That all goes back to last year, though, and the whole Horse business only blew up recently.'

'Hmm.' Libby was still frowning. 'I bet it was somebody at Marsham's who set it up, though.'

'Well of course it was! There are proper sales documents, aren't there? But then there's the solicitors.'

'Yes.' Libby took out her phone. 'Here they are, look. Hardy and Co., Canterbury.'

'And were they the solicitors who dealt with the scandal?'

'I don't know!' Libby looked surprised.

'Ask Philip. I bet they aren't.' Fran sat back, looking triumphant.

'You think,' said Libby slowly, 'that the whole thing was a set-up?'

'Makes sense, doesn't it?' Fran looked up at the sky and thought for a moment. 'First of all, someone inside Marsham's decides to sell the Horse.'

'Why?'

'I don't know, do I?' Fran sounded irritated. 'Anyway, they get hold of dodgy solicitors to set up the sale. And then' – she sat forward – 'then the London couple offer to buy it, in order to sell it to the developers.'

'Couldn't the developers have offered to buy it themselves?' suggested Libby. 'Oh, no. Marsham's wouldn't have done that. Even if it was a dodgy member of staff in the first place, by that time they all knew about it, didn't they?'

'Yes. It's a bit like creative accounting – if you're clever, you can hide anything.' Fran nodded wisely. 'What Ian needs to do is send in those forensic accountants again.'

'But it isn't accounts,' said Libby.

Fran waved this away. 'I bet they could find it.'

'So.' Libby sat back with her head on one side. 'In that case, the developers must be in on it. They must have got hold of the Marsham's person and – what? Paid him? Blackmailed him?'

'Or he – or she – saw an opportunity and got in touch with the developers after the application had been turned down.' Fran finished her tea. 'That makes sense.'

'And the London couple weren't real buyers but employees of

Speedwell?' Libby shook her head. 'Is that really how big business works?'

'You do hear of all sorts of dodgy dealings, don't you?' said Fran. 'I think it would be worth Ian looking into it.'

'But,' said Libby, 'Ian's looking into the murder of Malcolm Hodges, not the firing of the Horse.'

'It's all linked.' Fran shook her head. 'Everyone thought that – even before they discovered that Hodges had been killed in the Horse.'

'And that was a bit of a turn-up for the books, wasn't it?' Libby grinned. 'A completely random connection. And what do we think about that? Given that there was something definitely dirty about the sale of the pub, had Hodges found out? Was he blackmailing Speedwell?'

'Maybe he was,' agreed Fran. 'That makes sense, too.'

'Doesn't get me any nearer exonerating Marsham's, though,' said Libby. 'You're right – I should talk to Philip again. Ask him about these Hardy people. He'll know.'

'Hardy and Company?' said Philip, who had rung Libby almost as soon as he received her text, which she sent the minute she arrived home. She sat down at the kitchen table.

'That's what Portia said. What I wanted to know was – were they the company solicitors, or were they new?'

'Well, I can tell you quite categorically, they are not Marsham's solicitors, who I've worked with for years.' Philip was silent for a moment. 'Tell me what your thoughts are.'

Libby repeated the conversation she'd had with Fran. 'So it all looks very dodgy to us,' she concluded.

'I agree. And I thought it was questionable from the start.' Philip paused. 'I really can't see what you can do, though. I did point that out to Portia when she first asked me about you, but I think she's panicking.'

'Because she'll lose her job if they sell up?'

'Maybe. But I think what needs to be done now is to find out about

173

the couple who were the prospective buyers and see if they were connected to Speedwell. And you can't do that if even the police can't find them.'

'Exactly.' Libby sighed. 'I wish I hadn't talked to her now. She'll be hoping I can pull a rabbit out of the hat, and it'll be even worse when I can't.'

After another long pause, Philip said, 'Let me talk to Ian. He can authorise an inside search of Marsham's – again – and this bogus solicitor. Leave it with me, Libby. You go off and concentrate on your eighteenth-century smugglers.'

That's all very well, Libby thought, as she heaved herself up to go and find something for dinner. But I shall worry about it now.

The *Contraband* rehearsal went surprisingly well, Libby thought later. Partly because Judy and Cyd had been able to attend, and partly because first night was now within hailing distance and made everything seem far more real.

'Drink?' asked Judy as they were packing up. 'Do you fancy popping into the Pocket?'

'I shouldn't really.' Libby looked over her shoulder to where Ben was emerging from backstage.

'Drink, Ben?' called Judy. 'Libby's havering.'

Ben walked across the stage and smiled down at them. 'In the Pocket?'

'Yes.' Judy beamed and gave Libby a nudge. 'See!'

'Oh, all right.' Libby smiled sheepishly.

'Good. I wanted to have a chat with you, actually.' Judy slung her bag over her shoulder and linked her arm with Libby's. 'Come on, Cyd.'

'So what's it about?' asked Libby, as the four of them walked down the Manor drive.

'Couple of things, really,' said Cyd. 'You know we've been looking for somewhere to buy?'

'Yes?' Libby looked up.

'Found somewhere?' asked Ben.

'Well, yes, we think so. Just wanted to ask what you thought.' Cyd looked at Judy. 'Go on, you tell them.'

Ben and Libby exchanged puzzled looks.

'It's – ah – a bit . . .' Judy cleared her throat. 'It's a flat.'

'A flat. Yes. OK, so what do you want to know?' Libby frowned.

Judy took a deep breath. 'It's Edward's flat.'

'Eh?'

Libby and Ben both stopped dead.

'See? I knew you'd be upset!' wailed Judy.

'Don't be daft! Of course we're not upset – just surprised. Edward hasn't said anything.' Ben tucked his arm through Cyd's and resumed walking.

'But actually, only last week Ian said he thought he might be looking for a new neighbour, if you remember,' said Libby. 'So Edward's going to move in with Alice, is he?'

'Yes.' Cyd nodded. 'We bumped into him and Alice in Nethergate when we were down at the Alexandria the other day, and he mentioned it because he knew we'd been looking.'

'It's only one bedroom, though,' said Libby. 'Won't you want a spare room for guests?'

'He's got a study,' said Judy. 'Didn't you know?'

'No!' Libby was surprised. 'We've only been in the kitchen and the living room.'

'Well, we went and looked at it today and it's gorgeous!' Cyd sounded enthusiastic. 'But we were worried because Edward hadn't told you himself.'

'He would have done when we next saw him, though,' said Ben. 'I think it's a cracking idea. When will you be able to move in, do you think?'

'Oh, not for a couple of months,' said Judy, having recovered her equilibrium. 'Edward's got to sort things out with Alice and move all his stuff, and make sure he's still got his room at the uni, and it'll take at least a few weeks for all the solicitor's stuff to go through.'

'It's exciting!' said Libby. 'It doesn't seem that long since we went to the housewarming at Grove House, and now we'll have another one!'

'What was the other thing you wanted to talk about?' asked Ben.

'Ah.' Judy and Cyd looked at each other. Once again, Cyd took up the reins.

'We want to get married.'

'Oh wow!' Libby stopped again and threw her arms round Judy and then Cyd, while Ben tried to pat both of them on the back.

'Fantastic!' Libby began hurrying to cross over the high street towards Cuckoo Lane. 'Got any champagne in the Pocket, Ben?'

Judy and Cyd laughed. 'Let's save the champers for another time,' said Judy. 'We don't want to broadcast it too much yet.'

'Not until we've got it settled,' said Cyd. 'We thought we might see if we could do it where Peter and Harry had their ceremony. They've shown us the photographs and it looks lovely.'

'And then,' said Judy, as they arrived outside the Hop Pocket, 'we're hoping we can have it blessed in church.'

'Oh!' Libby was surprised all over again. 'Are you going to ask Beth?'

'Probably Patti,' said Cyd. 'We've been talking to her, too.'

Libby pushed down a twinge of jealousy as she pushed open the pub door.

'See, Lib?' said Ben, giving her a surreptitious nudge. 'You're a catalyst for bringing people together.'

Libby smiled weakly and followed him to the bar.

The Pocket was quiet. A few of the regulars were seated at the counter and a couple of the tables, and Simon's newest recruit, a Canterbury University student, was polishing glasses. Ben ordered the drinks and sent the three women to sit down.

'So Patti's happy to do the blessing, then?' Libby asked.

'Yes, but probably here at Beth's church. She said Beth won't mind.' Cyd looked at Judy. 'She's such a good friend, isn't she, Jude?'

Now completely flummoxed and feeling rather left out, Libby

smiled again and looked round for Ben, who arrived with the drinks.

'Cheers!' he said, giving Libby a warning glare. 'All the very best.'

'Well!' said Libby, as she and Ben walked home along the high street. 'That was a couple of bombshells, wasn't it?'

'Very nice ones,' said Ben. 'But you felt left out, didn't you?'

'I know, I'm sorry. I should be really pleased that all my friends get on so well together. And I am.' She sighed. 'It's me being annoying and selfish again, isn't it?'

'Oh, for goodness' sake, don't start that again,' said Ben.

Wednesday morning dawned brilliantly bright and sunny, and Libby, after giving herself a good talking-to, decided to go to the supermarket in Canterbury and stock up for the next couple of weeks. Lovely though the village shops were, there were certain things that only the supermarkets could provide, as she'd been reminded by her visit with Philip.

She had just parked the car when her phone buzzed in her bag.

Shouldn't be telling you this, said Ian's text message, *but we've just found another body.*

Chapter Twenty-Six

All thoughts of shopping fled. After staring open-mouthed at the phone for a moment, she texted back.

Where? Connected?

She waited a few more moments, then, as no reply seemed forthcoming, she gave up, collected her bags-for-life and went to find a trolley. Ian's reply came halfway through the frozen food section.

Not sure. What did Havilland tell you?

I'm in Sainsbury's, replied Libby. *Talk when home.*

In Canterbury? Come to the station was the rather peremptory answer.

Libby sighed, collected some frozen peas and made her way to the checkout. Anything she hadn't managed to buy she would do without.

'I've got frozen food in the car,' she announced, as she was shown into Ian's office, 'so don't keep me long.'

Ian's dark eyebrows rose into his hairline. 'I thought you'd be interested.'

'I am, of course,' said Libby, 'but—'

'And as my CHIS, I need to speak to you.' A smile tried to break out on Ian's face.

'All right, but I'll charge you for my spoilt dinner.' Libby plonked herself down in the chair by his desk.

'As it's Wednesday, and if you're not rehearsing, I could take you to dinner instead.' Ian leant back in his chair and swivelled to face the window.

'La, sir! How forward!' Libby grinned at his back. 'Come on then. What do you want to know.'

'Everything you talked about to Ms Havilland, please.' He swung back, now all business.

'So,' he said when she'd finished, 'it appears no one from Marsham's saw or had anything to do with this London couple?'

'Except whoever it was approved the sale, I guess.'

'Perhaps not even them,' said Ian. 'It looks as though the whole transaction was done through this suspect solicitor's firm.' He tutted. 'God alone knows what they were thinking of. Neither Philip nor I have ever heard of Hardy and Co.'

'What's their address? Portia said they were in Canterbury.'

'We haven't found it yet. I've got someone getting on to Speedwell, as I assume they would have had dealings with them.'

'Anyway,' said Libby, 'what's this got to do with your new body?'

There was a short silence.

'Well?' said Libby.

'I really don't think you should be talking about murder in quite that way.' Ian suddenly sounded remote. 'Whoever "my body" is, he was a human being.'

Libby shrivelled.

'Oh hell. I'm sorry, Ian.' She hung her head. 'I'll go.'

He sighed heavily. 'No, don't go. Just – please be careful. Haven't you always said murder isn't cosy? Nor is it a game. Don't lose sight of that.'

'No.' Libby swallowed an uncomfortable lump in her throat. 'I'm sorry.'

'Right.' Ian leant forward over his desk. 'What this has to do with this murder is that there was nothing on the body other than a smell of petrol.'

'Nothing? What – no clothes?'

'Yes, clothes.' Ian was back to being irritable. 'I meant no wallet,

179

cards or any other means of identification. And no suspicious items of jewellery, or cash – not that anyone steals cash these days – or anything else. Just a heavy smell of petrol.'

'And you think this might mean he was the one who set fire to the Horse? How far away was it?'

'Beyond Canterbury – on the way to Ashford. Where Speedwell are based.'

'Ah.' Libby thought for a moment. 'Not your case, then?'

'Not at the moment. We were informed, as someone remembered our fire and wondered if there might be a connection. Now I'm trying to find one.'

'I see. But no one could find this London couple, I thought, so how could you check if it is the same person? That's who you're thinking it might be, isn't it?'

'If we could find the woman it would help, but she's disappeared too.'

'Did you have their address?'

'Yes, Speedwell had it. But it was false. Turned out to be an animal sanctuary.'

'So really,' said Libby, fixing Ian with a gimlet eye, 'you already knew that the whole set-up was fake, didn't you?'

'Yes.' He stared back, daring her to comment.

They sat in silence for a moment or two.

'So now it's just a matter of who's the murderer, and who fired the pub, and are they one and the same? Or did one cancel out the other?' Libby chewed her thumbnail.

'What do you mean – cancel?'

'Did the murderer kill the fire-setter, or did the fire-setter try to cover up the murder?'

'Hmm,' said Ian.

'Right,' said Libby, taking a breath. 'In that case, I'm going home to put my shopping away.' She stood up. 'Let me know if you need anything else. And you'd better not commit to dinner this evening in case the murders take off.'

Ian nodded.

'Did you know about Edward moving?'

'Yes. I expect he'll tell you tonight. It wasn't my place to tell anyone.'

'Well, your new neighbours told me,' said Libby.

'My – what?' Ian stood up suddenly.

'Oh, didn't you know? Cyd and Judy are buying the flat.' Libby beamed and left the office in a hurry.

As usual, the Canterbury ring road was beginning to get clogged with traffic, and even though Libby only had to use a small section, it still held her up, and she was beginning to panic about her frozen peas by the time she reached home.

With a sigh of relief, she put the last item away, poured boiling water into a mug, sat down at the kitchen table and called Fran.

'It's very tenuous,' said Fran at length.

'It did strike me as someone trying to make things fit,' agreed Libby. 'And what's with calling me into the police station on a whim?'

'He's getting desperate,' said Fran. 'Didn't he say he was almost ready to leave the service and go private?'

'Mmm,' said Libby doubtfully. 'He won't, though. He wouldn't have the resources if he did that.'

'They don't seem to be doing him much good as it is.' Fran paused. 'But I suppose we could look into it.'

'What, this other body? How do you propose to do that?'

'I was thinking . . .' Fran spoke slowly. 'If we could get the address of that London couple . . .'

'It was an animal sanctuary.'

'Oh, yes. Well, the solicitor's office, then.'

'I don't think that exists either.'

'Well, they must be looking into that, then.'

'Yes, they must.' Libby stirred her tea thoughtfully. 'How about if I see if I can get Portia to show me any paperwork they have about the sale?'

'They'll have handed that to the police.'

'Oh.' There was another pause. 'We're stymied, then.'

'Back to the antiques boys?' suggested Fran.

'I guess so. I could always ask around and see if anyone knows that Jim Frost.'

Fran perked up. 'So you could! Wally Mayberry, perhaps?'

'Yes – and Fay. And Stan, I suppose.'

Fran laughed. 'He'll be thoroughly fed up with us!'

'You're coming too, then?' Libby gave Sidney a private grin. Fran was back on form.

'Of course. Sophie's still here, so I can get away from the shop. When shall we go?'

'No time like the present?'

'I'll pick you up,' said Fran briskly. 'Half an hour?'

Libby laughed. 'I'll see you when you get here.'

The drive to Shittenden took place in glorious sunshine, and made Libby wonder why she spent so much of her time indoors.

'I'm going to ring Stella and ask if I can go for a ride,' she told Fran.

'Stella who?' Fran squinted at the road ahead before turning left onto the Shittenden road.

'Stella! Cascade's owner! You know!'

Cascade was the pure white pony who had modelled with Cinderella's coach during last winter's pantomime. He lived with his owner, Stella Black, at Brooke Farm, along with stablemates Punch, whom Libby occasionally rode, Rajah, Charade and Dilly the donkey. And Alanna the stable girl, of course.

'Oh yes, sorry, I'm concentrating.' Fran slowed down and pulled in alongside the Fox and Hounds. 'Looks as though there are people here.'

'It is a country pub, and it is a sunny day in summer,' observed Libby. 'Pretty much a given, wouldn't you say?'

'All right, cocky.' Fran gave her a grin. 'Come on. I'm gasping for my tonic water.'

To Libby's surprise, Ricky gave her a cheerful wave from behind the bar, and Barney nearly pulled over the stool to which his lead was attached in his eagerness to reach her, tongue lolling as madly as his tail was whirring.

'This is nice,' she said, making a fuss of Barney while Fran hitched herself onto a stool. 'Where's—'

Fran gave her a kick.

'Where's Stan, Ricky?' she asked. 'Or are you bar staff today?' Libby straightened up. 'On the strength now, are you?'

'Baby bar staff, that's what Trisha calls me,' said Ricky with a grin. 'I'll get Stan.' He disappeared through a door at the back of the bar.

'Where's Debbie?' hissed Libby, peering round at the other drinkers.

'I don't know, and don't ask!' warned Fran. 'You nearly did just now.'

'I know, I know. But look!' Libby jerked her head sideways. 'Wally and Fay over in the corner. They're trying to ignore us.'

'Why, so they are!' murmured Fran. 'You stay here. I'll go over.'

Libby watched as Fran approached the little table under a window.

'Hello, Fay? How are you? And Wally! Who's in charge of Beer and Bargains today, then?' She smiled sweetly down at them.

'Ah – erm . . .' Wally cleared his throat. 'Fay, you remember Mrs – er – Fran?'

'Course I do,' muttered Mrs Hodges. 'Found Malc's body, didn't she?'

'Libby!' Stan's voice recalled Libby to the business in hand. 'Getting to be quite a regular these days!'

'Nice pub, Stan.' Libby smiled at him. 'We're actually on the hunt for information.'

'You don't say!' Stan tapped the side of his nose. 'Well, looks as though yer mate's finding it out!'

'They don't look too pleased about it,' said Libby. 'So I'll ask you. Have you ever seen or heard of someone called Jim Frost? Probably one of the antiques boys.'

Stan screwed up his eyes trying to remember. 'Tall bloke, skinny? Dark hair?'

'That's him!' said Libby excitedly.

'Nah,' said Stan. 'Never seen 'im.' He grinned.

'Oh, stop it.' Libby flapped her hand at him and turned to Ricky standing by and listening avidly. 'Can I have a half of lager, please, Ricky? And a tonic water for Fran.'

'Yeah, we know that Jim Frost,' said Stan, settling with his elbows on the counter as Ricky went to attend to the drinks. 'Only comes in once in a blue moon – and mainly used to be with Malc. Dodgy bloke, I always thought.'

'Yes, we thought so too,' said Libby, and explained about Frost's visit to Steeple Martin.

'Trying to find out what you knew, was he?' Stan waved away Libby's bank card.

'That's what it seemed like,' said Libby, as Fran wandered back to the bar. 'But for one thing, what *could* I know, and for another, how did he know my name?'

Fran hitched herself onto a stool and took a grateful draught of tonic water. 'Those two over there,' she said when she came up for air. 'They knew him.'

'They would.' Stan sent the pair in the corner a darkling glance. 'I can hardly tell 'em to go, not when they're long-standing customers, but I don't like all this stuff about murder. Not after the last lot.'

'I don't suppose they were behind Hodges' murder,' soothed Libby, 'but I'd like to know exactly what was going on.'

Stan came round the corner of the bar. 'You all right for a bit, Rick?' he said. 'We'll take Barney for a walk in the garden, all right?' He gave the boy a wink and undid Barney's lead. Libby and Fran followed him outside, where he let Barney off the lead, having shut the gate.

'Poo bags over there.' He waved. 'For visiting dogs.'

'Good idea.' Libby nodded approval. 'So what are you going to tell us, Stan?'

'I dunno much,' said the little man, perching his rear end on a table, 'but I reckon there was some buying and selling going on that wasn't all according to Cocker.'

'There's a phrase I haven't heard for a long time!' Libby gave him a grin.

'Buying and selling of antiques?' asked Fran.

Stan nodded. 'Now, far as I know, they was only bringing in ordinary domestic stuff, you know.'

'That's what we were told,' said Libby.

'But I think there was something else,' said Stan. 'Something them arts and antiques bods'd be interested in.'

Fran and Libby looked at one another.

'Something like Anglo-Saxon artefacts,' they said together.

Chapter Twenty-Seven

Stan looked puzzled.

'Eh?'

Libby looked uncomfortable. 'Something connected to – er – to the . . .'

'The Crooked Horse,' Fran finished for her. 'Do you think this Jim Frost was definitely involved with whatever was going on, Stan?'

'Yes.' Stan pulled a face. 'Not what I want in my pub, but as I said, difficult to turn people away if they aren't doing anything – I dunno – whatchamacallit . . .'

'Antisocial?' said Libby. 'No, I see that. When was this, though? Not that recently, surely? You haven't been open again very long.'

'They were in together that first week when we opened – you know, before the big flash opening you come to. That was before Malc disappeared. But mainly it was before Marsham's closed us down. Which was – what? Over a year ago now.'

Libby looked at Fran. 'When they were still meeting at the Horse.'

Fran nodded.

'Is this something to do with Malc's murder? Or the Horse burning down?' Stan looked between them with a frown. 'Not sure I follow you.'

'Could be both, Stan,' said Libby, 'but don't say a word to anybody. Even – er . . .' She looked over her shoulder.

'What, them?' Stan shook his head. 'Not a chance.'

'No – I didn't mean them,' said Libby.

186

'Ricky?' Stan's frown was back. 'Course not, poor lad.' His expression changed. 'Oh! Ah. Debbie.'

Fran glared at Libby. 'Well . . .' she began.

Stan looked up. 'We weren't really getting on,' he said slowly. 'See, I was so grateful when she . . . Well, when she . . .'

'I know,' said Libby.

He gave a little laugh. 'I just sort of realised it was all because I was grateful, if you know what I mean.'

Fran and Libby nodded.

'And then young Ricky and Trisha was getting on so well, and he started doing the odd shift here – well, it was difficult.' He gave them a pleading look. 'Don't say anything!'

'Course we won't,' said Libby, 'but I'm surprised Ricky didn't say anything. He never mentioned working here.'

'It's only been the last couple of weeks, really. Since uni's broken up.'

'How does he get here, though?' asked Fran.

'Ah, well. All part of the driving lessons,' said Stan with a grin. 'Trish collects him from Canterbury and takes him home after. Unless he stays here.'

'She's never said, either!' Libby shook her head. 'Why not? She could have popped in to see me.'

'Doesn't like to intrude,' said Stan. 'But I'll tell her. And she thought it might be difficult, with his mum living round the corner.'

'He didn't say anything when we were here for the opening, and neither did she,' said Fran. 'And Debbie was here then.'

'Course she was. I owe her a lot,' said Stan. 'But that's all it is.'

'Right, well, that's got that out of the way,' said Libby. 'Meanwhile, Jim Frost. Did you ever get any idea where he was from?'

'Not local, I don't think. London, maybe.'

'Hmm. Makes sense.' Libby nodded. 'Well, we'll see what else we can find out.'

'Carefully,' said Fran. 'I've already put the wind up Wally and Fay.'

Calling Barney, Stan led the way back inside.

'Bother,' said Libby. 'They've gone.'

'Yes,' said Ricky quietly, leaning over the bar counter, 'but there's someone here who wanted to speak to them.'

All three turned immediately, to be met with a cheerfully smiling man in jeans and a disreputable sweatshirt, his blond hair flopping almost Peter-like over his forehead.

'Hi, Stan, do you know where Fay Hodges might have gone? I was due to meet her here.'

'Hi — it's Ray, isn't it?' Stan held out his hand. 'You were in here with some of the lads a couple of weeks ago?'

'That's it!' Ray threw a curious look at the two women. 'I was going to look in Malc's old barn — see if there was anything I could take off her hands.'

Libby forced herself not to show a reaction to this and cleared her throat nonchalantly.

'Well,' said Stan, going behind the bar, 'these ladies might be able to help you there.'

'Eh?' said Libby.

'What?' said Fran.

'You could show Ray where the barn is, couldn't you?' suggested Stan, all wide-eyed innocence.

'Oh, I see!' Libby's face creased in a wide smile. 'Of course — what a good idea. Are you ready to go now?'

'I was going to have a drink, actually,' said Ray, looking rather taken aback. 'Could we hang on for a bit?'

'Of course,' said Fran. 'I'll have another tonic — what about you, Lib?'

'Oh, let me get these, please,' said Ray. 'If you're going to be kind enough to take me to the barn. Do you reckon Fay'll be there?'

'Sure she will,' said Stan. 'I reckon it was a misunderstanding and she thought you were supposed to meet there. Eh, Libby?'

'Er — yes!' Libby smiled brightly, while Fran tried to refuse Ray's offer of a drink.

Eventually they were all settled at the counter. Ricky had taken Barney out for a walk and Stan was serving the other customers in the bar.

'You're an antiques dealer yourself, are you?' asked Fran, raising her glass of tonic.

'I don't call 'em antiques,' laughed Ray. 'More like junk, really. But yes. I run what I call the junk market over near Whitstable.'

'I used to live near there,' said Libby. 'Whereabouts?'

'On the outskirts. Do you know Dungate?'

'Oh, the Dolphin! Yes, I know it.'

'Well, we've got a sort of outlet place over there now. You know the market garden?'

Libby nodded.

'We've got the junk market, the market garden and garden centre, and then the hop shop.'

'Hop shop?' repeated Fran and Libby together.

'You know there's a hop garden over near Whitstable? They've got a shop selling beers and things.' Ray beamed. 'We do quite nicely now.'

'We'll have to go over some time,' said Fran.

'Take your Ben,' Stan said, coming back to the conversation. 'Libby's old man's got a hop garden and a little brewery.' He tapped a pump behind the bar. 'This is his.'

After exclamations and explanations were exchanged, Ray finally decided he was ready to move off. Libby rushed to the Vixens before joining Fran in the car, where she was waiting to lead Ray's large white van to Hodges' barn.

'Why are we doing this?' she asked, buckling her seat belt.

'We want to talk to Ray,' said Fran.

'We won't be able to do that with Fay there. And Wally, probably.'

'We do it before we go in, or after we come out.'

'And what, exactly, do we ask him? He's not likely to give anything away.'

'Leave it to me,' said Fran. 'I've got a feeling he isn't mixed up in whatever-it-is.'

Libby gave her a sideways look and shut up.

*

The barn was as deserted as it had looked last time they arrived, and this time there was no other vehicle parked at the side. The only reminder – much, Libby thought, like the Crooked Horse – was a dejected piece of crime-scene tape fluttering from the big double door.

'Doesn't look like he ever did much business,' said Ray, joining them on the forecourt. 'Does Fay live near here?'

'We don't actually know,' said Fran. 'We've only been here once ourselves.'

'Oh?' Ray raised an eyebrow. 'You don't look like dealers.'

'No.' Fran looked towards the barn. 'We found the body.'

Ray uttered a strangled sound.

'You f-found . . . Malcolm's . . . How?'

Libby sighed. 'Fay said he was missing and asked us if we'd look into it.'

Ray took a step back. 'You're not . . .?'

'Police? No.' Fran smiled. 'Nor are we private investigators.' She fell back on Ian's own description. 'We're civilian investigators. We very occasionally help the police.'

Ray crossed his arms and frowned at them. 'You must have had some kind of interest. Apart from Fay Hodges asking you to track down her husband.'

'Do you think there might be something to find?' asked Fran.

Libby gasped.

Ray nodded slowly. 'I don't know,' he said. 'But I suspected they had something going on.'

'Who did?' asked Libby, surprised at the ease with which this information had been offered.

'Local junk dealers.' He heaved a sigh and leant against the Smart car's bonnet. 'The antiques boys, as they're known. Oh, it was all just smuggling in bits and pieces from France and Italy, but whenever I came over this way, I got the feeling there was something else. When I heard about Malc, I wondered.'

'And did you hear about the Crooked Horse?' asked Libby.

Ray looked surprised. 'Over Felling way? That was arson, wasn't it?'

'Yes. Did you ever go there?'

'No – bit off my patch. I know a lot of them met over there, but they never let me in on it!' He chuckled. 'I reckon they thought I was out of bounds. Being married to a copper.'

'No!' said Libby and Fran together.

'Yeah – why?'

'Do you know Ian Connell?' asked Fran.

'Oh, the dashing DCI Connell!' Ray threw his head back and laughed. 'The renegade cop.'

'The what?' Libby almost choked.

'He's a friend of ours,' said Fran with a smile.

'Oh!' Ray's expression was arrested. '*Now* I know.'

'Know what?' asked Libby.

'Who you are.' He looked smug. 'Do you know Clare Stone?'

'Yes,' groaned Libby.

'My missus and Clare are best mates.' He looked from one to the other. 'You know Rach as well, don't you?'

'Yes,' said Fran. 'But if that's the case, why on earth hasn't Ian asked you about this whole mess already?'

Ray frowned. 'I don't know,' he said slowly. 'I can only think he thought it would be prejudicial. Fiona – my wife – is on maternity leave just now, and DCI Connell isn't actually a friend. He knows Clare, but he met her through work. Fi and he have never worked together. He's just got a bit of a rep in the service.'

'Has he?'

'He goes his own way, apparently. Got suspended, too.'

'Yes, we know that,' said Fran.

'You're the ones he asks for help.' Ray nodded. 'Course.'

'So that's why we're interested,' Libby told him. 'But it doesn't look as though you can help.'

'I can't, I'm afraid.' Ray glanced round at the barn. 'And it doesn't look like you can help me, either.' He straightened up and pulled out his phone. 'I'll give Fay a ring, and if she wants to meet me, she can tell me where. And I'll see if I can find anything out for you.'

'About?' asked Fran.

'Whatever the antiques boys had going on.' He shrugged and turned away to make the call, then turned back fairly quickly. 'Voice-mail,' he said. 'I reckon she doesn't want to see me after all.'

'Oh well, it was worth a try,' said Libby with a sigh. 'You can find your way back to the main road, can't you?'

'Yeah, course.' He gave them both a grin. 'Got a number? If I find anything out, I'll let you know.'

Fran passed over yet another Harbour Street Gallery card, which Ray viewed with interest.

'Guy's your husband? Love his stuff,' he said. 'Artists and brewers – nice people to meet.' He grinned broadly. 'I'll be seeing you.'

'That was interesting,' said Fran, watching as Ray climbed into his van and gave them a wave.

'A little too fortuitous?' Libby was frowning.

'You thought that too?' Fran was still watching as the white van drove back onto the road and turned towards Shittenden.

'Does he really think we wouldn't ask Clare about him?' Libby opened the passenger door.

'He doesn't care.' Fran climbed in and started the car. 'He was far too free with his information.'

'But why? I can see he was probably fishing – more subtly than that Jim Frost bloke – but he must know someone would come after him.' Libby looked across at her friend. 'Let's ask Stan what he knows about him first. Then we can get a message to Clare.'

Chapter Twenty-Eight

'Did you find Fay?' Stan came out from behind the bar wiping his hands on a tea towel.

'No, the barn was shut up, and we realised we didn't know where she lived,' said Libby.

'And we want to know what you know about Ray, please.' Fran looked round at the other customers in the bar, who looked reassuringly unlike members of the antiques trade.

'Ray?' Stan looked startled. 'Why? He just came in a couple of times recently. Introduced himself, but didn't say anything else.'

'He doesn't seem quite on the level,' said Libby. She looked at Fran. 'Tell you what, we could go over and have a look at this little – what did he call it? Outlet.'

'And Ben could ask his friends over at that hop garden near Whitstable,' agreed Fran. 'He gave us so much information, didn't he? And all checkable.'

'Doesn't that mean he's kosher?' Stan was obviously puzzled.

'No,' said Libby and Fran together.

'Don't worry, Stan.' Libby patted his arm. 'You've done us a favour actually. We'll go and see what we can find out from what he said.' She looked round. 'Has Ricky come back? Does he want a lift?'

'Trisha's coming to give him a lesson later,' Stan said with a smile. 'Tell you what, shall I tell her to pop in when she drops him back to Steeple Martin?'

'We'll be in the Coach tonight, if she's later than eight o'clock.' Libby gave Stan a kiss on the cheek. 'See you soon.'

'Time's getting on,' said Fran as they went back to the car. 'I really ought to be going home, not gallivanting off to Dungate.'

'No, I agree,' said Libby. 'We'll get Ben to ask the hop people, and Tim can speak to the people at the Dolphin.'

'And we'll ask Clare. Or at least leave a message,' agreed Fran.

'I could call Rachel. I've got her personal number.' Libby beamed. 'Always useful being friends with the police.'

'You don't think this could possibly be dangerous?' Ben leant against the kitchen table and crossed his arms. 'This Ray knows who you are now. Come to that, so does Jim Frost, whoever he is, and Wally Mayberry.'

'Surely you don't think Wally's dangerous?' Libby peered at the rice in the microwave. 'You introduced us.'

'More fool me,' said Ben with a sigh. 'No, I don't, but the people he appears to be mixed up with obviously are. Whether one of them killed Hodges or not, the very fact that he *was* murdered means they aren't necessarily people you want to know.'

'Will you ask the hop person for me, though?' Libby got plates out of a cupboard. 'And ask Tim about the Dolphin?'

'Yes!' sighed Ben and took out his phone. He wandered into the sitting room while Libby, with a satisfied smile, took the rice from the microwave, the chilli from the cooker and sat down.

'You were right.' Ben came back in and sat opposite her. 'Yes – there is a hop shop, and a garden centre attached to the market garden, and they're just along the lane from the Dolphin. But there is no junk market, and therefore no Ray.'

'So why did he tell us all those porkies?' Libby piled rice onto her plate.

'And incidentally, how did he know Ian and Clare's names?'

'And Rachel's,' added Libby. 'And that Ian was a "renegade cop". He even knew he'd been suspended.'

'You must tell Ian. Did you say he was coming this evening?'

'It depends on the murders, I expect.' Libby forked up chilli. 'If he doesn't, we'll ring.'

They didn't need to.

There was a sharp rap on the door just as Ben was collecting his keys.

'Ian!' Libby stood back to allow him in.

'I'm sorry to burst in,' he said. 'Hello, Ben – sorry. But I didn't want to talk about this in the pub, if you don't mind.'

'About what?' Libby asked warily.

'What Clare told me not half an hour ago.'

'Clare? Clare Stone?' Libby waved him to a chair and perched on the edge of the sofa.

'Yes. Fran left her a message.' He scowled at Libby. 'Why didn't you tell me?'

'We thought you'd be busy. And Clare's told you, so now you know.'

Ian sighed.

'Would you like a drink?' Ben offered tentatively. 'Or are you driving?'

'I'm staying with Hetty,' said Ian, 'so yes please.'

'Scotch?'

'Please.' Ian's face relaxed. 'I honestly don't know how I haven't turned into an alcoholic knowing you lot.'

'Are you insinuating that *we* are?' asked Libby. 'If so, I'm offended.'

Ian laughed. 'That'll be the day.' He accepted a glass from Ben. 'Come on, then. Tell all.'

Libby did.

'So where does that get us?' she asked. 'This man knows the police and about practically everything you – and we – have been investigating. How?'

'He obviously has an in with the antiques boys,' said Ben, 'because he was in the Fox and Hounds with some of them. Stan met him.'

'That would be easy enough,' said Ian. 'All he would have to do was introduce himself to one of them as an out-of-town dealer. It's the fact that he knows about us – Clare, me and Rachel. That means he has inside knowledge somehow.'

'Perhaps he's someone who's been a person of interest in the past?' suggested Libby.

Ian shook his head. 'He wouldn't know all our Christian names, or my so-called reputation, if that was the case.'

'Perhaps he really is married to a cop,' said Ben.

'Although probably not one called Fiona,' said Libby.

'And no one will ever see him again,' Ian concluded. 'He's got everything he wanted.'

'But what *has* he got?' asked Ben. 'Fran and Libby didn't give anything away.'

'No, but he knows who they are now. So,' Ian turned a serious face to Libby, 'I think you must back away now. Whoever this guy is, and whether he's connected to the murderer, the people who set up the Crooked Horse fiasco, the antiques boys or all of the above, he's probably dangerous.'

'He didn't look dangerous,' muttered Libby.

'The worst kind,' said Ben. 'And if he isn't dangerous, the people he's working with are.'

'It's not just one person doing all this, then?' Libby looked at Ian.

'Hardly. You've already come across Frost and this Ray, and it looks as though the sale of the Horse was a complicated procedure that must have involved several people.'

'Someone from the developers?' said Ben.

'And someone from Marsham's.' Ian nodded wearily. 'Just think of what happened before. There are bad apples all over the place.'

'So we need to find the person inside Marsham's, basically,' said Libby.

'*You* don't need to do anything,' warned Ian.

'Suppose someone else comes looking for Lib?' Ben moved slightly closer to his best beloved.

'If they ask around, they won't get any answers,' said Ian. 'You can spread the word in the village, and Graham and Mavis can do the same in Nethergate. And I shall be inviting Wallace Mayberry to a chat that will put the fear of God into him.'

'They might not bother to ask,' said Libby. 'People have got in here before.'

'Then we put new locks on everything and security cameras,' said Ben. 'It's not as if we can't afford it. And we've got security measures at the Manor and the theatre – and the Pocket, come to that. I don't honestly know why we haven't got them here.'

'I'll call Guy.' Ian pulled out his phone. 'And then we'd better go and join the others, or they'll send out a search party.'

Libby was unsurprised when, on the way to the Coach, her phone started buzzing inside her bag.

'I'm walking,' she said to Fran. 'On our way to the pub. Ian came to us first to tell us to cease and desist.'

'Ah. I wondered if he'd phone you first.'

'No, he came to find out exactly what had happened. Clare spoke to him as soon as she got your message, apparently.' Libby stopped at the door of the Coach and gestured for Ben and Ian to go in ahead of her. 'I can't really talk now. Shall I come down in the morning?'

'Yes, and we can plan a strategy.' Fran sounded quite upbeat.

'I don't think there's anything *to* plan,' said Libby. 'We've been warned off.'

'We'll talk about it in the morning,' said Fran. 'See you about – what, ten thirty?'

Libby sighed, agreed, put the phone away and went into the pub.

'We've been waiting for you,' said Anne, almost bouncing in her wheelchair. 'Where've you been?'

Patti gave her partner a jab in the ribs.

'Glad you're here,' said Edward from beside the bar.

'Hello, dear heart,' said old Brandon from the big chair by the fireplace. 'I hope you don't mind us infiltrating your Loonies again.' He

197

waved a hand at Cyd and Judy, who were squashed in between Patti and Peter.

Libby laughed and pulled up a chair on the other side of Peter, while Ben helped Edward bring drinks to the table and Ian pulled up more chairs.

'Full house this evening,' she said.

'Yes.' Edward remained standing. 'I have an announcement.' He looked at Ian. 'Much as I love you all, and my neighbour and friend Ian particularly, I have made the momentous decision to leave Steeple Martin.'

There was a chorus of 'Oh no!' from around the table.

'But as you can imagine, I'm not going far. Just down to Herons-bourne Flats.' He gave Libby a lopsided grin. 'You were right in the first place, Lib. Ian was playing matchmaker.'

Everyone looked at Libby, who felt a tide of heat washing up her neck.

'Anyway, I shall be moving into Marsh Farm, and' – this time he looked at Patti – 'Alice and I are getting married!'

This produced a veritable roar of approval. Amid all the congratu-lations and Edward's conjuror-like flourish of a bottle of champagne, Libby looked at Cyd and Judy, who were joining in enthusiastically. Patti caught her eye and nodded.

'And now,' Edward continued, flapping his hand for silence, 'I believe the new owners of number one Grove House would like a word.'

Cyd cleared her throat. 'Thank you, Edward,' she began, and had to stop for the further outbreak of surprise. 'Yes, Judy and I are going to be Ian's new neighbours, and I hope he doesn't mind.'

Cue laughter.

'You've all been so nice to us since we landed among you, we couldn't bear to leave.' She glanced at Patti. 'And we think we've per-suaded Patti to marry us too!'

The noise after this announcement was such that a few customers from the other bar came in to find out what they were missing.

198

'Does it upset you a bit?' Libby murmured to Anne, who was smiling but unusually quiet.

'A bit,' she admitted. 'But we think there's hope on the horizon.' She looked at her partner fondly. 'We'll get all these weddings out of the way, and then – well, then we'll see.'

With this, Libby had to be satisfied.

Not surprisingly, the subject of antiques dealers, pubs and murders was not brought up for the rest of the evening. Libby managed to ask both Edward and Judy when their upcoming nuptials were likely to be.

'As soon as possible,' said Edward. 'We want to have the summer together before I have to start commuting back to Medway for work.'

'Have you still got somewhere to stay up there?'

'Oh yes, of course. But as I said, it means commuting.'

'And you two?' Libby asked Judy.

'Again, as soon as possible. We're going to have a two-vicar wedding here in the village!' Judy smiled at Patti.

'You and Beth?'

'Yes,' said Patti. 'Actually, Beth's supposed to be here this evening to join in the celebrations. So was Alice, in fact, but there was a child-care issue.'

'Oh dear.' Libby pulled a face. 'Never mind. I'll go over and see her in the next few days.'

Beth and John did finally make it, and after congratulating everyone and accepting a glass of champagne, Beth drew Libby aside.

'I think Patti might find a message on her phone when she looks at it,' she said. 'Moira's just called me.'

'Moira? Why?' Libby experienced a sinking feeling under her ribs.

'Her dig over near St Eldreda's has unearthed a genuine Anglo-Saxon hoard.'

Chapter Twenty-Nine

Libby was aware of her mouth hanging open.

'I know.' Beth shook her head wearily. 'It was a very garbled and excited message. If Moira has your number, she's probably left it for you, too. And I'm pretty sure she wasn't supposed to.'

'But . . . I mean, what?' Libby was trying to get her thoughts in order. 'They dug it up?'

'I assume so – I have no idea. And I'm afraid I wasn't going to ring her back and ask her.' Beth leant back in the chair Ben had vacated for her. 'I think you ought to tell DCI Connell, don't you?'

Libby looked over to where Ian was laughing with Edward and Peter.

'It seems a shame when he's relaxing for once.'

'He'll be cross if you don't.' Beth nodded towards Libby's bag, currently hanging on the side of her chair. 'Go on, look at your phone.'

Libby fished it out and saw the message indicated. 'OK,' she sighed. 'Here goes.'

She stood up and circled round the table.

'Here.' She thrust her phone at Ian. 'Beth thinks you should listen to this message. She got it too, and she thinks Patti has as well.'

Ian took the phone, frowning. 'Have you listened to it?'

'No.' Libby shook her head. 'Beth told me what it says.'

'How does she know?'

'It's a good guess,' said Libby. 'But I'll listen to it first if you like.'

Ian walked over to the window. Libby followed.

'I'll put it on speaker phone,' he said.

They both listened to Moira's excited voice telling them exactly what Beth had predicted.

'That *bloody* woman!' Ian exploded. Before the message had even finished, he took out his own phone. 'I'll have to deal with this, Libby, I'm sorry.' He looked across at Edward. 'And I'm sorry to spoil the party.'

'Edward understands,' said Libby. 'What do you want me to do?'

'Apart from murder that woman?' He smiled. 'Nothing at the moment. Let me make some calls. I'll speak to you before I go.'

'You were staying with Hetty. You can't drive,' protested Libby.

'Oh, I'll sort it. Go on, you go back. And thank Beth for me.'

Libby went back to Beth and waved at Patti, who stood up and joined them. Libby explained the situation.

'Why did she phone me?' asked Patti.

'She knows you took me over there and you know Sister Catherine,' said Libby.

'I wonder where it was,' mused Beth. 'And when did they find it? This message didn't come in until about three quarters of an hour ago, I would have thought they'd have packed up by then.'

'I know. It's odd, isn't it?' Libby looked over to the window, where she could see Ian pacing up and down outside. 'Perhaps he'll tell us.'

Proceedings were suddenly enlivened by the eruption of Harry into the bar.

''Allo, 'allo, 'allo!' he carolled. 'What's goin' on 'ere?'

Everyone rushed to tell him, and Harry immediately and indiscriminately tried to hug everybody, eventually finishing up with Libby.

'So what's up with Cranky Connell out there?' he asked.

'Something's happened in the current case, I think,' Libby prevaricated. 'Isn't all this good news?'

Harry raised an eyebrow, but smiled at Patti. 'You next, petal?' he murmured.

Patti blushed. 'You never know.'

Libby took Harry by the arm and dragged him over to where Peter, Ben, Edward and John were exchanging wedding horror stories.

'Look, the poor bloke's never done this before,' John was saying. 'Don't put him off!'

'I can recommend a good best person,' said Harry, slinging an arm round Libby's shoulders.

'I should think that position's already been filled,' said Ben.

'I haven't asked him yet,' said Edward. 'But I will.'

At this point, Ian re-entered and jerked his head at Libby.

'I can't tell you right now,' he said when she joined him, 'but if you could play it down with Beth and Patti? I'll let you know in the morning. And I'm afraid your friend Moira has some explaining to do.'

'What was all that about?' Ben asked after Ian had made his farewells and apologies.

'I don't know much,' said Libby, 'but I'll tell you what I do know on the way home. It's another can of worms, I think.'

Ian revealed the can of worms during Libby's breakfast the following morning. Libby provided a cup of not very good coffee and sat him down at the kitchen table.

'Ben's already gone to the brewery,' she explained, 'and I only gave him a very brief outline. I haven't spoken to Fran yet.'

'Well, I have absolutely no doubt that despite what I said yesterday, you will now find some way of ferreting about in the wreckage.' He sighed and stretched his legs. 'It appears that during the ongoing investigations at the Crooked Horse site, a fairly large cache of Anglo-Saxon artefacts was discovered.'

Libby gasped. 'And was that Moira's "hoard"?'

'It was.' He let out a mirthless laugh. 'And she did *exactly* what she was told not to.'

'Go on, then. I assume you're allowed to tell me, or you wouldn't be here.' Libby cradled her mug of tea in both hands.

'I doubt if I'm allowed to do anything of the sort,' said Ian, 'but you're better knowing the truth than picking up some garbled account from elsewhere.' He sat up straight and fixed his eyes on Sidney, languishing by the bread bin. 'Our scenes-of-crime officers were still at the site. Have you met our crime-scene manager? I say "our", but she's not ours at all – just my preferred manager, Alison. Well, she's a dogged little person, and felt sure there was more to find after we thought we'd finished. And of course she was right.' He looked at Libby. 'Do you remember when we discovered that room underneath the Fox at Creekmarsh?'

'Yes.'

'Well, Alison found one underneath the Horse.'

'Oh, wow!' Libby was enthralled.

'The thing is, no one had thought there would be anything like that – they didn't even have cellars because of the slippage. But there were a few steps down into a back room, behind the main bar, and a half-buried door.'

'What – it had slipped down below ground level?'

'Apparently. And there was a shelving unit in front of it.'

'For wine?'

'Probably would have been. Anyway, Alison found it, and lo and behold – a practically priceless collection of Anglo-Saxon artefacts.' Ian picked up his mug.

'How did Moira know, though?'

'Tara Nichols was still on site, so after Alison had reported to me—'

'You didn't tell me that!' Libby accused.

'No, I couldn't,' said Ian. 'But she did, and because Ms Nichols was still at her dig site, they went and hauled her off to have a look at what they'd found and, if possible, authenticate it. Which she did.' He heaved another sigh. 'Unfortunately, when she got back to the site, she told her volunteer diggers what had happened. She's over the moon, apparently, because it proves what she thought about the site and means there is probably more to be discovered.'

'So she told Moira. That was a bit foolish.'

'Indeed it was. She also warned Moira and the other person who was there not to say anything to anybody. But Moira took that to mean anybody but her own friends.'

'I expect she's proud of it, like Tara,' said Libby fairly. 'Still, she shouldn't have done it. It would have served her right if one of us had informed the press.'

'I'm surprised she didn't do that herself,' said Ian.

'Well.' Libby sat back and stared thoughtfully at the table. 'Do you think that was what Malcolm Hodges was doing when he was killed? Looking for this hoard?'

'I should imagine he was the one who put it there. I suspect he was there to retrieve some if not all of it. And it proves what we were thinking: that the dealers used the Horse to store whatever they found at the dig site, and did a lot of their selling from there. It must have been highly lucrative for them.'

'No wonder they weren't bothered about whatever they were bringing in from Europe,' said Libby. 'That was a useful cover.'

'And we ignored it, to all intents and purposes.' Ian was almost grinding his teeth. 'So now we have to round up all these so-called antiques boys and try and get the truth out of them.'

Silence settled in the kitchen, until Libby said, 'Do you think that's why Hodges was killed?'

'It's got to be, hasn't it?' replied Ian. 'Perhaps he was going to take the lot for himself.'

'Mmm.' Libby was frowning. 'That'll leave you with a whole army of suspects, won't it?'

'Among them the two gentlemen whose attention you've attracted. Presumably they wanted to know if the hoard was still there.'

'Yes! Of course.' Libby was much struck. 'And they knew Fran and I had been poking around, so they wanted to find out how much we knew.'

Ian sat back again, looking at her consideringly. 'So in order to keep you safe,' he said, 'perhaps we ought to announce the find.

Tara Nichols is going into our lab today to do some in-depth investigating, to make sure it's all genuine and to make sure it comes from the St Eldreda's site, so there'll be no harm in letting the press know.'

'But,' said Libby, wagging a finger, 'if you do that, all your suspects will suddenly disappear into thin air, betcha.'

'Of course.' Ian sighed. 'So what do we do? Keep it under our hats and hope they come after you so we can nab them in the process?'

'I think we do what we said yesterday. Make sure we're as security-conscious as possible and Fran and I don't ever go out alone – except in the village, of course.'

'You've been attacked in the village before now,' Ian reminded her. 'Steeple Martin isn't completely safe.'

'OK. I'll think about that.' Libby pointed at his mug. 'More coffee?'

'No thank you, I must get off. What are you doing today?'

'Going to Fran's.' Libby looked up at the clock. 'I said half past ten, so I'd better get a move on. I'm not showered yet.'

'Too much information,' said Ian, standing up. 'Be careful driving down there.'

'You think they'd attack me in the car?'

'Easiest thing in the world.' He grinned at her. 'But they'd keep you alive to tell them what they want to know.'

'Oh gee, that's a comfort,' said Libby.

Before she left for Nethergate, Libby called Ben. His voice sounded hollow.

'Are you at the top of a tun?' she asked.

'Yes, why?'

'You sound like it!' Libby laughed. 'Listen. Can you start organising those extra security measures you were talking about? Ian's just been here filling me in.'

'Oh. Serious, is it?'

'Fairly. I'll tell you all about it when I get home, but this morning I have to go and put Fran in the picture. I'll be careful, I promise. I was going to pop over and see Alice to say congratulations, but I don't think I'd better go out on the Flats by myself under the circumstances.'

'Oh blimey,' groaned Ben. 'Here we go again.'

Chapter Thirty

Remembering a few hairy moments in her recent past concerning villainous attacks, Libby left her phone on the passenger seat beside her, ready to press Ben's number if anything untoward should occur on her way to Nethergate. It was a pity, she thought, because it was another beautiful day, and normally she would have thoroughly enjoyed the drive.

She arrived at the top of the high street and relished for a moment the view over the town and the bay, with Dragon Island squatting in the middle, and the left-hand headland guarded by the traditional red and white striped lighthouse. So pretty, so very English and so deceptive. She drove slowly down, realising that the town was filling up almost daily now. Although, as she had said often to Fran, it no longer attracted the huge crowds it used to during high summer. Families wanted the more reliable weather of southern Europe or even the Caribbean these days.

She parked the silver bullet behind the Blue Anchor at the end of Harbour Street, and waved violently to Bert and George to make sure she had been noticed, in case there was a kidnap attempt between there and Guy's gallery.

'Hello!' Sophie looked surprised as she almost fell through the door. 'What's up with you?'

'Nothing!' panted Libby, forcing a smile. 'Nice to see you, Soph! Fran not here?'

'No, she said you were coming, so she stayed at home.' Sophie frowned. 'Are you sure you're OK?'

'I'm fine.' Libby took a deep breath. 'I'll get off, then.'

'Right.' Sophie resumed her seat behind the counter. 'Might see you at the weekend,' she added nonchalantly.

Libby opened her mouth, closed it again, nodded and left the shop.

'What's all this then?' she asked Fran as soon as the front door of Coastguard Cottage was opened. 'Sophie said she might see me at the weekend!'

'I did wonder if they might get back together, if you remember,' said Fran, amused. 'Tea?'

'Yes please. I've got an awful lot to tell you.' Libby followed her friend into the kitchen. 'And not all of it is pleasant.'

By the time Libby had covered the various revelations of the previous evening and earlier that morning, she was on her second cup of tea.

Fran was scowling out at her courtyard garden, where Balzac was sitting in his usual large flowerpot.

'So we've got to be careful in case we're attacked?' She shook her head. 'For heaven's sake! How many more times is this going to happen?'

'If you think about it, it stands to reason,' said Libby. 'We investigate murders. Murderers are dangerous people.'

Fran sighed. 'I know, I know.' She fixed Libby with a minatory glare. 'Perhaps this was why I lost interest for a bit.'

Libby grinned. 'Course it was.'

'What's Ian doing about it all?' Fran asked after a pause.

'He didn't tell me, but I assume he'll be looking for Jim Frost and Ray, and rounding up all the antiques boys he can lay his hands on. I know he's going after Wally. And probably Fay, as well.'

'Poor old Wally!' said Fran with a grin. 'He should never have left that little brooch on display.'

'Or that bronze figure. He is a bit of an idiot.' Libby giggled.

'But how's Ian going to prove that any of them knew about the hoard? Unless the whole lot of them have left fingerprints all over it?'

'I know. But at least we now know why Hodges was at the Horse when he was killed.'

'Hmm. But what about that other murder?' Fran leant her chin on her hand. 'Have they decided it's anything to do with this case?'

'I don't think so. I think the police who looked into it told Ian's lot as a courtesy, in case it was linked. 'But I don't see how—'

'It's the London bloke,' said Fran.

'What?' Libby stared at her friend.

'Of course it is. Where was the body found? Near the Speedwell head office, wasn't it?'

'Near Ashford. And it had a smell of petrol,' Libby said. 'Is this a moment?'

'I don't know. Ian only told you about it yesterday – did he say anything else last night? Or this morning?'

'No! But then an awful lot's happened in the last twenty-four hours. I expect the Ashford police have found out a bit more now, but just haven't told him yet.'

'Maybe. Let's see. If it is the London bloke, how does that fit in with the new information?' Fran got up and filled the kettle again. 'I'd suggest alcohol, but you're driving.'

'I drink too much anyway,' said Libby. 'And it's too early. Go on, how *does* it fit?'

'Well.' Fran sat down again. 'The body smelt of petrol. Which was why the Ashford police connected it to Ian's investigation. If it's the London bloke, does that mean he was trying to set fire to the Horse? And someone killed him to stop him?'

'But the Horse *was* fired,' objected Libby. 'So they didn't. Stop him, I mean.'

'No, but it wasn't damaged as badly as everyone thought at first, was it? So perhaps Hodges killed him to stop him burning the place down, which would probably also destroy the hoard.'

'OK – so who killed Hodges?'

'That stays the same – another of the antiques boys who wanted to stop him making off with the hoard.'

'Which they all felt was theirs by right.'

'Because it was some of them who dug it up.'

'Or was it a gang of nighthawks who then started selling it on to the antiques boys?' suggested Libby.

'I doubt it. If they were professional nighthawks they'd have a bigger market. As, I expect, our local boys did.' Fran nodded and got up to refill their mugs.

'Well, I don't see how we can do any more investigating, even if Ian hadn't warned us off,' said Libby. 'We went and saw Stan, and all that's done is alert that Ray. There's nowhere else to go.'

'What about Portia?' said Fran, waving the milk bottle at her. 'Couldn't she find out who it was inside Marsham's who signed off on the sale of the Horse?'

'That's exactly what she said she couldn't do,' said Libby. 'She wanted to do the investigating well away from the brewery.'

'Because there are people there who don't agree with her.' Fran frowned. 'Does that make sense?'

'I think so,' said Libby. 'There are people who said, with reason, that the best thing to do was get rid of the brewery. And I can see that there are some, including Portia, who don't want to, because it's an old established family brewery and it would be a shame for it to be bought up by the big boys.'

'Hmm. If only we could ask someone we met during the Marsham's business.' Fran sighed. 'We just need to know if that body really is the London bloke.'

'I don't see how that helps us,' said Libby. 'After all, it's not as if we know any of the people involved, do we? We haven't got any individual suspects, just the "antiques boys"' – she put air quotes round the words – 'and the developers. A whole company. Not actual *people*.'

'No.' Fran tapped her chin with a finger. 'What about that Frost person?'

'I suppose it's possible, if, as we said, some of the antiques boys were cross with Hodges . . .'

'Cross doesn't quite fit,' said Fran with a chuckle, 'but yes.'

'Or even Ray,' said Libby. 'Do you think they had a really widespread business going? Selling internationally?'

'Could be. The police were ignoring them, thinking they were merely *importing* domestic artefacts.'

'I expect the police have thought of all this, though,' said Libby. 'I don't suppose there's anything we can add.'

'No.' Fran looked at the table and sighed again. After a moment, she looked up. 'Did Trisha come and see you yesterday after all?'

'No!' Libby looked surprised. 'I forgot all about that – so much else happened.'

'I just wondered if she remembered anything about . . . well, anything.'

'Oh, yes. Wouldn't hurt to ask, would it? I'll go and see Ricky when I get home. Ask about his driving lessons.' Libby stood up. 'And make sure he knows all about the weddings.'

'If he's still living with Peter and Harry he will,' said Fran.

'I think he's doing part-time with Debbie. She has to look after Barney when he's at uni because Pete and Harry are busy.'

'I bet neither of them are happy with that.'

'Oh, it's not too bad. Debbie had the dog before, didn't she?'

'Mmm. Might be worth asking her, too.' Fran stood up and led the way to the front door. 'I'll watch you down to the car park.'

'Oh dear, do you think it's that bad?' Libby smiled sadly. 'Surely no one would attack me on Harbour Street?'

'Remember all the other occasions? Better safe than sorry.' Fran patted her shoulder. 'Go on. Drive carefully.'

Back in Steeple Martin, Libby didn't know what to do with herself. *Contraband* was on track, the minibus was booked for the Saturday-night concert at the Alexandria, no one was due at the Hoppers' Huts and Cyd and Judy were still in residence at Steeple Farm until their move to Grove House, so nothing needed to be done there. She had no way of finding anything out about the mysterious solicitors' firm, nor the traitor inside Marsham's, assuming that there was one, nor the developers. And was it, she asked herself, right to also assume that the London couple, one of whom might be the body discovered near Ashford, were employed by the developers?

She called Harry to see if Ricky was around, only to be told he and Barney had gone off to spend a few days with a uni friend, so that was a dead end. Instead she took a sandwich into the garden and sat down beneath the cherry tree. 'When you think about it,' she said aloud to Sidney, who had accompanied her, 'all of this seems an awful lot of trouble to go to just to acquire some fairly iffy land. I mean, what's so special about the area?'

'Were you talking to me, dear?' came a gentle voice from the other side of the fence.

Embarrassed, Libby shot to her feet.

'Ginny! No – sorry, I was talking to the cat!' She went to look over the fence.

'Not to worry, dear. I talk to him when he comes to see me too.' Ginny Mardle smiled up at her. 'How are you? Busy as usual?'

'Yes – you know! Show at the theatre coming up. Are you coming to the concert on Saturday with us?'

'Oh yes, dear! Looking forward to it. And those lovely girls are going to be in your next show too, Hetty says.'

'That's right – they were in the pantomime as well.'

'And then there's your latest murder, isn't there?' Ginny put her head on one side. Having been rather closely involved in previous cases, she was always interested in what she called Libby's shenanigans.

'Not really mine,' said Libby with a strangled laugh.

'Antiques dealers, Debbie said.' Ginny nodded wisely.

'Debbie Pointer?' Libby was surprised.

'Yes, dear. She comes over to Carpenter's Hall with her mum. Linda, you know?'

Carpenter's Hall was a community asset in Maltby Close, named for Frank Carpenter, Flo's late husband, where many of the village's more mature residents met regularly.

'I didn't know,' said Libby. 'Nice for her to have made friends, though.'

'Yes, but she should have friends of her own age, I say. Not a lot of old biddies like us!' Ginny let out a surprising hoot of laughter. 'Anyway, she said it were one of the antiques dealers she met at that pub she goes to. Over at Shittenden, you know? Her young Ricky goes, too.'

'Yes,' said Libby. 'So – antiques dealers. I must ask her about that.'

'We're having a little get-together this afternoon, dear. Why don't you come along? Do us good to have another young face!' Ginny peered up eagerly.

Libby made a heroic effort not to laugh at this and nodded. 'Lovely idea!' she said. 'Give me a knock when you're ready.'

Well, she said to herself as she made her way back indoors. Just when you think you've reached a dead end, Debbie comes up trumps.

Chapter Thirty-One

'Mind,' she said to Fran on the phone, 'she might not come up trumps. She might be just as dithery as she was when we first met her.'

'Worth asking, though,' said Fran. 'And I had another thought about Marsham's.'

'Yes? What?'

'Could you not find out from that place in Felling? That the chap at the Gate told you about?'

'Zack? What — you mean the Felling Business Community?'

'That's it. Where is it they meet?'

'Oh — the Shipwright's Arms, but we'd never get in there. It's owned by Marsham's and no longer a pub. They keep it for their own use.'

'Don't we know anyone who belongs to this business community?'

'There's whatshisname — you know, the parson who used to live at the Pocket.' Libby frowned. 'John. John Newman, that's it. And his awful Emma.'

'Would he know anything?'

'I expect he'd try and avoid me.' Libby grinned to herself. 'Listen — there's Nanny Mardle at the door. I'll report back.'

Mrs Mardle was obviously delighted that Libby was going with her to Carpenter's Hall, and chattered all the way there.

'How's Colin?' asked Libby, getting a word in edgeways. 'Haven't seen him and Gerry for ages.'

Colin Hardcastle had lived in the village as a boy and formed a strong bond with Mrs Mardle.

'Oh, he phones up every week mostly. But he's been very busy lately. You know they had property in Spain?'

'Yes, of course.'

'Well, they've expanded the business over here!' Ginny looked delighted. 'They've started buying up properties and turning them into – now what do they call it?' She frowned, putting a finger up to her cheek. 'Something housing.'

'Not social housing?' Libby almost yelped.

'That's it, dear!' Ginny looked startled.

'Oh, that's wonderful!' Libby actually clapped her hands. 'Do you remember all that fuss we had about people being turned out of their homes last year?'

'Yes, I think so,' said Ginny, looking as though she didn't.

'And Colin rented out the apartments in the old Garden Hotel instead of selling them?'

'Except for Linda's lovely flat.'

'Yes, well, she got in first.' Libby grinned. Ricky's grandmother was a considerable force to be reckoned with. 'So he's carried on! That's brilliant!'

Ginny nodded, still looking bewildered.

Carpenter's Hall was already quite full, and Libby was surprised to see the big doors at the back open.

'Turning it into a garden, see?' said Flo, noticing her interest. 'Might as well. Nothing else out there, and be nice to sit outside in the summer. What we get of it. Lots of 'em keen on gardenin'. Not me, though.' She put her head on one side and squinted at Libby. 'What you doin' 'ere anyway? Turned seventy overnight, 'ave yer?'

Libby laughed. 'Ginny invited me,' she said. 'And Debbie comes, doesn't she?'

Flo jerked her head. 'Oh, 'er. Wet weekend in Blackpool, that one.'

Libby looked round anxiously. 'She'll hear you!'

'Nah. Out in the garden with 'er mum. Go on, go and see.'

Ginny had gone off in search of tea, so Libby made her way out into the garden, which at the moment was little more than a patch of earth with a lot of small plants dotted randomly about. At a long bench hard up against the side of the building stood Linda Davies, Ricky's grandmother, and Debbie.

'Well, hello, Libby!' Linda looked delighted to see her, Debbie not so much. 'Haven't seen you since we went over to the Fox and Hounds.' She threw her daughter a disparaging look. 'Have we, dear?'

Debbie gave Libby a weak smile. 'I don't go there so much now.'

'It was nice of you to help Stan get back on his feet.' Libby hoped she wasn't putting her foot in it. 'But I suppose it's up and running, now.'

'No.' Debbie looked down at the small pot in her hands. 'I quite liked it over there.'

Ouch! thought Libby. 'You met some of the antiques boys there, didn't you?' she said aloud.

Debbie brightened up. 'Oh yes! Picked up some nice little bits as well.'

'You . . .' Libby swallowed. 'They were selling stuff, were they?'

'Not many of them.' Debbie looked self-conscious. 'Just this one – as a favour to me, really.'

'I told you, Debs, he was taking advantage of you,' said Linda sharply, pushing a sad-looking seedling into a pot of compost.

'Oh, they all have shops, Linda,' said Libby. 'I expect he was – er – collecting stock.'

'I didn't like the look of it,' said Linda. 'Just an old piece of china it was.'

'And the little bronze statue!' Debbie bridled. 'I love that.'

Libby took a firm hold of herself. 'Who was it who sold you those bits and pieces?' she asked. 'I know some of the antiques boys.'

'Oh yes, you would,' nodded Linda. 'It was one of them got murdered, wasn't it?'

'Well, it wasn't that one,' said Debbie quite firmly. 'It was Wallace Mayberry sold me my pieces,' she added to Libby. 'He's perfectly respectable. Has a shop in Nethergate.'

216

'I know it,' said Libby, relieved. 'Beer and Bargains – nice little place, isn't it?'

Debbie perked up. 'It is, isn't it? I went over there last week. There were a couple of the other dealers there as well. I'd met one of them before.' She went faintly pink. 'Really nice he was.'

Libby was beginning to feel quite overwhelmed with all this information. 'Oh yes?' she managed to croak.

'Of course, I hadn't met them all before,' Debbie went on confidentially, turning her back slightly on her mother. Libby didn't blame her. 'But they were all very nice.'

Libby smiled. 'Good to make friends away from the village, isn't it?'

Debbie rolled her eyes and nodded. 'You can say that again!'

'I hope you're happy here, though?' Libby made to go back inside.

'Oh yes! I love my little house – and Anne's such a good neighbour.' Debbie beamed. 'I'm driving her to Patti's this evening.'

Libby had forgotten that Debbie now lived next door to Anne Douglas. Two more different people she couldn't imagine.

'That's lovely,' she said. 'Well, I'll leave you to your potting-up. See you both soon!'

She escaped back to the kitchen and the large brown teapot, manned by Una from Steeple Lane.

'Hello, duck!' Una beamed. 'Nice to see you.'

'And you, Una. Can I have a cup of tea?'

'Course you can. Been talking to that Debbie?' Una lowered her voice.

'Yes.' Libby raised her eyebrows.

'Reckon it was her sent that bloke round to us all, you know.' Una poured dark brown tea into a white china cup.

'Eh? What bloke?'

Una looked up. 'Oh, I thought p'raps that was what you were talking about. Bloke trying to buy gold. Like you hear about on the telly.'

Now Libby was completely confounded. This was a definite step too far.

217

'G-gold?' she repeated.

'You know! They go round asking for your gold rings and such. And give you ninepence ha'penny for it.' Una shook her head and handed over the tea.

'And there's been someone doing that here?'

Una nodded, tucking in her multiple chins. 'Been up to Dolly and a couple of the others. We wondered how he knew where to go.'

'Why do you think it was Debbie who told him?'

''Cos she was talking about the nice little bits she bought from this bloke at that pub she goes to.'

'Well,' said Libby, rallying, 'Flo used to buy little bits from the dealers over at the Crooked Horse. This bloke could have heard of the village from her.'

'Never.' Una looked offended. 'Flo'd never say anything to anybody.'

Libby could attest to that. 'What did he look like, Una? Do you remember?'

'Course I do, duck! Not gaga yet, am I? Tall he was.' Una was thoughtful. 'Quite nice-looking.'

Not much help, thought Libby. Jim Frost could be called nice-looking, though.

'I expect you were all too clever to be taken in, weren't you?' she said, accepting the tea. 'Do I have to pay for this?'

'Course not, duck!' Una beamed again, good humour restored. 'Lovely to see you.'

Libby wandered back into the hall and found a seat near Hetty, who was talking to Edie Osbourne-Walker.

'Did Lewis bring you over?' Libby asked, giving them both a kiss on the cheek.

'No, dear, your Adam did,' said Edie. 'Good lad, 'e is.'

'Oh, ah.' Libby collapsed back into her seat. 'Het, did you ever see this bloke Una was telling me about? Trying to buy up gold jewellery?'

'Didn't come anywhere near the Manor,' said Hetty. 'Why?'

218

'I just wondered.' Libby took a sip of tea, a theory beginning to form in her overcrowded brain.

'Reckon 'e was one of those antiques boys Ben was goin' on about?'

'He told you about the person asking about me?'

Hetty nodded. 'Same man?'

'I just wondered,' Libby repeated.

'This to do with the old Horse?' asked Edie.

Libby shrugged. 'We don't know. Lots going on at the moment.' She made an effort and smiled. 'How are you, Edie?'

After another ten minutes of inconsequential chat, Libby decided honour was satisfied and got up to leave. Immediately, Ginny hurried across the hall.

'Did you speak to Debbie, dear?'

'Yes thank you, Ginny.' Libby smiled down at her neighbour. 'Thank you for bringing me.'

Ginny beamed. 'Pleasure, dear. Any time.'

Libby left quickly, waving goodbye to Flo and hurrying down Maltby Close, keen to share her new information with Fran. Who was rather surprised to hear from her again so soon.

'Yes, but listen! I've got news!' Libby proceeded to impart the results of her visit to Carpenter's Hall.

'Goodness!' said Fran. 'So you think the person going round trying to buy gold was Jim Frost?'

'It seems such a coincidence. And Una's description could have matched.'

'Did she say he was asking about you?'

'No. I rather gathered he got short shrift from everyone.'

'And Debbie bought some pieces from Wally Mayberry. Hmm. Was he getting rid of the evidence?'

'I think this was before recent events,' said Libby. 'When she was still going to see Stan a lot. Although she might have been down to Beer and Bargains since then.'

'Well, interesting though it all is, I don't see how it gets us any

219

nearer to the arsonist or the murderer,' said Fran. 'Worth passing on to Ian, though.'

'Yes, I thought so, except I don't want him harassing all our old ladies.'

'I seem to remember they rather enjoyed being in the thick of it before.'

'True. Well, I'll send him a message anyway. And I thought I might offer to take Debbie down to Beer and Bargains again. See what happens.'

'That's very noble of you. Quite a good idea, though. Shall I come?'

'If you want to. Doesn't Sophie mind spending so much time in the shop?'

'Not in the least. She's waiting to start a new job, so she's got nothing else to do.'

'Oh dear. Is she going away again?'

'No – it's at the university in Canterbury.' Fran laughed. 'So she'll still be near Adam.'

'Oh. It *is* on again, then?'

'Yes. She told me after you'd gone this morning.'

Libby pushed down a spurt of jealousy. Fran seemed to know more about her son than she did.

'Ah,' she said. 'He gave Edie a lift over here today, did I tell you?''

'No, Sophie did. He stayed with her last night and went home via Creekmarsh this morning.'

'Right.' Libby cleared her throat. 'Well, I'd better get on and send Ian this text. Both numbers, do you think? Work and personal?'

'Covers all bases,' said Fran. 'Let me know what happens.'

Chapter Thirty-Two

Libby sent a laborious text message to both Ian's numbers and wondered what to do next. It had been a busy couple of days and now there was nothing left to do. And many of the things she wanted to do, she wasn't allowed to. She'd had a vague plan to go over to the Heronsbourne Flats, congratulate Alice and then go for a ride with Stella at Brooke Farm. She hadn't seen her favourite pony, Punch, for weeks. But Heronsbourne Flats was a largely unpopulated marsh, except for the sheep, and she'd been attacked there before, so that was out. She'd already risked life and limb, according to Ian, by walking back from Carpenter's Hall on her own, and going the back way to see Ben at the brewery also involved woodland and open fields, highly propitious for an attack on an unsuspecting female. She could walk up the Manor drive to the theatre, but even that wasn't safe. People had been jumped there in the past too. She sighed. Life was suddenly very dangerous.

Eventually she decided to do some online research into Anglo-Saxon hoards, and took the laptop into the garden. She had just got to a very interesting article about a hoard found in Appledore, near Ashford, when her phone rang.

'Portia!' she said. 'Any news?'

Portia gave an uncertain laugh. 'I was going to ask you that.'

'Oh, right.' Libby racked her brains. 'Not really – or not about the Crooked Horse exactly, anyway.'

'Oh.' Portia sounded depressed. 'Well, I do have one bit of news. Whether it's any use I don't know.'

'Anything's better than nothing,' said Libby brightly and untruthfully. 'And you never know.'

'Well, you know I said no one knew who had authorised the sale of the pub?'

'Yes?' Suddenly Libby was all interest.

'One of the girls in the estates department did know something about it after all.'

'Goodness!' gasped Libby. 'Why hadn't she spoken up before?'

'Because she's been in St Lucia on honeymoon.'

Libby couldn't help laughing. 'So she told you – when?'

'Today. She's not back at work until Monday, but she got back to England last night and checked her emails this morning.'

'I assume she didn't check them while she was away?'

'No, she said they wanted a complete break. She apologised, but of course it wasn't her fault.' Portia was sounding more and more depressed.

'So what did she tell you? She knew who'd authorised the sale?'

'Not exactly. She said that someone got in touch with the department saying it had been authorised. And when she pointed out that we'd had rather a lot of trouble recently, he said he quite understood and he would bring all the paperwork to the office.'

'Bl—' began Libby. 'Right. And did he?'

'Yes. And he produced ID and everything.'

'And who was he?'

'Ralph Hardy, solicitor.' Portia let out a wail. 'So it was true!'

'Hang on, hang on,' said Libby. 'Not necessarily. All this girl saw was someone saying he was a solicitor. And I know from our mutual friend Philip Jacobs that there *is* no solicitor's firm called Hardy and Co.'

There was a short silence. 'Oh,' muttered Portia.

'What's the girl's name? Can I talk to her?'

Portia sighed. 'Yes, of course. Shall I ask her to ring you? Or do you want to come in again?'

'No – she's not at work, so it would be better if she rang me.' Libby paused. 'Don't worry, Portia. This could actually be a breakthrough.'

'Really?' Portia sounded more cheerful. 'All right. I'll call her now. Thank you, Libby.'

Libby heaved herself out of her deckchair and went into the kitchen to make tea. Although actually, it was time to be thinking about dinner, she supposed, and went to peer into the fridge.

She had just decided on Bob the butcher's special sausages when her phone rang again.

'Mrs Sarjeant?' asked a hesitant young voice.

'That's me.' Libby perched on the kitchen table.

'My name's Livia Bolton – I mean, Renshaw.'

'Oh yes! You're the lady from Marsham's.'

'Lady's stretching it a bit,' said the voice. 'Yes, I work for Marsham's. Portia Havilland asked me to ring you, as a matter of urgency, she said.'

'Well it is, sort of,' said Libby. 'And please call me Libby. You know Portia has asked me to look into the sale of the Crooked Horse?'

'Yes. And before I got married – you knew I'd just got married?'

'I did.' Libby noted the pride in the girl's voice. Some people still liked to get married then, despite what Patti had said.

'Well, I knew the sale had been stopped, but I knew nothing about what happened next.'

'When did you first hear about the proposed sale?' Libby went into the sitting room and picked up her theatre notebook and a pen. 'How long ago?'

'The first time? Wow. That would have been back when – when we had all that trouble. You helped with that too, didn't you?'

'Yes. So it was being talked about then?'

'Yes, but everything stopped, of course. But then this man called the office and said that the sale had been agreed. Just before I got married. I didn't know what to do, and I didn't know who to ask. I thought I'd missed something and it was my fault. So I rather dithered, I'm afraid.'

'I can imagine,' sympathised Libby. 'I would have done too.'

Encouraged, Livia went on. 'So he said if it would make me feel better he would bring the paperwork in. I said he could email me, but he said surely it would be better if I saw the real thing.'

'Emails can be traced,' said Libby. 'Even if they go through dozens of IP addresses.'

'Oh yes, of course. I didn't think of that.'

'With your wedding coming up, I don't suppose you did,' said Libby.

'Anyway,' Livia took a breath, 'he came in.'

'Did anyone else see him? Anyone but you?'

'I met him in reception and took him straight into a meeting room, so I don't think so.'

Libby nodded to herself, remembering when she had met Portia in that same reception. 'And then?'

'He showed me all the paperwork. To be honest, most of it didn't mean much to me, but he said the purchasers had signed the – er – deed of sale? Would that be right?'

'Possibly,' said Libby. 'But you didn't see their signatures?'

'No. He said he'd leave it with me for our directors to sign too. And then he left. He said the purchasers were very keen to go ahead and were looking forward to a new life in the country. I did remember to ask if they had applied for change of use.' She sounded proud of herself.

'And I expect he said it was all in hand.'

'Exactly. I was a bit of an idiot, wasn't I?'

'I don't think so.' Libby thought for a moment. 'You would have expected someone more senior to take over and know what to do. Not your fault at all. And how long was this before your wedding?'

'Oh, not long. Everyone knew about it, and poor Jenny Richards had been told she had to leave the pub. And then suddenly someone realised it wasn't a proper sale.'

'That would have been when you heard the developers were going to buy it.'

'That's right.' Livia sounded upset. 'There was a right barney. Everyone blaming everyone else – including me – but by that time I was getting married.'

'Right.' Libby had another think. 'Now, can you remember what this man looked like? Anything at all about him? And did he leave a card?'

'No, but the address of the offices were on the paperwork. Canterbury, I think. And there was even an address for the purchasers.'

'Yes, we know,' said Libby. 'Both were false.'

'Oh.'

'Never mind. What did he look like?'

'Ordinary. Tallish, very smart. Smiley. Fair hair that was a bit long. Not all over, but long at the front, you know?'

Libby's breath caught in her throat. 'Flopped over his forehead, did it?'

'That's right!' Livia sounded pleased.

'OK,' said Libby after a minute. 'So you never saw anyone from the developers?'

'Oh, no! Well, the last I knew of what was going on, the developers had only just come into the picture. We never saw the purchasers, either.'

'No.' Libby paused again. 'Look, Livia, I think the police might want to talk to you about this. Would you mind?'

'The police?' Livia's voice rose in a squeak.

'Nothing to worry about, but they'll need your information from the horse's mouth, so to speak. They won't be able to take my word for it. And this could be crucial to finding the murderer of the person who was killed in the pub, and whoever set fire to it.'

'Oh. Right. OK, then. What do I have to do?'

'May I give the police your name and phone number?'

'Well, I – er – yes, of course.'

'Good.' Libby smiled in relief. 'I don't know when they'll be in touch, I'm afraid, but fairly soon, I think. Is this the number to use?'

'Y-yes. Will I be in trouble?'

'Good heavens, no! You're helping. And thank you so much for calling me this afternoon, Livia. Next time I come to see Portia, I must see you too.'

Sounding happier, Livia rang off. Libby closed her eyes, took a deep breath and rang Ian's work number. It went to voicemail. She swore under her breath and sent Fran a message.

She had just put the sausages in the oven when her mobile rang, followed almost immediately by the landline. She picked up her mobile on the way to the landline.

'Fran – Ian's on the landline. I'll ring you back,' she said, picking up the house phone.

'You were engaged,' Ian's voice accused.

'Trying to ring you again,' Libby lied. 'You got my message.'

'Of course. Tell me.'

Libby told him.

'It's the man calling himself Ray, isn't it?' she finished up. 'It's got to be.'

'Sounds like it. I wonder if we could get her to do a photofit? You too, come to that.'

'Ooh, that'd be fun!'

'It's not meant to be fun.' Ian was sharp.

'OK. Sorry. But it would be a good idea.'

'It would, if only we had someone to match it to.'

'Oh. Oh yes.' Libby wandered back to the kitchen. 'I suppose . . . No, that wouldn't work.'

'Suppose what?' Ian was still sharp.

'I was wondering . . .'

'Yes?' Impatient now.

'Well, do you think the person behind all this is something to do with the developers and not the antiques boys?'

'Behind the fake sale of the pub and the arson, yes,' said Ian slowly. 'Why?'

'Could Fran or I get inside the developers' offices? We could perhaps identify him.'

'And he could identify you, too,' said Ian. 'We've already discussed that, haven't we? It's dangerous, Libby.'

'Oh yes.'

'No. Leave it with us. Can you text me this Livia's number? And thank you for your help – but please, don't do anything else!'

Libby called Fran back just as Ben came through the door, and gave them both the latest update with the phone on speaker.

'Ian's right, Lib,' said Fran. 'It's getting more dangerous by the minute. Frankly, I don't know who's guilty of what, but they'll all be getting desperate by now, so I think we stay safe from now on.'

'Just what I've been saying,' agreed Ben. 'And I can give Guy the details of the security company I'm using if he wants it.'

'Why can't you give it to me?' asked a peremptory voice.

Ben shut his eyes and swore under his breath. 'Sorry, Fran. Do you want the details now?'

Libby grinned and took the sausages out of the oven.

Chapter Thirty-Three

On Friday morning, Libby's second cup of tea was interrupted yet again by her mobile. She collected it from its night-time position next to the television and unglued her eyes.

'Fran? What's up?'

'Bert just knocked on my door.'

'Bert? As in boat Bert?'

'Yes. And – they've found the *Jan Bishop*.'

'They – what? Hodges' boat?'

'Yes.'

'Bloody hell, Fran! Who found it? Do they mean the police?'

'No – they did. George and Bert. They were out on the *Sparkler* together looking for new places to stop on their tours and found this little beach. And there it was.'

'Bloody hell!' said Libby again. 'When? Have they told the police?'

'They hadn't. They found it first thing this morning and they think it drifted in on the high tide. They've towed it back here in case it drifted off again. They wanted to know what to do.'

'You've told them to tell the police? Why didn't they do that straight away?'

'They thought they'd have to wait for ages for the police to send someone out. They were probably quite right. Although I expect they'll get into trouble for moving it.'

'I think they did the right thing. It must have been drifting around all this time and avoiding being seen.'

'I doubt if it did it on purpose!' Fran sounded amused. 'Anyway – I gave them Ian's number and they phoned him while they were here. They've been told to go and wait with it.'

'Do you think I'd be safe to come down?' Libby went back to her tea. 'I'll be very careful driving.'

'Oh, I think so. But tell Ben.'

'I shall. I'll be as quick as I can. Although by the time I get there it might have been removed. See you in a bit.'

Libby finished her tea, called Ben, then dashed upstairs to have the quickest shower in history. She took a slice of bread – no time to toast it – in the car with her and resisted the temptation to drive hell-for-leather through the village. She wouldn't be much use if she crashed the car.

All the way to Nethergate she once again kept a wary eye out for suspicious vehicles lurking and arrived safely in Harbour Street only just over half an hour after speaking to Fran.

It was, however, not quite what she had expected. The whole of the hard, the Blue Anchor, the Sloop and the car park were cordoned off, and needless to say, the rest of Harbour Street was packed with cars. A Kent and Coast outside broadcast van was parked illegally in the square outside the Swan, and Libby realised that there was no way she was going to get any nearer. Reluctantly she drove up to the other car park at the end of Victoria Place.

Hurrying back towards the square, she was hailed by a familiar voice.

'Libby! What's going on?'

Her heart sank.

'Hello, Jane,' she said turning to see Jane Baker coming down towards her from Cliff Terrace.

'Is this something to do with the murder at the Crooked Horse?' asked Jane, catching her up.

'Why on earth would it be?' Libby tried to look innocent while inwardly cursing Jane's sensitive newshound's nose.

'Because Malcolm Hodges' boat was missing. And now there's

massive police activity around a boat in our little harbour.' Jane put her head on one side. 'And if anyone knows, you do.'

'I honestly don't know.' Libby made a face. 'I just know a boat's been found. That's all.'

'Oh well, it'll be out on the wire soon enough.' Jane hunched a shoulder and turned to go back up to Cliff Terrace. 'Let me know if you hear anything?'

'If I'm allowed to.' Libby gave her a friendly grin and resumed her descent to the square.

Harbour Street itself wasn't cordoned off, she was pleased to see, but it seemed that no one was actually doing any business. They were all standing outside trying to see what was going on.

'Did Ian come?' Libby asked, coming up with Guy, Sophie and Fran outside the shop.

'No, Clare came, and that young DC – Bodie, was it?' Fran shook her head. 'And loads of others, of course. They called in to me first and then went off to George and Bert. They've got a police launch there now.'

'That was quick.'

'And the coastguard,' added Guy. 'Most excitement Nethergate's seen for years.'

'They've got the CSI people on the boat now,' said Sophie, standing on tiptoe.

'I wonder if it's Ian's favourite crime-scene manager,' said Libby. 'Alison, he said her name was.'

'It's not necessarily a crime scene, though, is it?' said Fran.

'If you two are going to discuss the ins and outs, I'm going back to work,' said Guy.

'And I'm going up to the flat. I can see everything from up there,' said Sophie, grinning at her stepmother.

'I suppose I'd better go in behind the counter, then,' said Fran.

'Do you think they'd let me get to Mavis?' Libby asked. 'I'm starving.'

'I doubt it, but you can try. I'll put the kettle on,' said Fran.

As expected, Libby was turned back by a uniformed officer, and waved helplessly at a furious-looking Mavis standing in her doorway.

'Sophie's making you toast,' Fran greeted her as she came back into the shop.

'Thank you.' Libby heaved herself onto her usual stool and stared gloomily out at the packed street. 'I wonder what they'll find.'

'I expect they'll look for DNA, but they aren't likely to find any except Hodges', are they?' said Fran.

'No.' Libby pondered. 'What do we think happened? Someone killed him, then went and set his boat free from the St Aldeberge Cut.'

'And then walked all the way back to the Horse from there? That's a hell of a long way.'

'Why did they go back to the Horse?'

'To get rid of the body.'

'No.' Libby frowned. 'They put the body in their car – that's the murderer – drove it to the cut, set the boat free and then drove the body to the barn.'

Fran nodded slowly. 'Makes sense. And Hodges would have had his keys on him, so they could open the barn and dump him.'

'So you're right,' said Libby. 'There won't be any DNA apart from Hodges' on the boat.'

'It was quite clever really,' said Fran, putting a mug of tea in front of Libby. 'The boat being gone from its mooring really confused everybody, because they thought he'd gone off in it.'

'Well, he had.'

'You know what I mean. No one thought to look any closer to home for him.'

A clattering on the stairs heralded the arrival of Sophie bearing a plate of toast in one hand and a jar of marmalade in the other.

'There's Marmite if you want it,' she offered.

'No thanks, Sophie, this is great.' Libby smiled and took the plate. 'Very kind of you to feed a starving old lady.'

'One does what one can for the aged,' replied Sophie, and disappeared back up the stairs.

'You know what,' said Libby, after demolishing the first slice of toast, 'if that's the way it happened, it couldn't have been the developers behind the murder.'

'Why not?'

'They wouldn't have known about the St Aldeberge Cut or Hodges' barn. So it had to have been one of the antiques mob.' Libby tutted. 'I really can't keep saying "antiques boys". It's completely inappropriate.'

'Unless there's something we don't know,' said Fran. 'And after all, there must have been a lot going on behind the scenes that we haven't been told.'

Libby frowned. 'Then why does Ian keep asking for help?'

'Because there are little areas where our – your – intelligence is better than theirs. You know perfectly well he bowed to your superior knowledge of pubs. And people will talk to us when they won't if they're questioned by the police. Things come out in conversation. And let's face it, Ray, or Ralph, or whoever he is, would never have presented himself to the police the way he did to us.'

'But did that do any good?' asked Libby. 'He'd already met Livia.'

'Yes, but it was linking him to Ray that made everyone realise he was one of the bad guys.'

'Well, once they found out that Hardy's was a fake company, they would have known that.' Libby thought about it. 'But I suppose we *have* helped.'

'And George and Bert came to me. If they hadn't, they might not have said anything to anybody.'

'That's true. They didn't really want to be involved when we first asked about the boat, did they?'

'No. So they might have just left it where it was and ignored it.'

'OK. We're helpful.' Libby finished her last slice of toast. 'What shall we do now?'

'I'm going to have to stay here in case we get any trade,' said Fran. 'And you shouldn't be wandering around on your own, so unless you want to go home, you might as well stay here too. You could have a go at rearranging the window if you like. We need more seaside-holiday items in there now the season's picking up. Like your pretty peeps.' Fran gave her friend a wink, and took the mugs back to the little kitchen.

Libby was on her knees placing paintings on a satin-covered mountain range of boxes when the door opened and a voice said, 'In prayer, Libby?'

She dropped a small picture and swore.

'That's no way to encourage customers,' said Ian. 'Hello, Fran.'

Libby crawled out of the window and managed to straighten up.

'Hello, Ian. Any news?' asked Fran.

'Very little.' Ian went further into the shop and sat on Libby's stool. 'I just wanted to ask you what our two mariners said to you this morning.'

Fran looked surprised. 'The same as they said to you. I was there when they phoned.'

'They didn't give you any extra little bits of information?'

'Like what?'

'What they were doing out that early in the morning?'

'Scoping out places to stop on their boat trips,' said Fran. 'Why? Don't you believe them?'

Ian sighed. 'I just wondered why they hadn't noticed the boat before.'

'Ian!' Libby and Fran said together.

'Your manor is at least half coastal,' said Libby. 'Don't you know about tides?'

Ian frowned. 'Of course I do.'

'You know that things move about a bit?' said Libby.

'Up and down the coast?' added Fran.

'Oh!' said Ian, enlightened. 'Of course! That's what they meant when they said they had to bring it in or it would have gone!'

'Exactly!' Fran laughed at Ian's annoyed expression. 'It's obviously been wandering all over the place for the last couple of weeks.'

233

'Yes. But there's one odd thing,' said Ian.

'What's that?' the women asked together.

'You know the theory is that the boat was set free from the little mooring below St Aldeberge?'

'Yes.'

'Well, that was obviously thoroughly checked, and there was no sign of a rope, yet the rope on the boat itself had been cut.'

Chapter Thirty-Four

Fran and Libby looked at one another, puzzled.

'What does that mean? It *wasn't* set free from the cut?' said Libby.

'There should be the other end of the rope somewhere,' said Ian.

'Perhaps it's just worked loose?' suggested Fran.

'Hardly. Boat owners are very good at knots.'

'Of course. That's why it had to be cut.' Libby nodded. 'Which presumably means the person who set it free wasn't a boat person.'

'Not necessarily,' said Fran. 'It could have been done in haste.'

Ian stood up. 'If you haven't anything to add, I'll be off. Thanks for your help, Fran.'

'I didn't really do anything,' Fran muttered.

Libby grinned.

'So what do we think this means?' she asked after Ian had left. 'Everybody's got it all wrong?'

'Looks like it.' Fran leant her elbows on the counter. 'And it looks as though neither of our groups of potential murderers had anything to do with it.'

'Really?' Libby came back to her stool, abandoning the window display. 'How do you make that out?'

'When you think about it, both lots – if we agree that Ray the antiques dealer is really Ralph the phoney solicitor – have been trying to find out what exactly happened.'

'I thought they were all trying to find out what we knew,' said Libby.

'Well, yes, what we knew and what actually happened. Let's face it, at least some of them want to know about the hoard and if it's been found, don't they?'

'Yes, but what about the developers?'

'They'll want to know if they're going to be able to go ahead.'

'No they won't.' Libby shook her head firmly. 'They know they can't. Marsham's pulled out of the sale and there'd be an outcry from the nature reserve people. So what do *they* want to know?'

'Just how much the police know, then.'

'If we – and the police – assume that the arson attempt and the excavator were something to do with Speedwell, they'll want to know if they've left any proof behind. And that's what I reckon Ray was after.'

'Why did he want to know about Hodges, then?' asked Fran. 'Why go through all that rigmarole about Fay and the barn?'

'He'd want to know about the whole investigation, wouldn't he? All threads of it. He wouldn't know about the hoard, so . . .'

'If he didn't know about it, what was he trying to find out about, then?' Fran shook her head.

'Oh Lord, I don't know!' Libby stretched. 'I think I'm going up to talk to Wally. You never know, he might open up.'

'I think that might constitute what Ian calls dangerous,' warned Fran.

'Not on a Friday morning with lots of people around.' Libby slid off the stool. 'You know where I'm going, and I'll keep in touch by text. Also,' she wagged a finger in Fran's face, 'Wally will have seen all the police down here, so he's unlikely to try and abduct me.'

Fran sighed. 'In that case, I'd better come with you.' She went to the foot of the stairs and shouted, 'Sophie! Can you mind the shop for a bit?'

A muffled shout was followed by clattering on the stairs once again.

'There's nothing happening out there that I can see, so I might as well be down here,' Sophie said. 'Are you going detecting?'

'No,' said Fran.

'Yes,' said Libby.

Outside, they paused to see if there was any new activity at the harbour, but there were fewer uniforms and boiler suits in evidence.

'Looks as though the boat's gone,' said Libby. 'I wonder if Ian will tell us what they find.'

They walked back to the square, then up the high street to Marine Parade and Beer and Bargains.

'Oh good – it isn't closed,' said Libby.

'Did you think it might be?' asked Fran.

'I thought he might be keeping out of sight.' Libby pushed the door open.

This time, there was no effusive welcome. Wallace Mayberry was sitting behind his counter looking miserable, while every table, inside and out, was empty.

'Bit early for a drink,' he said gloomily as the women approached, 'but I don't suppose that's what you're here for.'

'You're right there, Wally.' Libby smiled at him. 'Did you see what was going on at the harbour this morning?'

'Couldn't bloody miss it, could I?' He blew out his cheeks. 'Malc's boat, weren't it?'

'It was. Know anything about it?'

'Course I bloody don't.' He sighed deeply. 'That were genuine, you know. When Fay wanted to know where he'd gone.'

'I'm sure it was,' said Fran. 'And you were worried, weren't you?'

Wally nodded, eyes on the floor.

'Wondered if he'd taken off with the hoard, I expect,' said Libby, crossing her fingers. She was pretty sure Ian would be furious with her.

'Oh shit.' Wally put his head in his hands.

'He hadn't,' said Fran.

'No, he was bloody dead, wasn't he.' Wally pulled himself upright. 'Well, you might not want a drink, but I do.' He stood up and fetched himself a glass. Holding up a whisky bottle, he looked at the two women. 'Sure?'

'Sure,' they both said.

They waited while he poured himself a generous measure and sat down again.

'So what's happening down there, then?' he asked.

'Bert and George found Hodges' boat,' said Fran.

'Where was it?'

'Drifting,' said Libby. 'Someone set it free.' Best not mention the cut rope, she thought.

'Why?' Wally frowned.

'To make everyone think he'd gone off in it,' said Fran. 'And everyone did, so it worked.'

'I don't get it.' Wally shook his head. 'Why would anyone kill him? When we heard they'd found the stuff, you know, that we dug up—'

'So it was you who dug it up?' interrupted Libby.

'Yeah. Some of it.' Wally looked shifty. 'Malc said it was ours 'cos we found it. Finders keepers, y'know?'

Libby raised her eyebrows. 'If you say so.'

'Well, anyway. We thought that's what'd happened. He'd been offed because he was gonna scarper with it, like. Don't make no sense otherwise.'

'No, it doesn't,' said Fran. 'Tell me, Wally, did you ever meet the people who were going to buy the Horse?'

Wally looked surprised. 'Yeah – course. Young chap and his missus. First of all we thought they was just, y'know, tourists. Chatted to us all, they did. Then we found out they was going to buy it, after the brewery closed it down.' He shook his head again. 'This was ages before Malc went missing. We all wondered what we were gonna do with the stuff.'

'You used to sell from the pub, did you?' asked Libby.

'May have done.' He looked away.

'You know you're going to have to tell the police all this, don't you?' said Fran gently. 'And it wasn't just you, was it?'

'No.' He shook his head violently. 'It was that fu— sorry, that Jim Frost. Him and Malc.'

'Ah!' Libby nodded. 'Jim Frost. He came looking for me, you know.'

'Did he? Cheek!' said Wally, unaware of any irony.

'So you can't think of any reason why someone would kill Hodges or set his boat adrift, then?' asked Fran.

'Me? No!' Wally looked outraged. 'Course not.'

'And where would we find Jim Frost?' Libby asked.

'You don't want to go anywhere near that bloke.' He drew himself up. 'Nasty piece of work.'

'So you don't know?' said Fran.

'London, I think.' He put his head on one side. 'Or Medway, maybe.'

'OK, we'll leave him to the police,' said Libby with a grin. 'And thanks, Wally.'

'You reckon they'll open up the old Horse again after this?' he asked as he saw them to the door.

'They might. But you can hardly carry on doing business there, can you?' Libby gave him a grin, patted his arm and left.

'Well!' she said as they began to walk back down the high street. 'I wish he'd talked to us sooner.'

'He'd hardly have done that when they were all hoping to get the hoard back – or at least find out what Hodges had done with it,' said Fran. 'But we were on the right track. Now we'd better let Ian know.'

'So my idea of going to see Wally wasn't so stupid after all?' said Libby.

Fran didn't deign to answer.

Neither of them was surprised when Ian failed to reply to Fran's text.

'Perhaps we should go and see if Clare's still at the harbour and tell her,' suggested Libby.

'I don't suppose it's that urgent.' Fran let them into Coastguard Cottage. 'And I'd rather not draw anyone's attention to the fact that we disobeyed orders and went to see a suspect.'

'Is Wally a suspect?' wondered Libby, following her friend into her kitchen.

'Person of interest,' said Fran, peering into her fridge. 'I don't think I've got anything for lunch.'

'Is it lunchtime already?' Libby looked at her watch.

'Not quite, but I usually get something for Guy.' Fran led the way back to the sitting room. 'It looks as though they've taken the tape off the hard, so we could go and see Mavis.'

'And talk to Bert and George,' added Libby.

Mavis greeted them with ill-concealed relief.

'Thought I was going to have shut all day,' she grumbled. 'What did they want to do that for?'

'Just so they could investigate,' said Fran.

'Boat was in the sea, not up here. Tea? Coffee?'

'Are you doing sandwiches yet?' asked Libby. 'Early lunch.'

'Tuna?' Mavis nodded. 'Fran?'

Several rounds of tuna and ham and cheese ordered, Libby and Fran moved over to where George and Bert sat looking glumly down at the *Dolphin* and the *Sparkler*.

'You haven't got the "Boat Trips" board out,' said Libby.

'Not allowed to go out, are we?' George gave Fran a hard stare. 'Wouldn't'a said nothing if we'd known.'

'You know you would,' said Fran. 'What did the police ask you?'

'Wanted to know why we hadn't said anything sooner! Bloody fools!' Bert burst out.

'Yes, we put them right on that,' said Libby with a grin.

'There weren't nothing on it, anyway,' said George more peaceably. 'Although I heard them talking about DNA.' He looked at the women quizzically. 'And something about the rope?'

Libby shrugged and Fran shook her head.

'Why won't they let you go out?' asked Libby.

'Might want to talk to us again,' said Bert. 'As if we was going to run away to France or something.'

'It's just that they wouldn't be able to get hold of you quickly if there was something they'd forgotten to ask,' explained Fran.

'Should'a thought of everything first time round, then,' said Bert, hitching a shoulder.

Libby giggled.

Graham, the manager of the Sloop Inn, put his head outside and waved.

'Something to do with you two, all this?' he called.

Libby went over to him.

'Not really – George and Bert found a boat.'

'They told me.' Graham smiled. 'And they told me they'd told you.'

'Ah well – little helpers to all the world, that's us,' said Libby. 'It's to do with the murdered antiques dealer.' She thought she was safe saying this – if Graham didn't know already, he soon would.

'Malcolm Hodges.' Graham nodded. 'He used to come in here.'

'Oh! You knew him?'

'Oh yes. He was a regular.'

'Recently?' Libby felt a familiar tingle of anticipation in her solar plexus.

'Yes. He used to bring – well, clients, I suppose they were. Away from the old Crooked Horse.'

'Yes – too many competitors there, I suppose,' said Libby.

'I expect so!' Graham laughed. 'Mind you, the last lot he brought over didn't seem like clients. Young couple, they were. It was business, though.'

Libby stared at him. 'Young couple,' she repeated. 'From London?'

'Oh, that I wouldn't know. Not local, though. Didn't know the area. I think he was introducing them to the delights of our corner of Kent.'

'Haven't the police asked you about Hodges already?' Libby was trying to process this.

'When they came and asked if anyone had seen his boat, yes. And Bert and George told them he never moored here. But no one came near me this morning.'

241

'Graham,' said Libby after a moment, 'would you mind if I passed this on to DCI Connell?'

'That your pet policeman?' Graham grinned. 'No, of course not. Think it's important?'

'I think it could be, yes,' said Libby. 'Very important.'

Chapter Thirty-Five

Fran was collecting the sandwiches when Libby left Graham.

'We've got to send Ian another message,' she said urgently.

Fran frowned at her as she handed over cash.

'Thanks.' Mavis nodded. 'Still like cash better.'

Libby summoned up a smile. 'Thanks, Mavis.'

'Come on then – what is it?' Fran pulled her away from the Blue Anchor. 'Don't broadcast it to everybody.'

Libby repeated Graham's information.

'I can't understand why they haven't spoken to him already,' she said. 'What were they *doing*?'

'They didn't think he would know anything about the boat, so why would they?' said Fran reasonably. 'I think it's down to him, really. He knew the police were asking about Hodges – why didn't he say he knew him?'

'Mmm.' Libby started walking towards Coastguard Cottage. 'But when they asked about the boat first time round . . . Oh, I don't know. Anyway, Ian – or Clare – ought to know about this young couple.'

'I agree. I'll try and call Clare when we get in.'

'Or,' said Libby, stopping and turning round, 'why don't we tell that nice young policeman over there? He'd have a better chance of getting through.'

Fran gave her a surprised look of approval. 'Good idea. Come on.'

The nice young policeman was only too pleased to take the details, and asked if Graham would come out to speak to him, as he wasn't supposed to leave his post.

'Of course,' said Libby. 'Someone could come along and – er . . .' She looked round. 'Do something,' she finished lamely.

The officer grinned. 'Exactly. So could you ask the gentleman to come out and speak to me?'

Mission accomplished, and leaving Graham chatting happily with the officer, Libby and Fran returned to the shop and made a start on the sandwiches.

'Do you think we'll hear anything from anyone?' Libby asked when they'd finished eating and more tea had been made.

'I doubt if we're very high on the priority list,' said Fran, 'and they'll be checking Wally Mayberry as well as Graham's information. No one will have time for us.'

'No, I suppose not,' said Libby. 'But we might have provided vital information. I mean, Wally confirmed that all the – oh bother – *antiques boys* knew about the hoard, and it was Hodges and Jim Frost who organised the whole scheme . . .'

'Whatever the scheme was,' said Fran.

'Whatever,' Libby carried on, 'and they might be able to confirm from Graham's info that the body was the London bloke.'

'That's definitely who you think it is?' Fran looked amused.

'Well of course! Young couple, not from round here . . . And you said it was when I first told you about it.'

'Yes, but what were they doing with Hodges?' asked Fran. 'They were supposedly in cahoots with the developers. The antiques dealers didn't want to lose access to the burial site, so why would Hodges be encouraging the sale of the pub?'

'Oh yes.' Libby subsided. 'Blimey, it's complicated.' She thought for a moment. 'Perhaps he was trying to persuade them *not* to buy? Showing them Nethergate and saying they'd do better buying here than out in the wilds of the Dunton marshes?'

'Possible,' admitted Fran. 'What did Wally say? They used to go in the pub and chat to everybody – obviously checking out the lie of the land.'

'And that's where Hodges picked them up and said, "I'll show you a much nicer area!"' Libby was getting excited and warming to her theme. 'Not realising that they were in cahoots with the developers.'

'So they were in cahoots all the time, do we reckon?' asked Fran.

'I thought that was established,' said Libby. 'Wasn't it?'

'I'm not sure of anything any more. Let's just wait until Ian and his merry band sort it all out. They must be quite close now.'

On the basis that Cyd and Judy wouldn't be available again that evening, Libby cancelled the *Contraband* rehearsal and suggested a nice quiet night in front of the television. Ben was suspicious.

'What are you planning?' He handed her a pre-prandial glass of wine.

'Nothing.' Libby sighed. 'Let's watch the local news. See if it says anything about the boat.'

They sat through the entire half-hour of regional news from Kent and Coast, but there was no mention of boats, Malcolm Hodges or even Nethergate.

'I don't understand it,' said Libby, as she went to rescue the chilli from the cooker. 'The Kent and Coast van was there when I arrived.'

'But what actually happened?' said Ben. 'The police simply collected the boat, asked Bert and George where they found it and left. Not really worth a news item when you think about it.'

'I suppose so.' Libby dished up rice. 'But I want to know what's happening.'

'Of course you do.' Ben smiled at her. 'And I'm sure somebody will tell you – eventually.'

Libby glared at him. 'Don't patronise me.'

Friday evening passed, as promised, quietly. Ben confiscated Libby's phone after an hour of watching her scrolling through it every five minutes, and she reluctantly settled down to watch an old episode of *Midsomer Murders*.

'They always come across a startling fact right at the end, don't they?' she said as they got ready for bed. 'Do you think that's what's going to happen here?'

'Perhaps it already has,' said Ben, climbing into bed. 'Now for goodness' sake, woman, forget it!'

But Libby couldn't. She tried not to toss and turn too much, but it was almost two hours before she managed to fall asleep, and consequently she woke late in the morning feeling decidedly grumpy.

'Cheer up!' said Ben, putting a mug of tea down beside her. 'We're going to the concert tonight, remember.'

'Oh, so we are.' Libby struggled to sit up. 'Another Loonies' outing.'

'But without Harry and Peter,' said Ben, sitting on the side of the bed.

'I wonder if Linda's coming.' Libby blew on her tea.

'Ricky's grandma? She might be – she's joined the old biddies club, hasn't she?'

'Don't let Het hear you call them that,' said Libby.

Ben laughed. 'Why not? That's what they call themselves.'

'Hmm,' said Libby. 'What time are we leaving?'

Saturday morning was mostly taken up by costume fittings at the theatre. Although by this time the Oast had assembled a fair amount of its own costumes, which were occasionally hired out to other companies, Libby had found out last Saturday morning that there weren't quite enough eighteenth-century seadog or riding officer outfits, and a whole vanful had been brought down from a London costumier. Excited cast members flocked into the foyer, and Libby was kept busy making tea and coffee.

It was getting towards midday when her phone rang in her pocket.

'Mrs Sarjeant?' asked an unfamiliar voice.

'Yes?'

'DC Bodie here – we met at the – er – barn.'

'Oh, yes. Hello.' Libby frowned and went out into the little garden.

'I – um – I'm sorry to disturb you, but DI Stone wanted a word, if you don't mind.'

'Oh, she's finished her course, has she? Put her on.'

'Er – no. She wants to see you in person.'

'Does she?' Libby's heart sped up. What was this?

'She wondered if you'd be at home in about an hour?'

'I can be.' Libby looked back into the foyer. 'What's it about?'

'I'm afraid I can't say,' said DC Bodie, sounding pompous. 'We'll see you in an hour, then.'

Libby immediately rang Fran.

'Yes, someone's coming to see me too,' said Fran. 'It's obviously about what we told Ian yesterday. They want statements.'

'All very formal,' grumbled Libby.

'It has to be, Lib,' said Fran. 'Shall we liaise later?'

'OK,' said Libby. 'And I'll see you tonight, anyway.'

Libby was just setting out mugs, the big kettle simmering on the Rayburn, when a knock sounded on the front door.

Clare Stone and DC Bodie stood outside, Clare looking remarkably cheerful.

'Have I got to congratulate you, Clare?' asked Libby, standing back to let them in.

'You don't *have* to,' replied Clare with a grin. 'But yes, fully fledged DI now.'

'So has Ian retired back to his desk?'

'No chance!' She laughed. 'Sorry to burst in on your Saturday like this, but we need a statement about the information you passed on yesterday.'

'Yes, we thought that would be it,' said Libby. 'Kettle's on – tea or coffee?'

'I'll have tea, please,' said Clare. 'And DC Bodie's a coffee snob, so he'll probably have nothing.'

Poor DC Bodie went a pretty shade of pink and fumbled with his regulation tablet. Libby went into the kitchen and poured water onto teabags.

'Sit down, then,' she said, putting her head back into the sitting room. 'Won't be a minute.'

'Is that a script?' asked Clare, peering at the pile of folders on the little table in the window. 'What are you doing at the moment?'

Libby explained about *Contraband*, then brought the two mugs in and sat down on the sofa. DC Bodie sat upright at the table, looking uncomfortable, while Clare settled in the armchair opposite Libby.

'Can you run through exactly what you did yesterday?' she asked. 'And do you mind if we record this? Start with your visit to Wallace Mayberry.'

Libby tried to recall as accurately as possible the details of Wally's revelations, and then Graham's surprising information. Once or twice Clare asked for clarification, but mostly she let her tell it uninterrupted.

'Right,' she said when Libby ground to a halt. 'So it appears that the couple who were supposed to be buying the Crooked Horse had been visiting for some time and getting friendly with the regulars, particularly the antiques dealers.'

'It seems so,' agreed Libby. 'But we wondered why.'

'So that they could say they'd become fond of it and wanted to buy it when it went up for sale,' said Clare. 'That's what the thinking is at the moment.'

'So they must have been put up to it. By the mysterious seller at the brewery, or the developer?' Libby wondered.

'A combination, we think,' said Clare. 'No one's been identified either at Marsham's or Speedwell, all of whom are terribly shocked.' She pulled a face. 'Believe that if you will.'

'I know a fair amount about Marsham's,' said Libby, 'but nothing about Speedwell. I should have looked them up. Are they a large concern?'

'Not really. Premises on the outskirts of Ashford, and owned by an old family firm of builders. Not that the family run it any more.'

'So they probably *are* shocked,' said Libby. 'Does it look like some-one there is behind it all?'

Clare shot a glance at DC Bodie, who was looking disapproving. 'Mrs Sarjeant's helped us several times in the past, Julian,' she said. 'She's safe.'

DC Bodie said nothing. Libby hid a grin.

'So there *is* someone you're looking at?' she said.

'There might be.' Clare grinned back.

'And have you asked Wally Mayberry and Graham at the Sloop if they could identify the body found the other day?' Libby asked.

Clare laughed. 'You know I can't tell you that!' She stood up. 'Thanks for the tea. We'll be in touch.'

Well satisfied with this, Libby also stood up. 'I shall look forward to it.'

Her phone rang almost as soon as the two officers had left, but instead of Fran, it was Ben.

'Shall I buy you lunch at Harry's?' he asked. 'It'll be too early to have dinner before the concert.'

'That would be lovely. And I can tell you what Clare wanted,' said Libby. 'I'll meet you there.'

She put the mugs in the dishwasher, made sure she looked vaguely presentable and rang Fran. Fran's phone was switched off, which she took to mean that she was in mid interview. Collecting her bag, she left the house.

Her phone rang again when she was just turning the corner into the high street.

'Libby.'

'Ian!' Libby stood still. 'I've just given my statement.'

'I know. And you asked Clare a question she couldn't answer.'

'Yes, sorry. I quite shocked poor DC Bodie.'

'You've been doing that to every fresh-faced young copper you meet for years,' said Ian with a sigh. 'Nevertheless, as it happens, I'm going to tell you the answer.'

'You are?'

'Yes, because it means we are beginning to close in – therefore, I want to reiterate my warning. Please be careful.'

Libby heard him take a deep breath. 'Both Mayberry and Graham identified the body found the other day as the man posing as the buyer of the Crooked Horse. And . . .' he paused, 'his DNA was found inside Malcolm Hodges' car.'

Chapter Thirty-Six

'I don't believe I've ever stunned you into silence before,' said Ian after a moment.

'Well,' said Libby, recovering herself, 'I'm gobsmacked.'

'We were quite surprised ourselves,' said Ian, sounding amused. 'We've now got to work out what it means. But I mean it, Libby. We're getting closer to what happened – and to the killer. And you know what happens then.'

'They get scared,' said Libby. 'But to be honest, Ian, what point would there be in coming after me or Fran? If the killer knows the police are getting closer, nobbling us would only make things worse.'

'Logically, yes. But who says killers think logically – at least at this stage of the proceedings? We don't think either of these deaths was premeditated – I'm pretty certain that only happens in crime dramas – so he or she is quite liable to lash out again.'

'She?' repeated Libby. 'A woman?'

'We can't rule anything out, you know that.'

'OK. I'll be careful. Are you going to ring Fran?'

'Yes. And you'll both be at the Alexandria tonight, won't you?'

'Yes, why? You won't be able to join us, will you?'

He laughed. 'I very much doubt it. I shall be sleuthing along in my deerstalker, I expect.'

'Right.' Libby giggled at the image. 'I'll see when I see you, then.'

Ben was already in the Pink Geranium, sitting in the left-hand window on the sofa with a glass of beer.

'Ian just phoned,' said Libby, plonking herself down beside him. 'Major developments.'

'They can wait until you've ordered,' said Ben, waving at the latest student waiter, who approached nervously. Libby beamed at him.

'Can we have a bottle of Merlot,' she asked, 'and I'll have—'

'You'll have *pollo con verde* and like it,' shouted a voice from the kitchen.

'*Pollo con verde*,' finished Libby.

The waiter scuttled off looking even more nervous, just as Peter emerged from the kitchen and came to join them.

'Am I intruding?' he asked.

'No, sit down. I'm just going to tell Ben what's been happening.'

'I'll fetch the wine and an extra glass, then,' said Peter.

Libby had just finished her report of the morning's revelations when the food arrived, and they were moved to the table in the other window.

'Is Ricky here today?' she asked. 'I was going to ask him if he'd come across any of the antiques dealers his mum met over at the Fox and Hounds.'

'As it happens, yes, he did.' Peter was frowning. 'And he wasn't very happy about it. Like his grandmother, he doesn't think his mother has particularly good judgement when it comes to men. And no, he's not here, he's having a driving lesson.'

'With Trisha? That's nice.' Libby tucked into her chicken.

'It is. And he's got the promise of a car if he passes his test.'

'From his mum?' Libby's eyebrows rose in surprise.

'No, Grandma Linda. She also offered to pay Trisha for teaching him.' Ben laughed.

'I bet that went down like a lead balloon!' said Libby.

'It did.' Peter smirked. 'The lady hasn't quite got the measure of us all yet.'

252

'So why wasn't Ricky happy about his mum meeting the antiques boys?' asked Ben.

'She seemed a bit smitten with one of them, apparently, even while she was still – what? Making a play for Stan? Is that how you'd put it?'

'I suppose so,' said Libby.

'Did he say which one it was?' asked Ben.

'He talked about it with Adam, and we all wondered if it was the tall chap who came in asking for you.'

'Jim Frost!' said Ben and Libby together.

'Very smooth, Ricky said. And he said you'd met him, too.'

'We did – over the road. You know that,' said Ben.

'No.' Peter shook his head. 'He said you met him at Stan's pub. This week.'

After this bombshell, Libby could barely be persuaded to finish her meal before rushing off to see Debbie.

'It's that Ray!' she said. Harry had come out to join them by this time and add his words of caution to Peter and Ben's. 'He's the fake solicitor, and I bet he's the one behind it all. He was posing as an antiques dealer at Stan's, and he didn't care a bit if he was exposed, did he, Ben?'

'It would seem so. He must have known you'd ask everyone soon as he left the barn.'

'So he must be the smooth talker our Debbie got cosy with?' said Harry.

'I doubt he'd let her get that cosy,' said Libby. 'But I also bet he was the one trying to buy gold and stuff from the old biddies, not that Jim Frost at all!'

'You told me not to call them that,' said Ben, grinning at Peter and Harry.

'Oh, stop it!' Libby stood up. 'Someone's got to warn Debbie.'

'Why?' Three surprised faces looked up at her.

'Because the police are getting closer and she can identify him! Ian warned me and Fran, and Debbie's even more at risk, I reckon.'

'She might be right,' said Ben to the other two. 'Have you got her number?'

'I've got Linda's,' said Libby. 'Hang on.'

'Whoa!' said Harry. 'Not a good idea. She'll go charging in like a bull in . . . well, you know. Tell Ian. Or Clare.'

'*I'll* tell Ian,' said Peter. 'Better under the circumstances.' He got up and went out to the kitchen.

'What circumstances?' muttered Libby. 'Does he mean better than me?'

Harry and Ben exchanged martyred looks.

Peter came back to the table.

'I had to leave a message,' he said, 'but I think Libby's right. If this Ray or whatever his name is knows the body's been identified, even if he can't possibly know anything else, he'll be panicking. And Debbie obviously knows him. She at least needs to be on her guard.'

'Anne!' said Libby, having a brainwave. 'She lives next door!'

'Phone her, then,' said Ben. 'I'll pour you another glass of wine.'

Libby smiled and took out her phone again.

'Hello!' Anne sounded surprised. 'To what do I owe the pleasure? Are we still on for tonight?'

'Yes, of course. Anne, listen – are you at home at the moment?'

'Not yet. I'm on duty today. Why?'

Anne worked in the big library in Canterbury.

'Oh, I wanted to get in touch with Debbie and I haven't got her number,' gabbled Libby.

'Hang on, I'll send it to you,' said Anne. 'Are you all right? You sound a bit – erm – *rushed*.'

Libby let out a strangled laugh. 'That's it! I am – a bit rushed! Thanks, Anne – I'll explain later.'

She rang Debbie's newly received number. But Debbie didn't answer, and it rang out.

'Didn't even go to voicemail.' Libby looked at the other three. 'What now?'

'I suppose we go down there,' said Ben, standing up with a sigh.

'We're probably panicking without a reason,' said Harry.

'But we know what's happened before,' said Peter, 'so, to use an overused cliché, better safe than sorry.'

'I can't come,' said Harry indicating the remaining diners, who were all trying not to notice what was going on at the big round table in the window. 'But come back here when you've seen Debbie.'

'Shall I get the car?' asked Peter as they left the restaurant.

Peter's car was always parked behind their cottage on the other side of the Manor drive.

'Good idea,' said Ben. 'We'll start walking, you catch us up.'

'*Am* I panicking?' Libby asked, as they set off along the high street.

Ben put his arm round her. 'A bit. But as Pete said, better safe than sorry.'

They had just passed Bob the butcher's shop when Peter drew up beside them. They both climbed in and Peter started off again towards New Barton Lane.

'What do we say when we get there?' asked Libby from the back seat. 'She's going to wonder what on earth we're doing.'

'Presumably, dear heart, we tell her exactly why we're there.' Peter crossed the junction at the bottom of Allhallow's Lane. 'And once we've done that, we can leave her to do whatever she sees fit.'

'Suppose she goes running to Linda?' said Ben.

'She didn't seem overly keen on Linda when I saw her at Carpenter's Hall,' said Libby. 'I think she rather resents her.'

'And yet Linda helped her move here,' said Peter. 'Can't say I like the woman, but she has her family's best interests at heart.'

He pulled off the road alongside a short terrace of converted farm buildings.

'Here we are.'

Libby climbed out. 'I've never been to Debbie's house before.'

'You do know which one it is, I suppose?' Ben gave her a dubious look.

'That one's Anne's, and there's only one next door, so that'll be it.'

Libby took a deep breath, went up to the smart blue door and rang the bell.

'Not in,' said Peter. 'We should have thought of that when she didn't answer her phone.'

'Where can she be?' Libby was agitated.

'She is allowed to have a life, Lib.' Ben patted her arm. 'She could be shopping, at the gym, at her mother's . . .'

'I know.' Libby tried to peer in through a window. 'I just have this feeling.'

'Can I help you?' said a light voice behind them.

They all turned quickly. A small blonde woman stood smiling on the pavement. 'Are you looking for Debbie?'

'Yes,' said Peter, recovering first. 'Are you a friend of hers?'

'Yes,' said the woman. 'But I'm afraid she's gone out.'

'You don't happen to know where?' asked Ben.

'I'm afraid not.' The woman was still smiling. 'I'll tell her when I see her.'

'Are you local?' Libby forced a friendly smile.

'I'm afraid not,' said the woman again. 'Nice to have met you.' And she turned and hurried away.

'Where's she going?' muttered Ben, setting off in pursuit. A car door closed quietly, and a second later a very new and silent car slid out of the alleyway at the side of the buildings.

'Round the back!' said Peter, and set off at a run.

Ben and Libby turned to follow.

They caught up with Peter as he was trying to wrestle open the back door of Debbie's house.

'Who the bloody hell was she?' he said through gritted teeth.

'And is Debbie in there, or was she in that car?' Libby thumped on the kitchen window.

Ben was on his phone again.

'No,' he was saying, 'we didn't get the registration number.'

'Try this,' said Libby to Peter, picking up a rather unfortunate stone garden ornament.

He gave a grim smile. 'It could do with a little alteration, couldn't it? Stand back.' And he hurled it at the kitchen window.

'I'll go,' said Libby, and manged to crawl in through the broken double glazing. Without waiting to open the door for the other two, she charged through into what was obviously a bedroom.

And found Debbie.

Chapter Thirty-Seven

After Debbie had been removed in an ambulance, thankfully still alive, and the attending – somewhat confused – police officers had taken statements from Libby, Ben and Peter, Peter was allowed to drive them back to the Pink Geranium.

Harry was waiting in the now empty restaurant, and shook his head over Libby's cuts and bruises.

'Well, we had to get in somehow,' she said, subsiding onto the sofa in the window. Her phone rang and she threw it on the table. 'Someone else answer that,' she said.

Harry picked it up. 'Yes, Ian, she's here. They all are. Yes, I'll tell them.'

'He's coming over.' He returned the phone to Libby. 'And now tell me what happened.'

Fortified by a new bottle of Harry's best red wine, they told him what had happened in New Barton Lane.

'Honestly, it wasn't very much,' said Libby. 'We'd only been there a few minutes when this woman turned up.'

'And who was she?'

'The other half of the London couple, I reckon,' said Ben.

The other three looked at him in surprise.

'Well, it stands to reason, doesn't it? You told me, Lib, that the woman had vanished, and she's the only female anywhere in the story.' He shrugged and picked up his wine glass.

'Why did she bother to speak to us?' said Peter. 'She could have just slipped out without saying a word.'

'I expect she thought she would delay us. If she said Debbie wasn't there, we wouldn't try and get in and find her.' Libby said. 'That makes sense.'

'What had she done to Debbie?' asked Harry.

'Head trauma,' said Ben. 'But we disturbed her by knocking at the door.'

'Had we better tell Linda and Ricky?' said Peter.

'I'll do it.' Harry stood up. 'I'll go over there, if you like.'

'No, I'll ring,' said Libby with a sigh, picking up her phone again.

'Give it here,' said Ben. 'She'll only harangue you.'

While Ben called Linda, Harry called Ricky and Libby sat with her eyes closed. When everyone had fallen silent, she sat up.

'So what's London woman's role in this? And why was she there?'

'If she is the other half of the supposed London couple,' said Peter, 'she's obviously trying to keep it quiet.'

'By trying to kill someone?' objected Harry.

'She must have thought Debbie was going to give her away – but when would Debbie have seen her?' Libby frowned at her wine and took a healthy sip.

The door opened.

'Can't leave you alone for a minute, can we?' said Ian, coming in followed by a once more reluctant DC Bodie.

Everyone sat up a bit straighter.

'Coffee, Ian?' asked Harry.

'Yes please, Hal.' Ian squeezed in beside Libby and gave her a kiss.

'Julian's looking disapproving again,' said Libby with a tired grin.

Ian looked surprised and DC Bodie very confused.

'Have you come to quiz us or tell us what's going on?' asked Ben.

'Bit of both,' said Ian.

'You can't have caught that woman already.' Peter frowned. 'Not possible.'

'Actually, it is – possible, I mean.' Ian smiled round at them all.

'I told Libby that we were getting close and the killer might lash out.'

'And she did!' said Libby.

'Well, no, she didn't.' Ian looked at DC Bodie, who was getting out his tablet. 'No need to record this. It's off the record.'

Bodie looked affronted.

'Explain.' Harry put down two mugs of coffee, then sat down, stretched out his legs and folded his arms.

'I'm afraid I didn't tell Libby everything.' Ian picked up a mug. 'After all her information, and Fran's, we managed to get Wallace Mayberry to identify the antiques dealer called Ray.'

'But how?' asked Libby. 'As far as we knew, there was no photo of him. We just guessed that Ray the antiques dealer and Ralph the solicitor were the same person.'

'I told you Mayberry identified the body found the other day, didn't I?'

'Yes.'

'And under questioning, he also told us about the man who came into the pub with the so-called London couple. Apparently the young man told him – on the quiet, Mayberry said – that this other person was his solicitor.' Ian smiled at the astonishment on the faces around him. 'I don't think for an instant he was supposed to say anything of the sort.'

'Yes, but he still couldn't identify him properly,' said Libby. 'The solicitor person, I mean.'

'No, but we know for certain now that this Ray was part of the scam.'

'So you need to go to Marsham's and the builders to see of any of them know him?' said Harry.

'But still without a photograph,' said Peter.

Ian sighed. 'Indeed.'

'And what did you mean,' said Libby, 'by saying it wasn't that woman who lashed out?'

'Did she have any blood on her?' asked Ian.

'Er – no.' Libby looked at Ben and Peter. 'Not that I could see.' The other two shook their heads.

'And Debbie came round.' Ian looked satisfied at this announcement. 'And whispered something about Ray. And "don't".'

'Oh, goodness!' Libby's hand went to her mouth. 'Poor woman.'

'Her mother's right,' said Peter. 'She really does have appalling taste in men.'

There was a short silence while everyone addressed themselves to their chosen beverages – even DC Bodie.

'So now you've got to find out who the woman is, as well as finding the man.' Harry shook his head. 'You don't make things easy for yourself, do you?'

'I don't do it on purpose,' said Ian. 'And unfortunately, I don't see how Wolfe and Sarjeant are going to be able to help in this case.'

'No.' Libby stared at the table thoughtfully. 'Neither do I.'

'Neither of them are going to turn up anywhere you're likely to see them,' said Ben. 'In fact they could just quietly disappear and they've got away with it.'

'Yes, but' – Peter leant forward – 'what was their motive in the first place?' He looked at Ian. 'They must have had a reason.'

'For murdering the London bloke? And Hodges?' said Libby.

'Yes. Go back to first bases,' said Peter. 'It looks as if the whole point of the exercise was to allow the builders to develop their estate. Is that right, Ian?'

'Seems to be.'

'And somehow the antiques boys got in the way, because they wanted their lucrative Anglo-Saxon site to remain available. Right so far?'

Ian nodded again.

'So Hodges was killed. And then the purchaser – or fake purchaser – also got in the way. Not clear on that, but that's the way it looks. So the fake solicitor and this mystery woman must both have some connection to the developers.' Peter sat back looking smug.

Ian smiled. 'More or less our thinking.'

'Well done, Pete.' Ben punched his cousin lightly on the arm. 'Worthy of our Lib, that was.'

'Thank you, I think,' said Peter with a laugh. 'Sorry, dear heart.'

'Oh, cheer up, petal,' said Harry. 'He's not going to take over yet.'

Libby smiled. 'I'm impressed.'

'So am I,' said Ian. 'And now I must go and get on with finding the bastards. Thanks for the coffee, Hal.' He turned to Libby. 'Are you still going to the Alexandria tonight?'

'Of course. Why wouldn't I?'

'No idea.' Ian grinned and stood up. 'Say goodbye, DC Bodie.'

'He needn't have come,' said Ben thoughtfully, watching as Bodie and Ian walked round the corner into the Manor drive.

'No,' said Libby. 'I wonder why he did.'

Harry poured the last of the wine. 'Because he was here and it made sense to confirm what he'd been told. Poor young copper, though. Ian was right, you've been making a whole generation of them uncomfortable for years.'

'It's good training,' said Libby, picking up her glass. 'Cheers.'

By the time the minibus drew up at the end of the Manor drive, messages had been received from Linda and Ricky to say Debbie was doing well and there was no lasting damage.

'Rick said he was right about that bloke, wasn't he?' Harry said over the phone. 'From what they've gathered from his mum, it was him that attacked her.'

Hetty reported that Linda wouldn't be coming with them to the Alexandria under the circumstances.

'Started off by blaming you,' she told Libby as she climbed into the bus. 'Soon put 'er right.'

'Cheek!' said Libby, outraged. 'She wanted to come to the village! We didn't ask her.'

'She brought it on 'erself,' said Flo, who had decided to come after all. 'After young Rick's dad, you'd 'a thought she'd know better.'

'Pity Stan at the Fox and Hounds steered clear,' said Ben, settling

262

the two ladies in the front seat. 'He'd have kept her on the straight and narrow.'

'But he saw through her,' said Libby. 'Poor Ricky.'

The sun was glinting off the top of the Alexandria's cupola as they approached along Victoria Place, and Libby reflected on the huge change the years had brought about to this monument to Edwardian pleasure. No longer a run-down carpet warehouse or bingo emporium, but home to proper seaside entertainment as it had been when Dorinda Alexander had had it built.

The auditorium was full and the stage was set with smart music stands bearing the Ray McCloud logo. The Steeple Martin contingent took their places, Fran, Guy and Sophie joined them, and Jane and Terry Baker came to sit behind, and Libby planned on thinking of nothing else but music for the next two hours.

At the end of the concert, which was rapturously received with a standing ovation, the musicians joined audience members in the bar. Cyd and Judy were somewhere on cloud nine. Libby and Fran were deep in conversation with a member of the Alexandria management committee when Hetty's friend Joe Wilson came up and indicated that he needed a word in private.

'Hetty was telling me about that bloke who tried to con all that gold and stuff outa the ladies,' he said. 'One of them antiques dealers, wasn't he?'

'Supposed to be, Joe, yes,' said Fran.

'Well, you know Wally Mayberry, don't you?'

'Yes,' said Libby.

'He does that.' Joe nodded wisely. 'Does all sorts, Wally. If you want to sell anything, he's your man. Anyway. He told me when I was in there having a beer the other day that this other bloke was muscling in.'

'Oh – right. We did think Wally knew him,' said Libby.

'He knew his girlfriend, too.' Joe gave them an eloquent look. 'And he said — get this — "Don't know what he wants more money for, his girlfriend's loaded." What about that, then?'

'Who is she?' Fran and Libby asked together.

'Old Speedwell's granddaughter, that's who. Inherited most of the business.'

'Speedwell?' squeaked Libby.

'The developers?' said Fran. 'Have you told the police, Joe?'

'Police? No! Should I?' He looked surprised.

'We'll tell them,' said Libby, pulling out her phone. 'Well done, Joe.'

'What did I say?' Joe asked Fran, still looking bewildered. 'Is this something to do with the murder at the old Horse?'

'Yes, Joe, and it's vital.' Fran smiled at him. 'You've saved the police loads of time.'

Libby was still trying to make a case for being put through to someone on the murder team. Fran took out her own phone and called Ian's personal number. To her astonishment, he answered straight away.

'I have vital news, Ian,' she said. 'Libby's trying to get it through officially, but I think you might do better.'

By the time the two women had finished their phone calls and insisted on buying Joe a very large drink, the entire Steeple Martin party, with the addition of Cyd and Judy, had formed an audience.

'How did you and Wally know Speedwell and his granddaughter, Joe?' asked Libby, while Fran explained what she could to everyone else.

'Used to work with 'em years ago — when I still lived in Pedlar's Row. Wally's known 'em for years, too. Good bloke, old Alf Speedy.' Joe smiled reminiscently.

Eventually the Steeple Martin minibus was ready to leave, and Libby bade goodbye to Fran.

'That's it, then, I suppose,' she said.

'Makes a change not to be in at the finish,' said Fran.

'Bit of an anticlimax,' said Libby.

'Don't say that,' said Fran with a shudder. 'Surely you've had enough of that type of excitement!'

And as she rode home through the summer night, Libby had to admit that she had.

Epilogue

DC Bodie called Libby much earlier than she would have liked on Sunday morning.

'DCI Connell has asked me to say he'll see you at lunchtime, Mrs Sarjeant,' he said, sounding thoroughly disapproving.

'Oh?' Libby tried to sound encouraging.

'Thank you, goodbye,' said DC Bodie.

'He's coming to Hetty's,' Libby told Ben, climbing back into bed. 'I assume we'll get the lowdown over lunch.'

'Makes a change,' said Ben. 'And at least no one decided to have a go at you this time.'

Hetty called during the morning to inform them that she had asked Fran and Guy to lunch and to stay overnight if they liked, and Peter called to say Harry was closing early so that he could at least attend the post-lunch post-mortem.

Libby was unsurprised on arriving at the Manor to find Joe Wilson also at the big kitchen table along with Flo and Lenny.

'Well, you did provide the final bit of the jigsaw,' said Libby, beaming at him, 'and now you'll hear the whole story from the horse's mouth.'

'The Crooked Horse, see?' cackled Lenny.

Flo quelled him with a stare.

Fran and Guy arrived next and had barely got settled with their first glasses of wine when Ian arrived, accompanied, to the combined and intense interest of the company, by Clare Stone.

'I'm sorry to butt in,' she said, looking embarrassed, 'but Ian insisted.'

'Good to 'ave yer, gal,' said Hetty. 'Ian'll do you a drink.'

'And I'm not saying a word until after lunch,' he said, fetching glasses. 'I don't want my digestion ruined.'

It was over an hour later, when Harry and Peter had arrived, the early strawberries and cream had been finished and coffee and brandy supplied to those who wanted them and more wine to those who didn't, that Ian sat back in his chair and said, 'Where shall I begin?'

'Who was it at Marsham's who wanted to sell the Horse?' asked Libby quickly, before anybody else could speak. 'That's the start of it.'

Ian smiled. 'That was the clever part. There never was anyone.'

'What?'

'No!'

'Bloody hell!'

'It was all Natasha Speedwell's idea from the start,' he went on. 'She wanted to build executive homes on what turned out to be the nature reserve. She had it in her head that it would be an ideal site for what you call DFLs to move into.'

'I can see why she thought that,' said Fran. 'Anyone coming down from London would probably not know about the slippage problems.'

'As you know, the application was turned down. So she turned her attention to the Crooked Horse. Assuming nobody there knew her, she recruited an old school friend to pose as her husband, and they . . . I suppose you could say they infiltrated the crowd at the Horse. And very subtly let it be known they were thinking of buying it. That's where Ralph Hardy, aka Ray, came in. He was — is — a struck-off solicitor, and the clever part is that when he managed to get in touch with young Livia . . .'

'Who?' came the chorus, and there had to be a pause while Livia was explained.

'To resume,' said Ian at last, 'the clever part was there never had been an agreement to sell. Livia assumed she hadn't been told, and by the time the paperwork came into the office to be signed, she was on her honeymoon. When – somehow – it came out that the intention was to sell on to Speedwell, Marsham's immediately backed out, but by then, the place had been closed.'

'Poor old Jenny,' said Flo.

'At this point, Malcolm Hodges entered the picture. He had already tried to persuade the bogus buyers to go somewhere else—'

'When he took them to the Sloop!' burst out Libby.

'Indeed. But when that didn't work, he broke into the Horse one night to retrieve the Anglo-Saxon hoard collected by the infamous antiques boys. He surprised our young buyer trying to set fire to the place on the instructions of his fake wife, who thought if it was irretrievably damaged, Marsham's would sell it anyway. She had by this time invested a good deal of money in the scheme, and Speedwell weren't doing very well anyway.'

'Old Speedy'd be turning in his grave,' murmured Joe.

'So, in a panic, we assume, Hodges was killed. Then Ralph Hardy was summoned, and he got the killer – whose name was Neville Taylor, by the way, not that it matters now – to load Hodges' body into his own car, which he drove to the barn, followed by Hardy. They unloaded the body into its own barn, then went down to the creek, set the boat free and left the car there.'

'That's why Taylor's DNA was in Hodges' car!' said Fran.

'That's it.' Ian nodded. 'Then our resourceful Hardy collected Taylor, drove him to a remote area near Ashford and killed him.'

'What about Taylor's car? He must have got to the Horse somehow?' said Guy.

'Hardy went back and moved it from the square in Felling the following day, while everyone was concentrating on the Horse and the arrival of the excavator, organised, of course, by Natasha. Are you all following this?'

'If we ain't, our Lib'll fill us in later,' said Flo. 'But cor – it ain't arf complicated!'

'So the antiques mob weren't really anything to do with it?' said Libby.

'After we found him, Hardy has been remarkably informative about them, no doubt thinking it might help his case,' said Ian, 'and I think there may well be a few court cases arising, but it appears most of it was down to Hodges and Jim Frost.'

'And the buying-up of old gold?' asked Joe.

'That was Hardy building a smokescreen – unsuccessfully, as it happens,' explained Clare. 'I've only been involved in the investigation for part of the time, so I'm not fully up to speed, but you're right.' She nodded at Flo. 'It ain't arf complicated!'

Everyone laughed and Ben got up to offer more drinks.

'Well, that seems to be it, then,' said Harry, beaming round at the assembled company. 'Can we get back to normal now?'

'What's normal?' asked Peter, eliciting more laughs.

'Well, you know,' said Harry, 'our normal humdrum lives until Sarjeant and Wolfe's next case. Got a timetable for that yet, petal?'

Acknowledgements
and a Letter from Lesley

The idea for this book came from a real life event reported widely in the media, so first of all, I'd like to thank that pub for givng me the idea. Next as always, the NHS, who've kept me going for another year. My friends, the Quayistas — they know who they are — whose encouragemnt means the world. Of course Toby and Isabel at Headline, and finally, my family, Louise, Miles, Phillipa and Leo, for ongoing support, lifts, errands and anything else I ask them to do.

And now I'm going to ask you, my readers, for a favour. If you've enjoyed Libby Sarjeant's latest outing, would you leave a rating with your preferred bookseller? There are a lot of books out there — thank goodness — and every rating, or even a review, helps out visibility. It is much appreciated, believe me!

Lastly, apologies once again to the police forces of Great Britain for taking such liberties with them.

And if you'd like to receive news of future books, books in progress and anything else going on in Lesley and Libby world, please sign up for my newsletter at lesleycookman.co.uk — and receive a free short story!

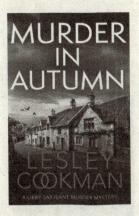

Libby Sarjeant is deep into rehearsals for the annual pantomime
when a body is found in a doorway two weeks before
Christmas – and Libby and her friend Fran are called into
action once again, when their investigation leads them
to a local brewery and the sale of many of its pubs.

With the help of a team of local publicans, can Libby
and Fran unravel the case before it's too late?

Available to order

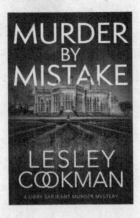

When a homeless man from the old-fashioned English
seaside town of Nethergate appears to go missing – and
the police are not available to investigate – amateur
detective Libby Sarjeant and her psychic friend
Fran are called in to search for him.

But it seems the case might be far more complex
than they anticipated – and when a second person
disappears without trace, Libby suspects there
must be a sinister connection between the two.

Following a murky trail to uncover the truth,
Libby and Fran find themselves uncovering
secrets hiding in plain sight.

Can they solve a puzzling mystery before
anyone else suddenly vanishes?

Available to order

ACCENT

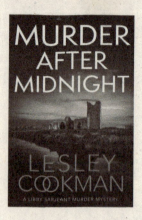

MURDER AFTER MIDNIGHT

LESLEY COOKMAN

A LIBBY SARJEANT MURDER MYSTERY

When a woman's body is found on the local
golf course after an illicit New Year's party, news
quickly spreads, and Libby finds herself being
tracked down by locals desperate to share
information about the victim, Jackie Stapleton.

But things are never that simple in Libby's world.
Whilst everyone had an opinion on Jackie, it seems nobody
really knew much about her. Libby's chum DCI Connell is
being more tight-lipped than usual, and even with her
friend Fran Wolfe's help, discovering a motive
for the killing is frustratingly difficult.

Is the murder linked to some distinctly dodgy dealing,
a dispute with the local golf club, or something far
more sinister – a ghost from Libby's past?

Available to order

ACCENT